To th...

The

Light

A Destiny Moments

Novel

All the Best!

Cindy Vincent

Also by Cindy Vincent

Bad Day for a Bombshell:
A Tracy Truworth, Apprentice P.I.
1940s Homefront Mystery

Swell Time for a Swing Dance:
A Tracy Truworth, Apprentice P.I.
1940s Homefront Mystery

Yes, Carol . . . It's Christmas!

The Case of the Cat Show Princess:
A Buckley and Bogey Cat Detective Caper

The Case of the Crafty Christmas Crooks:
A Buckley and Bogey Cat Detective Caper

The Case of the Jewel Covered Cat Statues:
A Buckley and Bogey Cat Detective Caper

The Case of the Clever Secret Code:
A Buckley and Bogey Cat Detective Caper

The Case of Too Many Clues:
A Buckley and Bogey Cat Detective Caper

The Case of the Perfect Pretty Picture:
A Buckley and Bogey Cat Detective Caper

The Mystery of the Missing Ming:
A Daisy Diamond Detective Novel

The Case of the Rising Star Ruby:
A Daisy Diamond Detective Novel

Cats Are Part of His Kingdom, Too:
33 Daily Devotions to Show God's Love

The Light

A Destiny Moments
Novel

Cindy Vincent

Whodunit Press
Houston

The Light

A Destiny Moments Novel

Published by Whodunit Press

A Division of Mysteries by Vincent, LLC

For information, please contact:

CustomerCare@mysteriesbyvincent.com

ISBN: 978-1-932169-99-7

Printed in the United States of America

Dedication

To Connie,
Wonderful Christian and cat mom,
Thank you for your friendship and encouragement.
May your light always shine!

"The light shines in the darkness, and the darkness has not overcome it." (John 1:5, NIV)

Chapter One

Libby Dawson barely managed to brush her teeth and wipe the makeup from her face, wishing she could just as easily wipe away the words that insisted on playing over and over in her mind since the day they'd gotten the news.

Stage Four.

Metastatic.

Words she never dreamed anyone would ever use when it came to her athletic husband, Devin. Not when he was just a year shy of his thirtieth birthday.

How could this be happening?

She plodded into the bedroom and dropped onto her bed. Between working all day and spending her evenings at the hospital, she was exhausted beyond anything she'd ever known in her twenty-seven years. She hadn't even been this tired years ago, when she'd worked full-time and put herself through college. At least then she'd still been able to think straight.

These days, she felt like she was operating on nothing but pure, raw emotion, with her brain being ping-ponged from one upset to the next. Her life seemed to be nothing more than a constant stream of reactions to the newest round of bad news. She was stretched beyond her limits, and to make matters worse, she hadn't slept one full night since they'd gotten the diagnosis.

And the prognosis.

If nothing else, at least she had the comfort of knowing that Devin would sleep well tonight. The doctors kept him heavily medicated, so he wouldn't feel the pain of the cancer that had spread through his body like wildfire. Of course, all that medication also meant he barely knew she was there most of the time.

It wouldn't be long now.

And in the next few days, she planned to take a leave of absence from work, so she could be with him over the holidays and spend every last moment with him. Because there weren't going to be many moments left. It would be their last Christmas together, though she guessed he probably had no idea what time of year it was. Naturally, she hadn't put up the tree and all the Christmas lights outside. Like they usually did.

Together.

Now, with every fiber of her being, she longed for the warm glow of those lights, and the way their life had once been.

Her eyes turned to his side of the bed. Empty now. Empty forever.

They had barely been married for three years, and here she was, being robbed of a lifetime together. This was not the way their story was supposed to go. And for that matter, this was not the way her *life* was supposed to go. She and Devin were supposed to live happily ever after, with a whole clan of kids and grandkids around them. A life full of joy and adventure.

But none of that would ever happen now.

She never dreamed she'd be a widow before she was thirty.

She pulled her long, golden brown hair into a messy bun and grabbed the box of tissues that she kept on her nightstand. Then she turned off the bedside lamp and let her head fall onto the pillows, settling in for another long, lonely night. It was strange how the hours could seem both endless and accelerated all at the same time.

If only she could sleep. It would bring such relief for even a few hours, and it would give her the strength to go on. It might even give her an ounce of normalcy.

Though she knew things would never be normal again. Not now. Not ever.

And not in this cold, empty bed.

So instead of drifting off to sleep, tears rolled down her cheeks, just like clockwork. And she wept, exactly like she did every night, in big, sobbing gulps.

"Why, God? Why?" she cried out into the darkness. "Why did this have to happen? God, where are you?"

But she had barely spoken the words when the bedside light went on.

All by itself.

"Huh?" she said as she sniffled and blew her nose. "I guess I didn't turn it off completely."

So she reached over and turned the switch to make sure it was fully off this time. Then she leaned back onto her pillows, bracing herself for the steady stream of tears that no doubt would come once more.

And the light went on again.

"Okay, this is weird," she said aloud.

Then she reached over and turned off the lamp.

But it simply went back on.

"Oh, great," she said. "Not only am I losing a husband, but now I'm having electrical issues. Just what I need."

Once again, she turned the light off and dabbed at her tears.

Only to have the light go back on.

As before, she turned it off and closed her eyes.

But the light merely went on again. Clearly, there was something wrong with her lamp. And of all the times for it to malfunction, why did it have to be now?

Regardless, it was pretty obvious that Libby had no choice but to unplug the lamp. The only problem was, it was plugged into a socket that was behind the bed. Their big, heavy bed that was a real chore to move at all.

Still, what choice did she have?

She leaned up on her elbow, ready to swing her legs out of bed and put her feet on the floor. But at that very moment, she just didn't have the energy to get up. Instead, she dropped onto her side, arm dangling over the edge of the bed. She decided to rest for a moment or two and gather the strength she needed to complete what suddenly felt like a Herculean task.

That's when Libby closed her eyes and took a few deep breaths.

And fell fast asleep.

For the first time since Devin had gotten sick.

Chapter Two

Libby awoke the next morning to bright sunshine coming in through her windows. Personally, she'd never been crazy about the wide-slatted blinds that covered the bay window of their bedroom. Those had been Devin's idea. She always thought they let too much light slip in between the slats during the summer. And summers in Destiny, Texas, a bedroom community of the greater Houston area, were beyond hot. Yet now that it was December, she actually enjoyed all that sunshine.

Especially since her bedside lamp was finally dark.

She stared at her lamp and blinked a few times, wondering when it had gone off. And for that matter, she wondered *what* had caused it to go off. Or to even go on in the first place.

Then again, considering her state of exhaustion, it was entirely possible that she'd simply imagined the whole thing. Or maybe she had dreamed it. But if that was the case, it also meant she'd been sleeping. And that's when she realized she'd gotten her first full night's sleep since the ordeal with Dylan's health had begun.

What a difference a little sleep could make.

"If only I could conk out like that every night," she murmured as she headed for the shower. "But somehow, I think the odds are pretty slim that it'll ever happen again . . ."

Yet that very night, after another long and emotionally wrenching day, Libby dropped into bed and turned off her bedside lamp. Then she leaned back onto her pillows, clutching a good supply of tissues. Ready for the nightly onslaught of tears.

And just as those tears started to fall, the light of her bedside lamp went on.

All by itself. Exactly as it had the night before.

"Okay, this time I know I'm not imagining things," Libby said into the empty room. "This is *actually* happening."

So she turned the lamp off once more and got settled in her bed. A few seconds later, the light stubbornly blazed on.

"Seriously?" Libby said aloud before she reached over and turned it off again.

Only to have it flicker on, mere seconds after she'd leaned back onto her pillows.

Much to her amazement, she and her lamp kept up this routine a few more times, in what was starting to feel like a strange kind of dance. And though she couldn't even begin to explain what was going on, one thing was quickly becoming crystal clear—this was a battle she wasn't going to win. Not to mention, a battle she really didn't have the energy to fight.

For the first time in weeks, she chuckled. "All right, lamp. You win. For now, anyway. I'll deal with you tomorrow."

Then she rolled over and fell fast asleep.

She awoke the next morning to find the light was off. Exactly as it had been the morning before.

Finally, after a third night of this unexplained phenomenon, Libby awoke feeling more rested than she had in months. And she also felt stronger than she had in a while, strong enough to face the day in front of her. And strong enough to face the fact that her husband was growing weaker by the moment.

Apparently, the change in her was obvious enough that her friend, Jessica, even noticed as they grabbed a cup of coffee in the employee break room that morning. "Libby, if I didn't know better, I'd say you must be sleeping again at night. Because I can see the blue of your eyes, instead of, well . . . so much bloodshot red. Did your doctor give you something? With all that you're going through right now, I would think that sleep must be super important."

"It's so true," Libby said with a nod as she poured a cup of coffee and added cream and sweetener. "And yes, amazingly, I have been getting some sleep. Finally. I can't even tell you how much it helps. I don't think I'd be keeping it together at all if I wasn't getting some sleep. But no, my doctor didn't give me anything, and I haven't been taking anything over the counter. Though . . . umm . . . there is something . . ."

"Something?" Jessica slipped her curly, red hair behind her ears and took a sip of her own coffee. "*Something* you want to talk about?"

"It's kind of hard to explain . . ." Libby went on. "And it's probably just my imagination anyway."

Jessica tilted her head, concern radiating from her dark eyes. "Oh, what's been going on?"

Libby sighed. "If I tell you, it will probably sound really strange, and you'll think I've completely lost it. So never mind. Forget I even mentioned it."

Jessica's mouth dropped open. "Fat chance. Now you've got me worried. You can't just dangle that out there and then leave me in the dark."

"Funny you should use those words," Libby breathed.

Then she bit her lip, wondering if she should confide in her friend and tell her the whole crazy story. But how could she expect Jessica to believe such an unbelievable tale, when she could hardly believe it herself?

Jessica touched Libby on the shoulder. "You know, I'm not letting you off the hook until you tell me. Besides, this is a time for you to lean on your friends."

"All right," Libby conceded. "But please don't laugh."

"I promise I won't," Jessica said after another sip of her coffee.

Libby took a deep breath, searching for the right words. "It's like this . . . every night, when I turn off my bedside lamp, it goes right back on. Then I turn it off, but it doesn't stay off. It goes on again. All by itself."

That's when Jessica gave her the same look that practically everyone had given her since Devin's diagnosis, a cross between pity and maternal concern. "Okay, well, that doesn't sound too serious. You probably just have a bad switch on your lamp."

Libby took a sip of her coffee. "Except that, no matter how many times I turn it off, the light keeps going back on."

"Did you try unplugging it?" Jessica asked her.

"No, not yet. Because I fall asleep before I can find the energy to get up and pull my heavy bed away from the wall and unplug the lamp. And . . ."

"And . . . ?"

"And in a weird way, that lamp makes me feel sort of . . . well . . . comforted. I'm not sure, but I think it might be the reason why I've been sleeping at night. And it's always off in the morning."

"So . . . it's a magical lamp?"

"No, no, nothing like that. I'm not Aladdin."

"Okay, not magical. But you're saying this lamp goes on by itself, puts you to sleep, and then goes off before you wake up. Honey, are you sure you're not just dreaming the whole thing?"

"Well, no . . . yes . . . maybe," Libby said, already regretting her choice to tell anyone about her lamp.

Jessica gave her a sympathetic nod. "You know, I'll bet it's just part of the grieving process. Watching Devin go downhill has been so heartbreaking that you're bound to have a few . . . umm . . . 'eccentricities.' Honestly, I don't know how you've managed to hold up as well as you have. You told me you went to a support group a few times. Maybe someone there has gone through something similar."

"I'm not crazy," Libby said with a laugh. "I know what I saw."

"I'm sure you do," Jessica said, patting Libby's hand. "But you've been under such an emotional strain. Almost like a rubber band stretched to the limit and about to . . ."

Libby raised an eyebrow. ". . . snap?"

"Or maybe your lamp just has a bad connection," said a masculine voice from behind Libby, at the entrance to the break room.

Apparently, Jessica wasn't the only one to hear about Libby's lamp. Did that mean the story would be all over the office before long? If so, would everyone at work think she'd lost her mind?

She turned to see bald, forty-something Bert walk into the room, carrying a platter filled with intricately frosted Christmas cookies.

"Why don't you just get a new lamp? You could order it online and have it delivered tomorrow," he suggested.

Libby shook her head. "The lamp was a wedding gift, part of a matching set, until Devin accidentally broke his one night. So I really don't want to get rid of it."

"Then you could fix it," Bert explained as he held the platter before her. "Any hardware store should sell a lamp kit. It'll have everything you need to replace the old wires and the switch. Just follow the instructions. It's pretty straightforward stuff."

Libby took a Christmas tree cookie that was glazed in green. "I suppose I could do that. There's a hardware store near my house. I'll run by tomorrow morning."

"Good idea," Jessica said. "You don't want a malfunctioning lamp in your house."

"Let me know if you need any help," Bert added. "And please take another cookie. Or two. Candace baked them and decorated them last night, and she gave me strict instructions to tell you to take a bunch. She's worried that you're not getting enough to eat lately."

Libby let out a little laugh and grabbed a second cookie, a reindeer this time. "That's so sweet of her. Be sure to tell her thanks. You are so blessed to have a wife like her."

"I'll say," Jessica put in as Bert held the platter in front of her now. "Marrying a gourmet chef was a good game plan. Wish I could find a guy who was a chef." She chose a big, blue snowflake cookie and took a bite.

"I highly recommend it," Bert said with a smile. "And anytime you need a good meal, Libby, you're welcome at our table. Candace says she'd be happy to cook whatever you like. And she's not kidding."

Jessica put her hand on Libby's arm. "Listen, honey, I know this is your last day at work for a while, and you won't be at the holiday party tonight. But don't worry about a thing while you're gone. We'll hold down the fort in the marketing department until you get back. In the meantime, call if you need anything at all. And I expect to hear from you anyway, you know. A lot."

"I know," Libby told them, fighting back the tears that immediately formed in her eyes. Tears that always seemed to be there these days. "That's so thoughtful of you both."

Of course, she truly appreciated the way so many people had offered to help her. More than she could ever say. But even with all the care and well-wishes of her friends, she had quickly learned that no one could take away the pain of slowly losing her husband. Grief was a journey she ultimately had to walk alone. Especially since Devin hardly even knew she was there these days.

And that night, when she went to visit him, he was in worse shape than ever. According to hospital rules, she wasn't supposed to cuddle up with him in his bed, but tonight, she couldn't help herself. She just needed to be next to him. So when the nurses weren't looking, she climbed on in.

She whispered a quick, "I love you," and for a moment, it seemed like he tried to mouth the words back, though she couldn't tell for sure. He was just so out of it. For that matter, he didn't even look—or feel—like Devin anymore. He was pale and gaunt and but a shell of the rugged guy she'd married. In a weird way, she felt like she had lost him already.

When she'd first found out he was sick, she had wanted him to live for as long as possible. So she could have every last moment with him. Yet now she hated to see his suffering. And it was clear that death would bring relief to his pain.

But not to hers.

She almost felt numb as she headed home late that night, driving past all the Christmas lights around town. And this time, when her bedside light went on right after she'd turned it off, she didn't even bother to fight it. Instead, she fell into a deep, dreamless sleep.

As always, the lamp was off when she awoke in the morning.

But, if nothing else, she knew her lamp would no longer be an issue by the time she went to bed again that night. Because

The Light

Bert and Jessica had been right—fixing her bedside light was a good idea. After all, there might be something seriously wrong with the wiring. And while she realized she hadn't exactly been operating on all cylinders lately, it wasn't normal to live with a lamp that went on or off by itself.

So she decided to take the advice of her friends. On her way to the hospital that morning, she stopped into the hardware store that wasn't far from her house.

Ritchie's Hardware Store and Lumberyard.

An elderly man with lots of thick, silver hair found a lamp kit for her right away. "I don't usually sell a lot of these at this time of year," he told her with a smile. "Instead, people are mostly buying replacement bulbs for their Christmas lights. But it sounds like you're replacing the hardware in an old lamp."

"I am," she nodded. "There's something wrong with it. I think it's got a short or something."

"Oh, yes, then you'll definitely want to get it swapped out," he told her kindly, before he explained the pieces of the kit to her and then went over the instructions. "What is the lamp doing? Have you seen any sparks?"

Libby shook her head. "Oh, no, nothing like that. It just goes on after I turn it off."

He stared at her for a moment. "That's odd. I assume you tried turning it off again."

She nodded. "Oh, yes. It stays off for about a minute and then it goes right back on again. But it's always off when I wake up in the morning."

His eyebrows went up. "Hmm . . . that is unusual . . . I don't believe I've ever heard of such a thing. Did you unplug it?"

"No," she sighed. "I was too tired. Since I haven't really been sleeping well."

"I would guess not," he said with a chuckle. "Not if your light stays on all night."

"That's the strange part," she confided. "I've actually slept better when my light stayed on."

He gave her a fatherly look. "So there must be something else that's been keeping you awake. Something on your mind."

Yet he had barely spoken the words when tears pricked at

her eyes and threatened to roll down her cheeks.

"My husband is in the hospital," she explained, sniffling. "He has cancer, and he won't . . ." Her voice cracked, and she just couldn't get the rest of the words out.

The older man put his hand on her shoulder. "Say no more. I know exactly what you're going through. I've been there myself. I lost my wife of forty-eight years to cancer. It was the hardest thing I've ever been through. How many years have you and your husband been married?"

"Not long," she managed to say, barely above a whisper.

"But long enough," he said softly. "And I'm sure it's doubly hard during the holidays."

"Yes," she murmured. "But I'd better be going. I've got to get to the hospital."

"All right, young one. You've got what you need, and you should have no problem fixing your lamp. In fact, with that kit, you can basically turn anything into a lamp."

"*Anything*?" she asked, suddenly surprised as she dabbed at her eyes.

"Pretty much," he told her. "As long as it can hold a socket and a light bulb. But in case you don't have time to work on your lamp right away, if I were you, I'd plug it into this remote-control system." He pointed to a packet with what looked like several small, oblong plug-ins along with a remote control.

"I've never seen anything like this."

"It's so easy to use. Just plug your lamp into one of the plug-ins from this kit, and then plug that into the wall socket. Then you can use the remote to turn the lamp on and off," he explained. "That should temporarily take care of your problem. Because you'll basically shut off any electricity going to your lamp. So it can't turn back on. Not unless you turn it on with the remote."

"That's a great idea," she told him as he handed the packet to her.

And, truth be told, it *was* a great idea.

"In fact," he went on, "you can even plug all the lamps around your house into these. Then when you go to bed at night, you can simply press the buttons on the remote and turn them all off from your bedroom. If you need to turn on a light in the middle of the night, just hit whichever button you've assigned to it on the remote. And it'll turn on."

"Wow, that sounds good. I'll do it."

"By the way," he told her. "I'm Mr. Ritchie and I own this store. So holler if you need any more help. Or if you just need to talk."

"I will. Thanks again," she told him, as she put the packet of remote-control plug-ins into her basket, alongside the lamp kit.

Then with a quick wave, she headed for the checkout. But along the way, she couldn't help but notice the collection of brocade lampshades on a shelf. On impulse, she added a maroon drum shade to her basket.

Though she had absolutely no idea where she might use such a lampshade.

Oddly enough, she left the store feeling just a little bit lifted. Minor though it might be, she had faced a household problem head-on. And with the help of some friends and a very kind store owner, she'd found a solution.

A solution to the kind of problem that Devin would've taken care of in the past. Something she never would've done on her own.

Yet here she was, about to deal with a lamp that wasn't working properly. It may have only been a small victory, but it was a victory, nonetheless.

Because tonight, she would be in control of her lamp.

And whether the light stayed on or off would be entirely up to her.

Chapter Three

Caleb MacKnight strolled into Ritchie's Hardware Store and Lumberyard with his supply list in hand, ready to deliver it directly to Mr. Ritchie himself. After all, the store owner was not a fan of receiving such a large and varied order as this one by text or email. Instead, he preferred to actually speak to his customers, either in person or over the phone. Just to clarify that he was ordering the precise items that someone needed or wanted. He even made cost-cutting suggestions when he could, and he let people know about any new products that might help with their latest construction projects.

Yup, Royce Ritchie was practically a legend in the home-building community, and he was famous for respecting the hard work of craftsmen and general contractors like Caleb. And though Mr. Ritchie's hair had changed from dark auburn to sparkling silver over the years, he remained the same old-fashioned guy with old-fashioned ways.

Which suited Caleb just fine.

Though to him, Mr. Ritchie was so much more than simply the man who'd been supplying building materials to Caleb's father for decades. And the man who now supplied materials to Caleb's brothers, as well as to Caleb himself, ever since he'd joined the family business. No, Mr. Ritchie wasn't merely known for dispensing high-quality building supplies. He was also known for dispensing good advice.

Amazingly, his advice spanned all kinds of subjects, which pretty much covered the many curveballs that life could send hurtling right at a guy. And this morning, Caleb had one of those curveballs zeroing in on him like a guided missile heading for a target. So if there were ever a day when Caleb needed some wise advice, well, today was that day. Because frankly, he didn't know where else to turn at the moment. Normally, he would've talked to his brothers. Or his father. But he didn't have the heart to tell them what had happened. Not when his latest relationship fiasco had gone so wrong that it could cost him and the family business dearly.

The thought of it made him sick to his stomach.

To think, he'd only joined their home-building business a few years ago, on his twenty-seventh birthday. Now he wished he never had, since the business would be better off without him if Fallon went through with her threats. And when his father and brothers found out—if they found out—they'd be angry at best, and completely disappointed at worst.

Disappointed in him.

He cringed at the thought. He hated the idea of letting his family down. Besides that, he wondered how he could have been so blind. His brothers had told him from the start that Fallon was bad news. If only he'd been able to see it then, too. So why didn't he?

If nothing else, at least he'd had the smarts to avoid the beautiful woman who was walking out of the store just as he was walking in. Sure, he'd noticed her, so pretty and yet so teary-eyed and sad. His natural instinct had been to ask her what was wrong and if she needed help. But after dealing with Fallon, he'd officially sworn off rescuing damsels in distress. Especially since he had a history when it came to saving hapless females.

The only problem was, while he may have believed he was rescuing said damsels from fire-breathing dragons, it turned out he was actually saving the fire-breathing dragons themselves. In disguise, of course. And according to his track record, he couldn't see the subterfuge until it was too late. Not surprisingly, those same dragons didn't bother holding back their ire or their fire once they had their claws firmly hooked into him. And he'd been burned more than once. Fallon was a testament to that.

If only he could find the kind of lifelong love that his grandparents had. Growing up, he'd heard the stories of how they fell in love and stayed in love despite all the ups and downs and horrors of World War II. He'd been told the tales of his grandfather's heroism, flying B-17s and making bombing runs over Nazi Germany. Risking his own life every single time he went. When the war was over, he came back and married his sweetheart, and the two of them built a life, a home, and a family together. He had loved and admired them with every fiber of his being. And he was there when they passed away, just months apart from one another.

Still in love after all those years.

Was it too much to want that same kind of love for himself?

Maybe that was his problem—he belonged in another era. His grandparents' era. And the modern women he seemed to attract weren't as interested in him as they were in what he could do for them.

Or what they could *get* from him.

Caleb headed toward the heart of the store and spotted Mr. Ritchie right away.

The older man smiled and waved to him. "Hey, Caleb! How're you doing? Got another order already? Business must be good. And so close to Christmas, even."

"I sure hope so . . ." Caleb said, running his fingers through his dark, curly hair. "Because I think I'm going to need the money."

Mr. Ritchie tilted his head. "That sounds ominous. Spent too much on Christmas? Everything all right?"

"Well . . . umm, no, Mr. Ritchie. Not exactly." Caleb hesitated for a few seconds, trying to come up with the right words to say.

"What's going on, son?"

All of a sudden, Caleb felt foolish and weak. Because this wasn't the first time he'd come to Mr. Ritchie for advice. And more than anything, he wanted to hide at that moment, but since he was a pretty tall and muscular guy, hiding wasn't exactly his strong suit. Plus, there was the fact that his problem wasn't going to solve itself. Or go away on its own.

Meaning, he needed to buck up and face the situation.

So he took a deep breath and closed his dark eyes. "Do you remember when I told you about that girl I was dating? Fallon?"

Mr. Ritchie smiled and nodded. "Oh, yes, I remember you talking about her. You thought she might be the one."

Caleb sighed. "Yup, I did. At the start anyway."

"As I recall, it sounded like the two of you had a lot in common."

"Uh-huh, I thought we really hit it off," Caleb told him. "In fact, when I look back now, I realize it was kind of eerie how much we had in common. If I liked something, it seemed like she liked it, too. And for once, it was nice to meet someone who was interested in what I do for a living. And who complimented me on all kinds of things. In the beginning, I thought she was a very optimistic, positive person."

"But I suspect things changed," Mr. Ritchie murmured.

"Oh, yeah, things changed, all right . . . oh, boy, did they ever."

"What happened?" The older man asked as he leaned his tall, thin frame against a cabinet, his eyes never leaving Caleb's face.

Caleb stared at the floor and shook his head. "Well, I guess I noticed something was off when it seemed like she didn't want to talk about her own job. At first, I wasn't too concerned about it, since I guessed she didn't really want a major career in life. And she wanted to be a stay-at-home mom someday instead. Which I was okay with. But then I realized that every time I even mentioned her job, she would change the subject and talk about the houses I had in progress."

Mr. Ritchie crinkled his brow. "So something must have been up. Where did she work?"

Caleb shrugged. "She said she worked in a grocery store as a cashier. But she absolutely didn't want me to visit her there. She said she'd get in trouble if I did."

"Hmmm . . . well, I suppose that makes sense," Mr. Ritchie said. "But then what happened?"

"The day after Thanksgiving, she claimed she'd lost her job," Caleb explained. "That's when she started crying. And crying and crying and crying. Practically nonstop."

"I'll bet you were pretty worried about her."

"I really was. She even made hints about committing suicide, so I was almost afraid to leave her alone."

Mr. Ritchie's eyes went wide. "I can imagine. Did she try to find a new job?"

Caleb shook his head. "No. She refused."

"My goodness. What did you do?"

"I didn't know what to do. She would call me up in the morning and say she didn't think she could go on. And she wondered if she could hang out with me all day. But I couldn't just drop my projects and stay with her. So I agreed to let her come with me to the houses I was building. And she went with me from job site to job site."

"Hmmm . . . how did that go?" Mr. Ritchie asked, folding his arms.

"Not the best," Caleb said with a groan. "My brothers were pretty annoyed, since she kept telling us that we needed to change our designs. And she was constantly telling us how to decorate and stage each house. Her advice was terrible, and never anything we would ever use. So believe me, we *didn't* use it."

"I don't blame you. Did she have any background when it came to decorating? Or designing? Like your mom?"

"No, absolutely none. Aside from watching home improvement shows."

"Wow, so that was pretty brazen of her to tell you and your brothers what to do."

"Yup," Caleb agreed. "Especially on the day when she cornered some customers. She started talking to them about tearing down walls and changing the whole layout of the house. Load-bearing walls, I might add. My brothers and I had to say something to her and get her out of there."

Mr. Ritchie gasped. "Was she still crying while she dished out her unsolicited advice? And while she was talking to your customers?"

Caleb glanced up at the ceiling for a moment. "Now that I

think about it . . . no, she wasn't. I guess she quit crying every time she stepped onto a job site. But when we told her not to talk to customers, she started crying again. So my brothers basically avoided her, since nobody knew how to handle her. Or what to do. This went on for several weeks."

"Sounds very stressful. And frankly, a little suspicious."

"Well, I wish I'd been a lot more suspicious about it," Caleb confessed. "Because, long story short, she's now claiming that she was actually employed by our company, and that I owe her for her work. And she's demanding that I pay her."

Mr. Ritchie's mouth fell open wide. "But you didn't officially hire her, right?"

"Never. Not at all. I only took her with me because I was worried she might harm herself. But little did I know, she documented all the hours she spent with me and at what project. And she's claiming that her so-called advice qualifies as actual employment. On top of that, she's threatening me. If I don't give her the money she's asking for, she promises to drag our company name through the mud. All over social media."

"Do you think she could do that?" the older man asked, his eyes wide in disbelief.

"Absolutely. People get trashed and their reputations get ruined on social media all the time. She could post all kinds of negative reviews and have stuff all over the Internet and I wouldn't even know where she posted all her lies. Especially since plenty of people use fake accounts, and they get other people to repost their posts. And even if I did manage to dispute lots of the stuff, our company's reputation would still be tarnished. She's got pictures of our construction sites to prove she was there. And I didn't realize it, but she even recorded a few conversations where she was giving us advice. Of course, she cut out the parts where we told her, 'No way.'"

"Holy cow . . . what a manipulative young woman. Have you told your father and brothers about her threats?"

That's when Caleb felt his mouth go dry, and he hesitated once more. "No, I haven't. I feel so bad about all this, and it's my fault for getting involved with Fallon in the first place. Even when they told me she was trouble. Now *they* could be the ones to suffer the consequences for my mistake. They don't deserve this. MacKnight and Sons Custom Homes doesn't deserve this. And I don't have the heart to tell them."

Mr. Ritchie shook his head. "There's no way you could have predicted something like this would happen."

Caleb rubbed his forehead. "And what's a guy supposed to do when a woman is crying? I couldn't just walk away. So there I was, jumping in with both feet to rescue her. I am such a fool. Now I don't know how to fix this. A very big part of me thinks I should just pay her and be done with it."

Mr. Ritchie put his hand on Caleb's shoulder. "I wouldn't suggest it, son. There's a word for what this young woman is doing. It's called extortion. It's a crime, and people who commit crimes like that are crooks. So you can't believe a thing they say. Meaning that, even if you paid her, it doesn't mean she won't demand more payments. Or go through with her threats."

"Then what can I do? I'd really love any advice you can give me, Mr. Ritchie," Caleb said, feeling sick to his stomach once more.

Mr. Ritchie spoke in a calm, firm voice. "First, I'd suggest that you stall. You can make it sound like things will be shut down over Christmas. And you could tell her that you're waiting to get paid on another job before you can get your hands on any cash. While that's going on, I would avoid seeing her in person. Again, you can use Christmas as an excuse. Make it sound like you've got family plans and obligations. Which you probably do. In the meantime, I think you need to tell your father and your brothers. Let them know what's going on."

Caleb cringed and tried to take a few deep breaths—unsuccessfully—before he quietly agreed.

"After that," Mr. Ritchie went on, "I'd suggest you contact a customer of mine. A guy named Matt Doychek. He's a private investigator."

"A private eye? Why would I need someone like that?"

Mr. Ritchie raised an eyebrow. "Because, if you ask me, this girl sounds like a real smooth talker. Like she's done this before, and she's got her game down pat. My guess is that Matt will run a background check on her. And, depending on what he finds, you can see what he recommends from there. He's really sharp, and he'll know what to do."

"Well, all right. I guess I could call the guy. This is such a nightmare. I can't believe I stepped in it like I did."

"Don't blame yourself, son," Mr. Ritchie said kindly. "And even though you're not the one at fault here, I think you'd better take the bull by the horns and deal with this right away. Otherwise, it could plague you for a long, long time."

Which weren't exactly the words that Caleb was hoping to hear. Including the part about hiring a private investigator. Even so, he'd come in for advice, so he figured he'd better take what he'd been given.

He sighed as Mr. Ritchie ran off to get Matt's information. All the while, he wondered over and over again how he'd gotten himself into this situation. He had no idea that dating Fallon would turn into such a disaster. He also wondered how it would play out, since, no matter how he looked at it, he didn't really *see* a way out. Frankly, the future looked incredibly bleak to him. How in the world would he ever get out of this mess?

Though he didn't know the answer, he did know one thing—his days of rescuing damsels in distress were over. Done. In the rearview mirror.

Because, no matter what happened, he would never, ever, *ever* jump in and rescue a woman again.

Chapter Four

By the time Libby got to the hospital that morning, Devin already had visitors, since his parents and sister had flown in from Sioux Falls late the night before. It was a complete reversal from their usual holiday plans, when Libby and Devin would fly north to be with his family and enjoy a white Christmas.

Devin's dad smiled up at her from the chair in the corner, and his teary-eyed mom and sister nodded to her from their own chairs on either side of the bed. His mom held one of Devin's limp hands, while his sister grasped a huge bunch of tissues and dabbed at a steady flow of tears. In contrast, Devin lay there silently with his eyes closed, completely incoherent.

Of course, Libby had a pretty good idea of the shock his family must be feeling, after seeing how quickly Devin had gone downhill. He barely even looked like the man he had once been. He had lost so much weight, and his cheeks were completely sunken in. Not to mention, the healthy, vibrant color of his skin had been replaced by a waxy, yellowish tone. At least her own parents, who lived but a few hours away, had been able to visit more often. So they'd witnessed the decline in shorter increments. Though just barely.

Now Libby merely stood there for a moment or two, taking in the scene, one that quickly turned into the strangest reunion she'd ever been through. Normally she would have jumped right in and welcomed Devin's family to town, gushing over how glad she was to see them. But this time she held back for a few seconds, and they did, too, since everyone was well aware of what this visit signified.

It was the beginning of the end.

Especially since they weren't even staying with her. Instead, they had booked a hotel in the Texas Medical Center, to be closer to Devin.

So rather than the usual "How was your flight" and "Merry Christmas" kind of talk, there were quiet, tearful hugs all around.

"How are you holding up?" Devin's dad finally asked her, running his hand through his short, salt-and-pepper hair.

"The best I can," she said as she took the chair he offered. "I don't think Devin knows we're here anymore," she added in a whisper.

"Oh, honey," said Devin's mom as she reached for Libby's hand. "I'm so sorry you have to go through all this. At your age. I can't believe how fast the cancer took his body."

Libby looked into her dark eyes that were surrounded by dark circles, her chestnut hair pulled back into a slipshod ponytail. A far cry from her usual polished appearance.

"I can't believe it, either," Libby told her. "And I'm sorry you have to go through it, too. Devin loves you all so much."

"And he loves you, too, Libby," Devin's dad added. "He did from the moment the two of you met."

Which made Libby smile, at least for a couple of seconds.

And so the morning went, with everyone quietly talking of good times with Devin. While they wept and while they waited. They waited for those brief moments when Devin would open his eyes and seem to know that Libby and his family were there. And they waited for any updates from the doctor. And of course, they also waited for the inevitable.

Around one o'clock, Devin's dad stood up and stretched. "Anyone up for some lunch?"

When Devin's mom and sister waved him off, he turned to Libby. "Come on, dear daughter-in-law. You've been here since day one. Why don't you take a break? Come with me for a few hours. I hate to eat alone. And you look like you could use some food."

Libby was about to wave him off, too, since she wasn't the least bit hungry. But she also knew how much he was suffering, and the idea of him eating by himself tugged at her heart.

"I'd love to go," she lied. "Lunch sounds wonderful."

So they said quick goodbyes and headed for the elevator, passing several Christmas trees as they walked through the lobby. Symbols of the season that were strangely comforting and yet surprisingly painful all at the same time. They found a quaint café near the hospital that specialized in gourmet burgers, and they ate in companionable silence, lost in their individual thoughts and yet joined together in their grief. Much like the rest of the people in the large room that appeared to be filled with families and loved ones of patients, judging from the tired and anxious faces around them. No doubt these people were awaiting the outcome of some medical procedure or diagnosis. Or watching the life of a loved one slowly fade away, like Libby and her father-in-law had been doing.

"Devin would hate all this sadness," her father-in-law murmured, shaking his head. "With everyone crying and grieving. Even in the worst of times, he managed to find some joy. Like he was allergic to misery and refused to experience it. He raised the spirits of everyone around him."

Libby nodded and bit into her burger. "That's Devin, for sure. He's always had such a good attitude, even after we got the bad news. He refused to be down. It's like he isn't even afraid to, well, go . . ."

"Go on? To Heaven?" her father-in-law supplied.

"Yes," Libby said, just above a whisper. "And if anyone would be going to Heaven, it would be Devin."

"I have no doubt he will. You know he called everyone as soon as he got the diagnosis and told them what was coming. And that he didn't want anyone to be sad."

Libby nodded. "I know. He said he'd had a great life, even if it was short."

Her father-in-law ate a couple of fries. "And you played a very big part in that, Libby. He also wanted to make sure you were taken care of. He told people to watch over you."

Libby stared into her iced tea. "I believe it. He's that kind of a guy. It's hard to even think about going on without him. How about you and the rest of the family?"

"It's going to be a long road. Especially for my wife. I don't think the loss of a child is something you ever completely get over."

"I can imagine. I'm losing my husband, and I'm not sure I'll ever get over this myself."

"You know we're here for you," he told her. "Whatever you need. We won't stop being your family."

"Thanks," she said, knowing that he meant it.

When they had finished their lunch, he spotted an antique mall across the street. "Mind if we take a look? I think a little distraction might do us good."

"Sure," Libby answered. "Devin always loved going into places like that. Most of our furniture is refinished and repurposed."

He laughed. "Ah, yes, Devin's 'finds.' Proof that one man's trash is another man's treasure."

Something that made Libby laugh in return. "He was always so excited whenever he found something. He could see the beauty in a piece, though I couldn't. Not at first anyway. But I always loved the finished product."

Her father-in-law smiled, and together they walked into the store. Right away Libby noticed the richness of the smells that filled the huge ground floor of the building. A combination of furniture oil and perfume popular in another era. It was a place full of things that had belonged to people who had lived their lives and had already gone on. A place full of history and somebody's memories.

Libby grabbed a shopping basket while her father-in-law chatted with the clerks at the front counter. It was only a matter of seconds before they were deep in conversation.

And while they talked, Libby began to wander the aisles, from booth to booth, her eyes darting from a 1940s china hutch to a walnut secretary desk. And from century-old books to 1920s toys.

She was halfway up the first aisle when something caught

her eye, drawing her in like a magnet. Yet for the life of her, she couldn't explain her reaction, and she couldn't seem to turn away. So she stepped into the booth for a closer look.

Before her was a large, plastic container full of vintage rhinestone jewelry. All in very nice condition and all sparkling up at her. On a whim, she grabbed the pieces that stood out to her the most and put them in her basket. And that's when an idea started to take root in her mind, and she moved on to a container full of old silverware. She picked out a variety of forks and teaspoons and added them to her basket, too. Then she spotted some beautiful mother-of-pearl buttons and other shiny trinkets in other plastic containers. She picked out a bunch and put them with the rest of the stuff she'd already gathered.

Her father-in-law joined her and nodded to her basketful of things. "Looks like you've got some 'finds' of your own. Are you working on a project?"

She crinkled her brow. "I don't know . . . maybe. An idea popped into my head, and I can't seem to let it go. Have you ever made a lamp?"

"No, I can't say that I have. But I think you just need a base and something upright that you can run a cord through and hold a socket. Like these old thread bobbins right here," he said, pointing to a collection of round, hollowed-out wooden spindles that ranged from about twelve to eighteen inches in length.

"These look great," Libby murmured as she grabbed up a bunch of the bobbins.

Her father-in-law glanced around the booth. "Hardware stores do sell lamp kits that will have everything you need for the electrical part. And they're easy to use."

Libby nodded. "I bought one this morning. To fix my old lamp. But making a new lamp might be kind of fun."

"Sounds interesting," he told her as they continued to wander from booth to booth, and Libby continued to add things to first one basket and then to a second basket that her father-in-law brought her.

By the time they checked out, Libby left with a box full of stuff and a brain that was absolutely buzzing with possibilities.

Her father-in-law offered to carry the box for her when they left the store. "If you need any help building your lamp, or with anything else, don't hesitate to ask. You're still my daughter-in-law. Devin couldn't have found a better person than you to join our family."

Once again, Libby felt tears stinging at the back of her eyes. "That's so sweet of you to say. Thank you so much. And if you guys need anything, be sure to let me know. Because I know you're going through the same stuff that I am."

He sighed. "We are. And like it or not, we've got to figure out a way to cope."

Libby paused at the crosswalk as they headed for her car. "That's something I haven't figure out. At all. I'm not sure how to cope right now."

He rattled the box full of stuff as they crossed the street. "But you've got a new project. And oddly enough, it might be a very good way to deal with things. Lots of people pour their heart and soul into new projects or creations when they're grieving. It can really help. And don't forget, everyone grieves in their own way. There is no right or wrong way, though I'm sure plenty of people will tell you what you're supposed to think and feel. And when."

"That's the same thing they told us in my grief group."

"Yup. And we have to realize that it's okay to go on living, even after our loved one has passed on. You know, Libby, you're still very young. You may get remarried someday. And it's okay if you do."

Libby shook her head. "I can't even imagine it. I just can't. To tell you the truth, I don't see much of a future for me at all."

Chapter Five

That afternoon, Caleb headed to one of the houses that he had under construction, a project that was his and his alone, one that his father and brothers weren't involved with at all. And though the house only had studs for walls and not a bit of drywall yet, and it was only roughed in where the plumbing fixtures would be attached before long, it was exactly the kind of home that Caleb wanted for his own one day. The style was his favorite—a modern version of the Colonial Revival period homes from the 1920s. Though in reality, the only modern things about the place were the kitchen and the bathrooms. Everything else that he had planned could've easily belonged in a bygone era. A wide curving staircase. Architectural embellishments and niches. Detailed woodwork with extra wide baseboards and crown molding. Tray ceilings and coffered ceilings.

"God is in the details," he murmured aloud as he walked through the foyer.

And while the house was far from finished, in his mind's eye, Caleb could already picture what it would look like when it was completed. Yet even at this stage, just entering the soon-to-be home made him happy. Building houses like this one was a crowning achievement.

"It should be," he said with a chuckle, "considering how

much *crown* molding that will be going into the place."

More than anything, he loved building houses like this one, places that were absolutely loaded with character. Rather than the cookie-cutter homes that plenty of people requested after watching home remodeling shows on TV. Most of which featured houses that were done according to the latest trend—minimalism.

And as far as Caleb was concerned, minimalism needed to be *minimized*. Not to mention, all those plain white or gray walls were way overrated and did nothing but create a sense of coldness.

Instead of the kind of warmth that a home should have.

No, he'd take a nice aged yellow or buttercream paint color, or even a relaxing sage green, any day of the week. Something that would emphasize all that white woodwork and make it pop, instead of blending in with all-white walls.

Thankfully, the customers who'd hired him as their general contractor to build this house shared his vision. In fact, working with this couple, Mitch and Alyssa Van Sant, had been a dream come true. And while he'd been building this home for their family, they'd practically become like family to him. Something that wasn't all that common in the construction industry.

Now he pictured their four kids sliding down the banister next to a twelve-foot Christmas tree in the huge foyer. A wonderful family in a wonderful home. More than anything, he hoped to build a house just like this one for a family of his own someday. Along with the love of his life.

But that would probably never happen, not with his track record when it came to women. And not after this fiasco with Fallon. Apparently, he didn't know how to have a normal, healthy relationship. All he knew how to do was rescue, and the women he rescued were rats.

So for now, the most he could hope for was to simply enjoy the home he was building for another family.

He grabbed his phone from his pocket and started to make his rounds. He checked all the progress on the house, making sure his subcontractors had done a good job. He started with the first floor and then climbed the bare wooden stairs to the second floor. Along the way, he snapped a few pictures here and there of things he intended to look into later.

He was just about finished when he heard a strange noise coming from the attic. That's when his heart started to pound. He had been so meticulous when it came to overseeing this project and he'd personally inspected every piece of equipment that had gone into the house. So how could there possibly be a strange noise coming from . . . well, anywhere?

He pulled down the attic stairs to check it out, and finally heard the sound a little bit clearer. It was kind of high-pitched and squeaky, and it sounded like . . . meowing?

He quickly climbed the steps until he was eye-level with the floor. Only to be greeted by a fuzzy, little face.

Of a tiny, orange kitten.

A very *demanding* little, orange kitten.

"What are you doing up here, buddy?" he asked in pure astonishment. "And where did you come from?"

After all, there were no houses nearby. And the kitten was too little to have made it all the way from the nearest home, which was a couple of miles away. That meant the tiny creature must be lost. And it probably didn't belong to anyone.

Not only that, but it would've been quite a climb for the kitten to even get up into the attic of the big house. Still, it must have managed it somehow, probably while the front door was open and the heater was being installed in the attic. But regardless of how the kitten had gotten there, one thing was for sure, it would never survive if Caleb just left it there. So he picked up the tiny, longhaired feline and tucked it into his button-down shirt.

Naturally, Caleb's first thought was that the kitten might be dehydrated. And hungry. So he locked up the house in progress and took the little creature to his truck.

Then he poured some water from his water bottle into the lid of his coffee container and set it on the passenger seat next to the kitten. Right away, the little one started to lap it up.

"Well, I guess you're old enough to be away from your mama," Caleb murmured as he tore off a bit of his breakfast sandwich and gave the kitten a bite of sausage.

The kitten had a little trouble eating it at first, but after a few tentative nibbles, the tiny cat seemed to get the hang of it in a hurry. It polished off the piece that Caleb had set down and then latched onto his arm and went for more.

"Hungry little guy, aren't you?" Caleb said with a laugh as he tore off a few more small pieces and set them on the seat. "I hope you weren't stuck up there too long."

But the kitten was too busy eating to respond at all.

"I wonder if you're a boy or a girl?" he asked as he checked the kitten's hind end. "A girl, it would appear."

He rolled his eyes. "Oh, great . . . here I am, swearing that I'll never rescue another female again, and I didn't even make it two hours. Plus, I don't even like cats that much. So what am I going to do with you?"

Thankfully, he remembered the veterinary hospital about five miles down the road. "I'll drop you off there, little one. I'm sure they can find a good home for you."

So he jumped in his truck and drove straight to the vet center. He walked in, carrying the little cat in the palm of his hand, and was surprised to find the place was packed.

The redheaded receptionist behind the counter had a phone receiver squeezed between her shoulder and her ear, and she looked at Caleb warily. "Do you have an appointment, sir?"

"Umm . . . no," he answered. "I just found this little kitten and I can't keep her. I wondered if I could drop her off here, and maybe you know someone who could take her."

That's when the receptionist let the phone drop. "Are you kidding me right now? Do you know how many people out there want to dump off a cat or kitten they found somewhere?"

He raised a brow. "No, ma'am, I'm afraid I have no idea."

Her dark eyebrows formed a deep *V* as she continued to stare at him. "Well, let me tell you, there are a lot. Probably more than a big, dumb guy like you can count."

He gritted his teeth. "No need to be rude, ma'am. I merely asked a simple question."

"Then let me give you a simple answer. When it comes to cats and kittens, we are full up. Is there some reason you can't take that kitten in and give it a home?"

He frowned at her. "I work all day."

She put her hands on her hips. "Don't we all. Now tell me,

are you allergic to cats?"

"No."

"Do you have an apartment that won't allow pets?"

"No. I own my own home."

"Then congratulations. You just found your new best friend. Here's a list of all the things you'll need to get for her." Before Caleb could respond, she pulled a sheet of paper from a folder and shoved it at him.

He looked at her sideways. "Wait a minute. I know we have a city shelter. I'll just take this kitten there."

Now her eyebrows went straight up her forehead. "Fine, if you want it to be killed. Because the shelter is full up, too, and if you take that adorable kitten there, it will probably be euthanized."

With that, the little cat started to cry. At the top of its little lungs.

"What do you mean, 'euthanized?'" Caleb demanded.

"*Euthanized*. . . as in put to sleep. Because they don't have room for all the cats and kittens who are brought in there on a daily basis. So they euthanize whole bunches of them every week."

"That's horrible," Caleb said, chomping on his words, while the kitten continued to get more upset.

"Tell me about it."

Realizing that he was in a battle he wasn't going to win, Caleb grabbed the supply list she'd given him and stomped off, tossing a sarcastic "Thank you, ma'am" over his shoulder as he left. Though he hadn't succeeded when it came to unloading the tiny kitten, one thing was for sure—nobody was going to be euthanizing it. Not on his watch.

Which meant that, like it or not, he now had a cat.

Something that seemed to suit the new kitten just fine. Because she started to purr up at him like he was the greatest being on the planet.

"Well, kiddo, I guess it's just you and me," he said as he drove to the nearest pet supply store.

A gray-haired saleslady greeted him with a smile and reached out to pet the kitten. "It looks like you have a new baby."

Baby?

That's when he suddenly realized how ridiculous he probably looked, being such a huge guy holding such a tiny pet. No doubt, a German Shepherd or a Bull Mastiff would've fit him better.

But a kitten who fit in the palm of his hand? Not hardly. And now as the lady led him around the store, smiling all the way and gathering everything on his list, he could hardly believe that one little cat could need such a big cart full of stuff. Including a giant climbing tree.

Finally, the lady turned to him, her smile never dipping. "She's a lucky cat to have such a wonderful pet dad."

Pet . . . dad?

For a moment, he almost started to hyperventilate.

"Now I'll need to get her identification tag printed," the woman went on. "What is this little one's name?"

Which was when Caleb's mind went completely blank. "I dunno. I haven't named her yet."

"Well, you do need to give her a name."

"Wow, I have no idea what to call her . . . Say, what's *your* name?" he asked, glancing at the woman's name tag.

"My name is Ginger," the woman replied.

"Ginger," Caleb repeated. "Sounds good. I like it. I'm going to call this cat Ginger."

"Oh, very nice," the woman said, clearly flattered.

Then she plugged some letters into a machine, along with Caleb's phone number, and had them printed on the heart-shaped tag.

When it finished printing, she pointed to some collars. "What color of collar would you like for Ginger?"

Again, Caleb was at a loss. "I don't know. What would you suggest?"

"Something glamorous for this little girl. Something sparkly, I'd say," she answered, pulling a silver, rhinestone collar from the rack. Then she attached the newly printed tag to the collar and put it around the kitten's neck. "There you go, sir. Enjoy your new cat. You can check out at one of the registers in the front."

"Thank you, ma'am," Caleb managed to say, remembering

his manners at the last minute.

Still in shock over it all, he took Ginger the cat and all her stuff and headed for a register. As he watched the thin, young man ring up his purchases, he began to get more and more nervous.

Finally, the cashier turned to him and said, "That'll be six-hundred and eighty-seven dollars, sir."

Now Caleb really did start to hyperventilate. "Six-hundred and . . . say what?"

This time the cashier simply pointed to the amount on the screen.

"All for a kitten?" Caleb gasped.

The young man just nodded silently while Caleb got out his credit card.

Then he tucked the kitten inside his shirt again and walked out of the store with all the supplies. "So, not only do I rescue another female, but she also manages to bilk me for big bucks," he said out loud. "I will *never* learn."

He put the giant climbing tree in the bed of his truck and set the rest of the stuff on the back seat. Then he pulled the small litter box from a bag and set in on a rear floor mat. He poured in some kitty litter and set the tiny cat on top. She glanced up at him with great adoring eyes, before she started to dig in the litter and proceeded to "do her business." Exactly like the lady at the store told him she would do.

The odor immediately filled the truck.

"Whew, little cat. For something so tiny, you sure pack a wallop in the potty department," he said, feeling oddly conscious of the language he was using.

Like a father being careful what he said around his kids. Which didn't make any sense, considering the little cat had no idea what he was *actually* saying.

Then Caleb used his newly purchased pooper-scooper and scooped out clumps from the litter and dropped them in a bag. He put the kitten back inside his shirt and deposited the bag in a nearby trashcan.

Next, he pulled out the soft-sided pet carrier that he'd just purchased and carefully set the kitten inside. He put the carrier on the passenger seat before getting in and driving out of the parking lot.

Right away, Ginger started to cry with the voice of a cat ten times her size.

That's when Caleb rolled his eyes and hit the brakes. "I can't believe this. Even if it's only a cat who's crying, all that crying still gets to me. I really am a sap."

He unzipped the pet carrier and put the kitten back inside his shirt once more.

Ginger immediately started to purr and cuddled up to him. He was halfway to the design center for MacKnight and Sons Custom Homes when he heard the kitten let out a heaving breath, which meant she'd fallen fast asleep. If only he could do the same, considering he was on his way to a meeting with his father and his brothers. To fill them in on his situation with Fallon.

Something he dreaded with every fiber of his being.

Even so, he knew he needed to step up to the plate and get it over with.

So he took a few deep breaths before he walked into the beautifully appointed conference room with Ginger still tucked in his shirt. After all, he couldn't exactly leave her in his truck, could he?

He was immediately met with jokes and jabs about his kitten. His three brothers, two older and one younger, all looked so much alike that it was obvious they were from the same family. And while Caleb shared their size and dark hair and eyes, he was the only clean-shaven one of the bunch, aside from his father.

Caleb was also the only one who wasn't laughing as his brothers teased him about Ginger, and his father just smiled and shook his head. Normally, Caleb would have given as good as he got, but not today.

And of course, the entire mood of the room changed once Caleb got down to business.

"Okay," he started, "I've got something really bad to tell you about, and since I don't know how to say it to make it sound any better, I'm just going to come out and say it."

His brother, Joshua, who was only a few years older than Caleb, rolled his eyes. "Now what did you do?"

Caleb cringed. "I stepped in a big mess, that's what. A very big mess. And I think you need to know what happened."

With all eyes on him, he told them the whole story about Fallon and her threat to extort him. His brothers stared in shock and anger, while his father sat stone-faced.

Caleb finished his tale with an apology, along with, "I think I'll just pay her off and make this all go away."

And that's when his oldest brother, Jacob, let him have it. "Of all the stupid, moronic things you've ever done!" he yelled. "We told you that girl was bad news!"

But he had barely gotten the words out when Ginger started to cry and howl and carry on so loudly that Caleb had to pull her out of his shirt and cuddle her in his arms to calm her down.

"Yes, I know," Caleb said in a loud whisper. "I messed up. Big-time. And I don't blame you for being upset. But don't upset Ginger. Say what you've gotta say but keep your voice down."

For a moment, Caleb's brothers just stared at him with their mouths wide open and laser beams practically shooting from their eyes.

"You're worried about upsetting a kitten?" Joshua yelled in a loud, furious whisper. "What about us?"

Caleb furrowed his dark brow. "Do you want her crying like that?" he whispered back. "Believe me, she doesn't stop."

"That's because you're spoiling her," his younger brother, Luke, put in, also whispering. "Here, let me hold her."

Just as he reached over to take Ginger, she looked up at him with those same adoring eyes and gave him a soft, little meow. "Aww . . ." he murmured as he held the tiny cat with one hand and cuddled her close.

She gave him a kiss on his bearded chin and snuggled in tight.

"Let's get back to Fallon," Joshua hollered in the same loud whisper. "Why didn't you listen to us? We told you that woman was going to cause problems."

"Believe me, I wish I had listened," Caleb went on. "I just didn't see what she was really like until it was too late."

"Well, we could tell something wasn't right," Jacob

whispered sternly as he took Ginger from his brother and held her next to his shoulder, like he'd held all three of his children when they were babies. "The thing is, Caleb, you're not the only one who's being hurt by this nightmare."

"I know," Caleb said as he hung his head. "Believe me, I know. I couldn't be more sorry."

"When does she expect this money?" Luke asked, still whispering.

"There isn't a definite date," Caleb said with a sigh. "I took Mr. Ritchie's advice, and I stalled her. I used the holidays as an excuse. I told her I'd be in touch a couple of days after Christmas."

"But she's not going to wait forever," Joshua said through clenched teeth.

And so it went, until Caleb's father finally raised his hand. "That's enough," he said quietly.

All the brothers instantly obeyed.

"Something is really odd here," Caleb's father said as he reached for Ginger and took her from Jacob. "This is much more than a love affair gone wrong. I met this girl, Fallon O'Malley, and she seemed way too slick as far as I was concerned. She is a very pretty girl, and I think she knows how to use that. She could turn on the charm when she needed to, and my guess is that she's a first-class manipulator. But people don't get to be that good without some practice. Frankly, I think we should take Royce Ritchie's advice and meet with the private eye."

Without speaking, Caleb simply nodded his agreement.

"And one more thing," his dad added. "What's been said in this room stays in this room. We aren't going to tell your mom just yet. I do not want Christmas to be ruined for her. Or any of your wives or kids. Understood?"

"Understood," all four brothers said together.

"And in the future, Caleb," Joshua added, "don't date a woman if we notice something's wrong."

That's when Caleb let out a sad laugh. "You're assuming that I will *ever* date again. As far as I'm concerned, I'm done with dating. I don't have a future. Not when it comes to relationships anyway. For a guy like me, there is no hope."

"For I know the plans I have for you,' declares the Lord, 'plans to prosper you and not to harm you, plans to give you a future and a hope.'" (Jeremiah 29:11, NIV)

Chapter Six

That evening, Libby left the hospital a little earlier than usual, to give Devin's family some time alone with him. And a chance to privately say their goodbyes.

"We'll call if anything happens," his mom had assured her with a hug.

Then Libby drove home on autopilot. Yet instead of being overwhelmed by her usual swirl of emotions, this time she only felt numb. Spent. She headed for a fast-food drive-thru and ordered a chicken sandwich and fries, more out of habit than actual hunger. And honestly, she wasn't even sure if she'd eat half of it. The smell filled her car and didn't whet her appetite one little bit. She turned back onto the main road and was just about to drive past Mr. Ritchie's hardware store, when an idea suddenly sparked in her mind. So she made a quick turn and pulled into the parking lot. She raced into the store, and amazingly, made it inside about ten minutes before closing time.

"You're back," Mr. Ritchie said with a kind smile. "Rough

day at the hospital? Then again, that goes without saying, doesn't it? Because they're all rough days."

"Very," she told him. "But thanks for asking anyway. It helps to know that people care about all this."

Mr. Ritchie nodded. "I know exactly what you mean. There may not be a thing they can do, but it still helps to know they're thinking of you. So what brings you in tonight?"

"Well . . ." she started to say, and then hesitated, since she wasn't entirely sure how to explain what she wanted. "I was wondering if you could cut some wood for me."

His eyes registered his surprise. "Most certainly, young lady. What kind of wood, and what are the measurements?"

"Hmmm . . . I don't know for sure, but I need something about this big," she said, demonstrating with her hands. "I've got an idea for a lamp."

"Okay, maybe you could draw a diagram of what you're thinking, and we can go from there," he suggested, handing her a sketchpad.

And so Libby did. Still on autopilot, she just let her fingers do the work. She drew and sketched until she thought she had a pretty good depiction of what she wanted to build.

"So you're going to need a base to attach to a big bobbin. Have you ever used a cordless drill before?"

Libby nodded. "Uh-huh. My husband showed me how to use his."

"Okay, then you'll need to drill holes and attach screws here and here," he explained as he pointed to her diagram. "And you'll need to drill a hole back here, to thread the lamp cord through."

"I can do that," she told him.

"And since it appears that you plan to cover the bobbin with burlap, you'll need a good adhesive for attaching it to the spindle. And then to attach all your things to the burlap. You'll also need some sandpaper to sand the wood base, and you might even consider a polyurethane or paint just to protect it."

And on it went, with Mr. Ritchie giving her instructions and suggestions. Then while he went off to cut her wood pieces, she gathered the other things she was going to need. Once she'd gotten all her supplies, she left the store feeling a sensation that she hadn't felt in a long time—anticipation. She actually had something to look forward to. It may have only been a small lamp project, but it was still something fun and creative. And though she probably should've simply fixed the lamp she already had, somehow, for some reason, she needed this new project.

But first things first. As soon as she got home, she set up the remote-control plug-ins like Mr. Ritchie had instructed her that morning. With a lot of tugging, and by really putting her back into it, she managed to pull her bed away from the wall. Just enough so she could attach the first plug-in to the wall socket, and then plug in her bedside lamp. Once that was in place, she tested the ON and OFF buttons on the remote control a few times. It all worked perfectly.

Smiling, she sat on the floor near the foot of the bed and used her legs to shove the bed back into place again. Then she plugged in four other lamps in various rooms of her small, ranch-style home, using the rest of the plug-ins. As before, she tested them out by hitting the ON buttons for all five of the lamps. Everything went on, just like it was supposed to. Then, using the OFF buttons, she turned off each lamp, one at a time. Again, the lamps reacted exactly like they should have. And just to make sure everything was working, she clicked each lamp on and off, and watched as the lamps did exactly what she'd set them up to do.

When she was done, she left the remote control on her bedside table. "There, no more lights going on unless I turn them on," she said to the empty room.

For a moment, she glanced at her bedside lamp, feeling an odd sense of fondness, like she was looking at an old friend.

I must be worse off than I realized, she told herself, rolling her eyes.

She immediately remembered something she'd learned in her grief group. That she should expect the unexpected, and that a person might not act like they normally would.

"Well, I'd say this counts," she said with a laugh.

But she'd barely spoken the words when thoughts of Devin came into her mind. She could practically envision him saying his usual, "It's not so bad. Now quit moping and get your fanny in gear." With an added, "Get to work making that lamp you've been thinking about all afternoon."

The thought of it made her laugh while tears rolled down her cheeks. Still, it was enough to spur her on, and she did exactly what she knew he would have encouraged her to do. She immediately wiped her tears and headed to the garage for Devin's toolbox.

"Use a drop cloth," she knew he would have said next. "Don't you dare ruin that kitchen table I spent a week refinishing."

So she covered the huge table with a drop cloth. Leaving room to work in the center, she spread out the supplies she'd gotten from Mr. Ritchie's store and the box full of "finds" from the antique store around the edges.

Then she got to work on her new project. She picked up the wood base that Mr. Ritchie had cut for her and quickly sanded it. As he had suggested, she applied a light finish, and while she waited for it to dry, she glued the edge of the burlap onto the length of one of the thread bobbins. Once it was dry, she wrapped layer after layer of the rough cloth tightly around it, until she had built the bobbin out a bit. After gluing the end, she set it aside to dry, too. Then she used Devin's pliers to pull the pins from the backs of some of the old jewelry she'd bought, so they'd be ready to be glued on. After that, she attached the bobbin to the base, drilled a hole in the bottom, and threaded the lamp cord through to the top. She attached the socket, ready for a bulb.

Then the fun part started. She simply picked up the first of her antique store items that caught her eye. She dabbed some epoxy on the back and then stuck it onto the burlap that was wrapped around the bobbin. She had to admit, it didn't look like much yet, but somehow, she knew it would by the time she was finished. So she picked out another piece and attached it, too. Then another and another. Once she got started, it seemed like she just couldn't stop. She kept on gluing and attaching. A piece here, another item there. Adjusting, adding, and building, as she created a colorful, sparkly collage all around the bobbin and the base of the lamp.

Amazingly, as she worked, the drama of her days left her,

while her mind stayed focused on her project, and she let her artistry take over. Once she had finished creating the lamp, she added some sparkly items to the brocade shade she'd bought earlier. Then she stood back and admired it all. She could hardly believe how beautiful it looked, and she was absolutely amazed by the work of her own hands.

It was the first joy she'd felt in quite some time. Not to mention, the first sense of satisfaction she'd had since her world had gone hurtling out of control, with Devin dying of a cancer that had metastasized in a heartbeat and did not respond to any treatment.

Exhausted, she left her work of art on the kitchen table to dry overnight and headed for bed.

Then she picked up the remote control on her bedside table and hit the OFF button for each of the lamps she'd plugged in earlier. One by one, the lamps went dark. Finally, she hit the OFF button for the plug-in that controlled her bedside lamp.

And it went off, exactly like it was supposed to.

"Tonight, I'll sleep like a normal person," she muttered as she leaned back and rested her head on the pillows.

And that's when she suddenly realized she was alone, all alone, there in the dark. And just like on the nights before her lamp had started to malfunction, her tears began to fall. And they would not stop.

"Oh, God, why? Why did this have to happen?" she sobbed into the darkness. "Where are you?"

But she'd barely reached for the box of tissues when her bedside light went on.

"Huh?"

Sniffling, she blew her nose before she grabbed the remote and hit the OFF button for her lamp. It went off, but suddenly she saw a light coming from down the hallway, probably from the lamp in her family room that she'd plugged in earlier.

So she hit the OFF button for that lamp and it went off right away. But then another light from the same vicinity immediately lit up.

"Wait a minute . . ." she muttered, jumping out of bed. "This isn't right."

She raced down the hallway to see the light in her home

office and her dining room was now on. So she used her remote to turn them off, only to realize her bedside lamp was now shining brightly.

Then she hit the button to turn it off, and while it immediately went dark, her hallway lamp went on.

And so it went, one light on and another one off. Sometimes two went on and one went off. She spent a good fifteen minutes just hitting buttons and trying to get all her lamps off at the same time.

Finally, when they were all on, except for her bedroom lamp, she laughed and hit the ON button for that lamp. That's when her bedside light went on, and the other four went off.

Despite herself, she couldn't help but laugh. Loudly. Her lamp fiasco wasn't something that was supposed to happen in real life. No, it was the kind of thing that only happened in a movie. A slapstick comedy.

"Okay, lamp, I give up. You win, once more," she said as she plodded off to bed.

She slipped under the covers and just stared at her bedside lamp for a moment, shaking her head. Then she rolled over and closed her eyes.

And fell fast asleep.

Chapter Seven

Never in his wildest dreams did Caleb ever think he'd be meeting with a private investigator. Not at his age. Though right about then, he felt a *whole* lot younger than his twenty-nine years. In fact, he felt more like a little kid, since his father had come to the meeting with him. Yeesh. If nothing else, at least he had some relief in knowing that his mother was still in the dark about this whole mess. Because his dad still insisted that they keep it quiet, so it wouldn't upset her, even though it was the day after Christmas. And like a dutiful son, Caleb went along with the plan.

Even so, it didn't help matters that he'd had no choice but to bring Ginger with him today, too. She was already so bonded to him that she cried incessantly whenever he headed out the door. And all that crying just tugged at his heart so badly that he couldn't help but go back and pick her up again. Oddly enough, they'd already fallen into a routine, of sorts. She rode around on his shoulder or tucked inside his shirt. She was fine either way, just so long as he didn't leave her alone.

So there he sat, with a tiny, sleeping kitten in the palm of his hand and his father sitting beside him, while Matt Doychek, the P.I., gave them the once-over from the other side of an antique desk.

A desk that went along with the rest of the furniture and

décor in his office, pieces that were mostly from the thirties and forties. Caleb's favorite era. Thanks to his grandparents, who taught him all about styles and elements from that time.

Apparently, the private eye sitting before them was also a fan of the forties. The fifty-something man was thin and muscular, with a military-style haircut. Caleb half expected him to plop a fedora on his head and wrangle his way into a trench coat at any moment. Because he had the man figured for being a big fan of *The Maltese Falcon*, and any other P.I. novel from that era.

Which suited Caleb just fine. Since he was a big fan himself.

Though he would have preferred to be sitting on the other side of the desk, instead of on the client's side.

Or rather, the victim's side.

Some big, tough guy he turned out to be.

Matt grinned at the kitten. "I see you brought a friend with you today."

Caleb sighed. "I found Ginger just a few days ago. Abandoned. And until I can find a good home for her, I can't leave her alone. She starts crying her heart out whenever I head for the door without her."

The P.I. gave him a knowing nod. "So you're a good guy. A hero type."

Caleb stared at his shoes. "Funny, but I used to think that was a good thing. My grandfather was a World War Two hero, and he was my hero, too. I grew up wanting to be just like him. Turns out it got me into trouble."

To which he almost expected the P.I. to respond with the famous Humphrey Bogart line, "I don't mind a reasonable amount of trouble."

Instead, Matt just shook his head and came back with, "Don't ever apologize for being a good guy. I'd still like to believe that good wins out over evil."

"Me, too," Caleb's dad agreed as he took Ginger and held her over his shoulder. "Though it's a different world now."

"Maybe," Matt said. "But people from the forties thought the same thing, with the rise of Hitler and the Third Reich. Did you know that authorities fully expected the U.S. mainland to be invaded by both Germany and Japan back in that day?"

"I'm sure that was the goal of the Axis forces," Caleb's dad put in quietly, now that Ginger was sound asleep.

"So there were bad people back then, too," Matt told them. "Which means we can always use heroes."

Somehow, his words made Caleb feel better.

"Speaking of heroes," Matt went on. "I see you were referred by Royce Ritchie. He's a great guy."

"The best," Caleb and his dad both replied at the same time.

Matt leaned back in his wooden, swivel chair. "So tell me your story in a nutshell. What brings you and Ginger and your father into my office today?"

Caleb let out a heaving sigh. "Well, here goes nothing," he began, before he gave a rundown of what had happened between him and Fallon.

To be honest, he expected Matt to be shocked by it all, but the P.I. hardly seemed fazed. "So you met a beautiful girl, started dating, and then after everything seemed perfect, things took a one-eighty. But I want you to think back for a minute. Did you ask her out or did she ask you out?"

Caleb did his best to recall the day when he'd met Fallon. "I asked her out. I think . . . I was with my brothers, eating lunch at the café down the street from our design center. We'd just had a meeting with a guy we thought was a prospective customer. But the meeting turned out to be a complete dud."

"How so?" Matt wanted to know.

"Usually, people have a lot of questions about our houses, but this guy had more questions about us," Caleb explained, with a quick glance at the ceiling. "In the end, we figured he wasn't a real customer at all. He was just some guy out looking for some information. Though who knew why."

Matt grabbed a notepad. "What was his name?"

"Logan . . . Logan Smith," Caleb told him.

Matt chuckled and wrote it down. "What'd'ya want to bet, that's a made-up name."

"I remember that guy," Caleb's dad put in. "He asked a lot of questions about our business. I even wondered if he might be an undercover IRS agent or something. He stood out from our usual customers. And I pretty much cut him off after he maneuvered his way around to asking personal questions."

"Such as?" Matt asked.

"He asked something casual like, 'Did y'all build homes for your own families?'" Caleb's dad responded. "Of course, Caleb's brothers and I said yes, since telling people that we happily live in our own custom homes can be a great sales tool."

"But I said no," Caleb went on. "Then I quickly explained it was because I was the only single guy in the bunch. And that I was late to join the company, since I spent time in the Army first."

"And this Logan guy zeroed in on that," Caleb's dad explained. "He wanted to know where Caleb had served and how he was adjusting to civilian life and all kinds of stuff. And sure, I realize we're very friendly here in Texas, but I don't think this guy was from Texas. His accent was off. Way off. Not only that, but I couldn't help but wonder why he booked an appointment and then only wanted to chat about other things."

"Stuff that had nothing to do with building houses," Matt mentioned.

Caleb's dad nodded while Ginger continued to sleep, still leaning against his shoulder. "That's right. And from that point on, he didn't seem interested in learning more about building a custom home."

"Can you describe the guy?" Matt asked.

"Yeah, I think so," Caleb said with a glance at his father. "He was quite a bit smaller than me, with reddish-brown hair, styled sort of scruffy. He had a scruffy beard, one that was a little thin yet. And he had dark blue eyes."

"Weird, angry-looking eyes," his father added. "The guy smiled a lot, but his eyes didn't show it."

Matt wrote some more in his notepad. "Then after you got suspicious about this supposed customer, you got rid of him, and you all went to lunch."

"All of us, but now that I think about it, I realize my brother Jacob wasn't with us," Caleb said. "He went home to have lunch with his wife and kids. And Dad didn't go, either, since he went off to have lunch with Mom."

"So it was just three brothers who went to lunch," Matt clarified. "Where was this Fallon? Was she there when you

47

went into the restaurant?"

Caleb shook his head. "No, I don't think so. I don't remember seeing her right off the bat. And believe me, I would have noticed. Because she's so pretty."

Matt raised an eyebrow. "Naturally pretty? Or 'she's-had-some-work-done' pretty?"

Caleb shrugged. "I'm not sure . . . Here, you take a look." He pulled up Fallon's picture on his phone and handed it to the P.I.

Matt whistled. "Salon highlights in her dark hair, veneers on her teeth, lips and nose done, forehead lifted."

"But why does that matter?" Caleb asked. "I think having work done is a personal choice. Especially if there's something that really bothers a person about their looks."

"It just depends," Matt said as he handed the phone back to Caleb, "on *why* she had things done to alter her appearance. It's one thing to do it for cosmetic purposes. It's another if she's trying to hide a previous identity, and she doesn't want to be recognized."

"Oh . . ." Caleb murmured.

"But back to the way you met," Matt went on. "I'm guessing it was at the restaurant. When did you first see her?"

Caleb thought back. "She walked past our table. A couple of times. Going to the bathroom, I think."

"Then what happened?" Matt asked.

Caleb looked at the ceiling, trying to recall the entire incident exactly as it happened. "She walked by again. That's when she spilled some iced tea on me."

The P.I. gave him a knowing nod. "I'll bet it made you jump up from your seat. And I'll bet she couldn't apologize enough. Plus, I'm guessing she already had a nice supply of napkins with her, and she made quite a show of trying to soak up the tea on your shirt. No doubt, while she had her hands on you."

"That's exactly what happened," Caleb told him. "Almost like she was giving me a back rub."

"Which most likely lulled you into a state of relaxation," Matt said. "And then I'll bet she told you she wanted to make it up to you, by buying you lunch."

"Dinner, actually," Caleb confirmed, with the memory

becoming more and more clear in his mind. "While she was trying to mop up the mess on my shirt, there was a little chitchat. She introduced herself, and then she got my name. After that, she insisted on making it up to me by buying me dinner. But in the end, I said that I would buy *her* dinner. Not only did I think she was sweet and pretty, but I didn't want her to feel bad for making such a clumsy mistake. So we got each other's numbers and made the date."

"How did it go?" Matt asked with a wry smile.

"*Fantastic*," Caleb said, emphasizing the word. "We had a wonderful time. So I asked her out again and again."

Matt leaned back in his chair. "And how about the conversation while you dated? I'll bet you've never had anyone compliment you so much in your entire life. I'll bet she only wanted to talk about your work, saying something about her work being so boring."

Caleb's mouth dropped open. "Yes, that's exactly what she did. How did you know? I always asked her about her job and her life, but now that I think about it, she always managed to steer the conversation back around to me."

"Which means you probably know very little about her, when you think about it," Matt concluded.

Caleb nodded. "It's true. And I remember eventually starting to feel like the relationship wasn't going anywhere. I couldn't put my finger on what was wrong exactly. Even though everything seemed perfect on the surface. But I just wasn't feeling it."

"And that's when the crying started," Matt interjected.

"Yup," Caleb told him, with a glance at Ginger who was snoring quietly. "And once that started, I felt sort of trapped. Like I was responsible for her and her feelings. And her life, for that matter."

Matt crossed his arms over his chest. "So those tears truly manipulated you."

"Oh, yeah," Caleb agreed.

Now his father jumped in. "But his brothers and I saw her turn them on and off. Like a spigot. And we saw her acting one way around Caleb and an entirely different way around us."

"Like she was trying to separate him from the herd, so to

speak," Matt added.

"And now she wants money," Caleb said quietly as he stared at his shoes.

"Which is probably all she was really after in the first place," Matt said. "She sounds like a skilled con artist."

"Yup, she does," Caleb muttered. "And I am such a moron for not spotting it right off the bat."

"That's how victims of these crooks usually end up feeling," Matt said matter-of-factly. "They're embarrassed and ashamed and they feel like it's all their fault. Like they should have seen what was going on, and not fallen for the scam. It can really shake a person's confidence, because they no longer trust their own perception to read or judge people."

"You've pegged it exactly," Caleb told him.

"That's why crimes like this are so underreported," the P.I. went on. "So it might surprise you to know that you're not alone. Tons of people get scammed every day. That's because these con artists are pros. They're experts at reading people and they know how to zero in on a target. They're criminals, pure and simple. Thankfully, you saw the light before you gave her any money."

"Saw the light," Caleb repeated as he dropped his head into his hands. "Oh, how I wish I'd seen the light sooner. Because I don't think I've ever felt so low in my whole life. But now what happens? What can we do about all this?"

"First, let's take a closer look at her," Matt told him. "I'd like to start with a thorough background check. Tell me, did you ever go to her place? Do you have an address for this girl?" Matt held his pen over his notepad.

"I always picked her up outside an apartment building, but I never went inside her actual apartment," Caleb explained. "She told me she was embarrassed about her place, after seeing the beautiful houses that I built. So she insisted on meeting me out front."

Matt shook his head. "Which means she probably doesn't even live there. Most likely, someone dropped her off there, or she drove over."

"I did see her car in the parking lot once," Caleb said. "I'm pretty sure it was hers, since I saw her drive it whenever she came to my place."

"Well, it's a start," Matt assured him. "Now I'll just follow her around a bit and see where she goes and what she does. So I'd like you to text her and ask her to meet you somewhere for lunch tomorrow. Somewhere public. Like a restaurant. And preferably a chain, where there's more than one location around the city."

"I've got just the place," Caleb said.

"Wait a minute," his dad interjected. "I don't think Caleb should be meeting her at all."

Matt shook his head. "He won't be. I just want her to think he is. So she'll show up and I can get eyes on her. Then I can follow her around and get her full information. But I will need him to go with me to point her out. He'll be staying in my truck the whole time."

"In that case, I'm okay with it," Caleb's dad agreed as Ginger yawned and stretched.

Caleb let out a long sigh. "I guess I am, too. I'll send the text."

"But one thing you should be aware of," Matt added carefully. "You may not like what you find out. My guess is, you'll need to brace yourself for the truth about her."

"Honestly, could it get any worse than it already is?" Caleb asked with a groan.

"Trust me," Matt told him. "It can get a whole lot worse. And I want you to be ready for it."

"All right," Caleb replied, wishing now, more than ever, that he'd never laid eyes on Fallon in the first place.

And needless to say, he wasn't exactly looking forward to it again.

Chapter Eight

Libby was still half asleep when she reached an arm over to Devin's side of the bed, just like she'd done hundreds of times over the past few years. But she jolted awake the second she realized the other side was empty. Then she started her day with the instant awareness of something she'd managed to forget while she was sleeping, that Devin was still dying and never coming home. She sighed and glanced over to see the sunshine seeping in around the slats of the blinds. As always, her bedside lamp was off. At least that made her smile for a moment.

She got out of bed and went through her morning routine on autopilot. But just before she left the house, she checked on the creation that she'd made the night before. It looked even prettier in the daylight. Excited to see it in action, she screwed in a light bulb and rolled the switch to the ON position.

"*Ooooh . . .*" was all she could say when she saw it lit up.

She could hardly believe her eyes. She'd made a lamp. All by herself. And a very pretty one at that.

She immediately reached for her phone and snapped off a few pictures. Okay, maybe a few *dozen* pictures, truth be told. Though the lamp probably wasn't everyone's cup of tea, it was certainly hers. And she couldn't stop looking at it.

On top of that, she had to fight the overwhelming urge to

make another lamp right then and there. That's when she realized there might be a downside to her newfound creativity—apparently, it was very addicting. Because she was already thinking of other lamps she wanted to make, and new ideas were running through her mind faster than she could type notes into her phone. Once she had them all down, she took a quick inventory of the things she had left over from her first project, to see what supplies she might need now. Though one thing was for sure—she was definitely going to need more lamp kits. And more wooden bases!

That meant her first stop of the morning would be at Mr. Ritchie's store.

He smiled when she walked in. "Nice to see you again, Libby. You're becoming my best customer. How did the lamp project go?"

"Wonderful, Mr. Ritchie. Absolutely wonderful. I loved putting that together."

"I'm glad to hear it," he told her. "Because it sounds like it made you happy. And if you don't mind a little advice from someone who's been in your shoes, it's important to take a break every now and then from all the sorrow and misery of grieving. Sometimes a good creative project is just what a person needs. Plenty of artists put all their emotions into their work, and it can really help a person deal with things."

"I can see that," she said quietly. "I think that's what I did last night."

"When a loved one is dying, we spend so much time taking care of them. But you've got to take care of yourself, too. Grieving can take such a toll on your mind and your health, and you've still got to go on," he told her. "But that's enough lecturing from me."

She smiled at the older man. "I really appreciate all your advice, Mr. Ritchie. It's helped so much. Dealing with Devin's situation has been, well . . ."

"I know," he said before she could finish. "I know just what you mean. And I'm hoping you took pictures of your new project."

"Yes, I took a bunch," she gushed. Then she quickly scrolled through her phone and pulled up the series of photos she'd taken of her lamp, complete with the lightbulb and decorated brocade shade.

Mr. Ritchie let out a low whistle. "That is a true work of art, young lady. I've never seen anything like it. So many beautiful details. And like they say, 'God is in the details.'"

"Thank you, Mr. Ritchie," she said, surprised at how pleased she felt having someone appreciate her work.

Especially since she'd never considered herself to be a real artist. Sure, she'd worked on plenty of flyers and ads for work, things that required graphic art skills. All on a computer. But she'd never actually built something from the ground up with her hands before. For some reason, it felt so much more satisfying.

"I've got a customer who would love a piece like this," Mr. Ritchie went on. "She's decorating an old Victorian home and she's been looking for a truly unique lamp. Are you, by chance, interested in selling it?"

For a moment or two, Libby was dumbfounded. The idea that someone might want to buy her lamp had never crossed her mind.

"Well. . . yes," she told him. "I can bring it by tomorrow. If she decides she wants it."

"Perfect," he said. "If you'll pass along your pictures, I'll show them to her and see what she thinks. But I already know what she's going to say. She's going to want this one and a second one, too. Recognizing, of course, that no two custom art lamps would ever be identical, since it probably depends on the kinds of items you can find for the collage part of it. But would you be willing to make another one if she wants a set?"

Once again, it was something that Libby hadn't even thought about. "Umm . . . sure. I can do that."

"Do you have any idea what kind of price you'd put on your lamp?"

She hesitated. "I don't even know where to start when it comes to pricing my work. What do you suggest?"

"Let's see . . ." he murmured as he stared at the pictures of the lamp again. "This piece would be one of a kind and *very* high-end. I could buy it for, say, three hundred dollars wholesale. Then I'd have to add my share and fees to resell it.

Does that sound reasonable to you?"

"Wow, that much for a lamp?" Libby gasped.

"Like this one, yes," he told her. "I've seen more expensive than that. In fact, that might even be a little underpriced. We could go higher if you like."

Libby waved him off. "No, no, that sounds good to me. In the meantime, whether you sell my lamp or not, I'm going to need more supplies. Probably a *lot* more supplies."

"Not a problem," Mr. Ritchie agreed cheerfully. "So it sounds like you're going to make more than just this second lamp?"

"Well . . ." Libby said, hesitating again, since everything seemed to be happening so fast. "I enjoyed making that lamp so much last night, that yes, I think I will make some more. Until I get it out of my system anyway."

"That's terrific," Mr. Ritchie told her. "I can give you a price break on those supplies." He pulled out a calculator and punched in some numbers, before he turned it around and showed it to Libby. "Does this sound fair?"

"Very," she told him.

About an hour later, Libby left Mr. Ritchie's store feeling oddly elated as she hauled a load of lamp kits and wooden-base pieces and much more out to her car. Including a bunch of lampshades in different colors. Mr. Ritchie went with her, bringing the overflow that she couldn't carry.

"I'll let you know what my customer says just as soon as I talk to her," he told her before she took off.

"Wow," Libby uttered to herself as she drove out of the parking lot. "I can hardly believe it. My first work of art and I might have already sold it."

From the little she knew of the art world, things like this just didn't happen.

Of course, the first person she wanted to tell was Devin, even if he had no idea what she was saying.

And so she did just that when she reached the hospital. This time, her in-laws left her alone with her husband while they took a break.

"I'm so amazed that I could actually make a lamp," Libby gushed to Devin's still form, while the equipment around him quietly whirred and beeped. "And a pretty one, too. I wish you could see it. I took pictures." Out of habit, she pulled up one of the photos on her phone and held it close to his face.

Much to her surprise, Devin opened his eyes. "The light, Libby. I saw it," he barely muttered.

"Yes," she said, squeezing his hand, excited to have him speak to her. "The light. I made a lamp."

"No, not that," he said, shaking his head. "I saw Nonna yesterday."

"Nonna?" she repeated. "Your grandmother? Devin, she passed away years ago."

Devin's face showed an expression of pure euphoria. "Nonna said it would be a good day to go flying. To the light."

"Okay . . ."

"I told her I would go," he whispered. "I told her I was ready. And I would go flying with her. So don't worry about me, Libs. I'm going to be fine. But you . . . you have to go on. You have to live your life. I want you to. I want you to be happy. I love you, Libs. You were the best wife a guy could ever ask for."

"I love you, too," she barely murmured before he nodded off again.

His words stayed with her that night when she went home, because she knew it had been goodbye. He believed he had seen his long-dead grandmother, and she had wanted him to go flying. Libby had a pretty good idea what that meant. She immediately started to sob, and yet through her tears, she also knew that he had been right—she did have to go on. She did have to live her life, even though his was ending. It was almost more than she could stand.

Without thinking, she spread all her new lamp-building supplies across the kitchen table, adding to the things that were already there from the night before. She also included more antique store items that she'd bought over lunch again today.

Then, while her heart ached for her husband, she started to create her second lamp. As she did, she cried, and she smiled as she relived so many memories that she and Devin had made together. Moments of joy and moments of sadness. Moments of discovery and moments of tradition. Their own special traditions, that they had decided on themselves. And it all came flashing back to her as she wrapped and glued and created. Fitting one piece into the next, and then another one into another spot.

And she decided she would just keep on making her lamps, until she had cried all the tears she needed to cry and relived all the memories she needed to relive.

Because, oddly enough, creating these lamps had suddenly become a lifeline for her. Lamps that would give off lovely, glowing light. Funny how light seemed to be having such a big impact on her life lately.

She didn't even balk when she turned her bedside lamp off later that night, and it refused to stay off. As it always did these days.

Instead, she just fell sound asleep, so she'd be ready to face the valleys of the coming days as she learned to navigate life on her own again.

Life without Devin.

Chapter Nine

Caleb gulped and stared out the windshield of Matt Doychek's truck. Funny, but even though the P.I.'s truck sat taller than most of the vehicles nearby, Caleb had to admit, it was still what someone could call "nondescript." *Completely* nondescript, as a matter of fact. In Texas, the truck blended in with all the other trucks in the parking lot. Plus, it was a charcoal gray that was nearly black, with just the right amount of road dust to make it nearly invisible and the last thing anyone would ever notice.

For a moment, Caleb almost had to laugh, considering he had once binge-watched *Magnum P.I.* with his dad. And when he compared the vehicle of a real-life P.I. to one of a fictitious, made-for-TV detective, well, they were night and day. Literally. Considering Magnum's red Ferrari stood out a mile, compared to Matt's truck that basically blended in with the asphalt.

Which meant they were free to sit there without being spotted as they waited for Fallon to show up. Of course, they'd gotten to the restaurant a good half hour ahead of time, so they could get into position in the lot next door and keep their eyes peeled.

But they'd barely arrived when Matt told Caleb to go take a selfie in front of the restaurant. "Make sure you look happy, like you're looking forward to seeing her."

Without asking why, Caleb went along with the idea.

Matt checked the photos once Caleb returned to the truck. He nodded his approval and handed Caleb's phone back to him. And then they sat there, waiting, with a perfect view of the front door. If nothing else, at least Caleb didn't have to worry about Ginger today. Thankfully, his dad had offered to take care of the little cat, to free Caleb up for this "stakeout."

Or whatever it was supposed to be called.

Matt pointed to the clock on his dashboard. "We'll give it ten minutes, and then I'll have you text her."

"Got it," Caleb said with a nod.

"Blue car at two o'clock," Matt murmured as he discreetly lifted a very compact pair of binoculars to his eyes. "Is that her?"

Caleb glanced in the direction that Matt had indicated, just in time to see Fallon's blue sedan pull in.

"Oh, yeah, that's her," Caleb said quietly as the car circled around the restaurant's parking lot.

Oddly enough, she passed by several open spots and kept on driving around.

"What's she doing?" Caleb wondered. "Looking for my truck?"

"Maybe," Matt responded. "But one way or another, she's checking things out. I'd say she doesn't trust you."

"That's weird. Considering she's the crook."

"And crooks are the most suspicious, distrustful people you could ever meet," Matt told him. "Probably because they compare themselves to everyone else, and they tend to believe other people are as dishonest as they are. As a result, they don't trust anyone."

"Must be an awful way to live."

"It's not the way I'd want to live," Matt said as Fallon finally pulled into a parking spot. "But you'd be surprised how much con artists enjoy what they do. They get a real thrill whenever they reel in a new mark. Like catching a prize fish. Though for them, it's more like winning the lottery."

"How bizarre," Caleb responded, keeping his eyes on Fallon's car. "I still can't believe someone can be that sweet and that much of a liar at the same time."

And frankly, Caleb didn't want to believe it, not even now. More than anything, he hoped and prayed that Fallon was simply a very disturbed and very misguided person. Instead of a con artist who was purposely trying to take advantage of him, like Matt and Mr. Ritchie and his father seemed to believe.

Yet for the life of him, he still couldn't see what they saw. Was he completely blind when it came to matters of the heart?

"Cut yourself some slack, kid," Matt told him, almost like he could read Caleb's mind. "People who con and steal for a living are really good at it. Like I said, you might want to brace yourself for the truth about her."

In response, the most Caleb could do was nod.

"Looks like she's texting someone," Matt relayed. "It might be you."

"Might be?" Caleb repeated.

Though he knew it wasn't him when he didn't receive a text within the next few minutes.

"Check out the other car that just pulled in," Matt said with a sly smile. "The black one."

"The one driving past Fallon's car . . . and pausing in front of hers?"

Matt raised an eyebrow. "That's the one. Did you catch the nod? It was subtle, but it was there."

"So . . . she's got an accomplice?"

"They often do. He can keep track of her, and he can provide a fast getaway. If she needs one."

Caleb's mouth dropped open. "But why? Does she think I'd try to hurt her?"

"I doubt it. But she might suspect a setup. Meaning, she might think you've already called the police. Or she could be nervous that you or your brothers might try to pull something, and she might not have a safe route to her car. This way, she's got someone waiting for her. Her partner can pull up and she can jump inside his car and be out of there."

And that's when it finally hit Caleb that Fallon's partner was a man. "Do you think that guy is her . . ."

"Boyfriend, probably," Matt supplied. "I doubt he's her husband. Marriage tends to leave a paper trail. By the way, did you notice something? She's not crying."

"No, she's not," Caleb said quietly, the reality starting to sink in. "It looks like she's still texting away. But apparently not to me."

"You've got that right," Matt agreed. "Though she does look up every now and then. Probably watching for you. I think it's time to send her a text."

Caleb took a deep breath. "Okay. What should I say?"

"Make it sound like you're a little annoyed. Ask her where she is. Tell her you're in the restaurant and you're waiting for her at a table."

So Caleb quickly typed in the message. "Got it. Went through."

A few seconds later, his phone went "*ping!*"

"She says she doesn't see my truck," Caleb relayed to Matt.

"Tell her you parked in the back. And you're waiting inside for her."

Caleb did just as he'd been told.

Seconds later, his phone pinged again, and he got another message. "Wow, listen to this," Caleb said. "She responded with, 'What's going on? Your truck isn't here. Is this some kind of a trick?'"

Matt shook his head. "Sneaky. She's testing you. Because neither she nor her accomplice have looked in the back. So send her a text that says, 'No. What's the holdup? I'm waiting here for you. You said you wanted money.'"

Once again, Caleb followed Matt's instructions.

But this time, Fallon didn't text back. Instead, she simply got out of her car and slammed the door.

That's when Matt smiled. "Be right back. If she texts again while I'm gone, tell her you're at a table in the back, on the right-hand side."

"Got it," Caleb responded.

"Keep your eyes on her partner," Matt told him as he handed his binoculars to Caleb.

Then he opened the door of the truck halfway and slipped outside.

Caleb put the binoculars to his eyes and watched as Fallon walked up to the restaurant. She turned once to glance at the man in the black car as Matt slipped around behind the rest of the cars. Caleb was amazed by the P.I.'s sleek movements, almost like a cat weaving its way around. And to top it off, Matt moved so quickly and so smoothly that he was barely even noticeable. He paused for a split second near the rear of Fallon's car and then slipped around closer to her accomplice's car. As he did, he was careful to stay in the man's blind spot.

Seconds later, Matt returned to the truck.

"That was quick," Caleb said.

"Just long enough to get a quick photo of each car and its license plate. Any signs that the guy in the black car saw me?"

"Not a one," Caleb told him. "He was busy watching Fallon walk into the restaurant."

"Good. Has she texted back?"

"Not yet."

"Then go ahead and send her another one," Matt said, taking the binoculars again. "Ask her where she is."

Caleb did as he was told while Matt started the truck.

Fallon's reply was immediate. "I'm here. Trying to find you! Where are you?"

"Ask her if she's at the right restaurant," Matt said with a grin. "The northwest location."

"Even though we're at the central location," Caleb said with a chuckle as he sent the next text.

Naturally, he got a quick reply in return. "I knew you were playing some kind of a trick," came Fallon's angry words. "You'll be sorry for this."

"Tell her you must have gotten your wires crossed," Matt instructed him. "Then tell her to stay put and you'll be there in twenty minutes."

So Caleb did. Then he and Matt watched as Fallon came stomping out of the restaurant, looking at her phone. She didn't bother to hide her frustration, and this time, gave an annoyed wave to her partner.

Minutes later, she drove her car out of the parking lot, followed by the man in the black car.

Then Matt put the truck in gear and took off after them, keeping a decent distance behind. "Keep your eyes on those cars," he told Caleb.

"Got it. Are we tailing them?"

"That's right, kid. Just like in the movies."

"Couldn't we just use a tracking device? Like stick one to the black car and then track him on a phone?"

Matt chuckled. "Nope. Unlike what you see in the movies, it would be highly illegal for us to do something like that. Not unless we owned the vehicle, or it had been parked in a public area."

"Oh."

"We're going to do this the old-fashioned way, kid. One that takes a lot of skill. And believe me, you're gonna love this," Matt added with a grin.

Great, Caleb thought, pretty sure he *wasn't* going to "love this" at all.

But apparently, this was his reward for trying to find the love of his life and daring to dream about being married and having a family and a dream house. Maybe even a dog. Instead, here he was, hanging out with a P.I. and tailing the guy who was the partner to the beautiful woman he once thought might become his wife. Fleeting as that idea may have been. Not only that, but instead of having a dog, he had a cat. Ginger. A tiny, orange kitten who managed to manipulate him with her conniptions.

Somewhere or another, he had *really* taken a wrong turn.

Though clearly Matt was taking all the correct turns as he effortlessly followed the black car from a distance, while it followed Fallon's car more closely. From what Caleb could tell, Matt's ploy had worked, and these two had let down their guard.

Before long, the two cars took the on-ramp to the I-45. So Matt did the same. That's when things got a little dicier, since the interstate was packed. As usual.

"Keep an eye on the black car," Matt told Caleb, passing him the binoculars. "Just in case they lose me."

But the fact was, they didn't. And that's when Matt's skills really started to shine. Because he smoothly switched lanes and passed other vehicles to keep track of both the black car and Fallon's car. Sometimes he even seemed to hide behind a big truck for a bit, before popping out and jumping into a different lane.

63

"Those two may have Texas plates, but I don't think they're from around here," Matt said, keeping his eyes on the road. "They sure don't drive like it. But as soon as I get an address, I'll have a good jump on finding out their real identities. Assuming the ones they're using now are fake. Either way, I'll run complete background checks on them and see what I find out."

"I'll be looking forward to it," Caleb told him. "Sort of."

"I hear ya, kid," Matt said, his mouth forming a grim line. "More than anything, I hate to give bad news to a good guy like you. So I hope the news I have when I'm done investigating is good. But I don't think it's likely."

Caleb sighed. "I don't think so, either."

Matt continued to follow the two cars as they drove past the downtown area, and then headed a long way south. Finally, Fallon's blue car and the black car aimed for an off-ramp. Without signaling, of course.

As they each took the ramp, Matt eased his foot off the gas and let his truck fall back. Then he carefully made his way over to the same ramp, allowing other cars to jump in front of his truck.

Caleb put the binoculars to his eyes. "They're at the top of the overpass and taking a left."

"Got it. This will be the tricky part, keeping up with them now. When we're a little more exposed," he said as he got to the top of the ramp and took the same left turn.

Once they'd crossed over the interstate, Matt even pulled into a gas station and paused for a few seconds while the two cars they were tailing stopped for a red light a half a block ahead. But seconds after the other cars took off, Matt entered the traffic again.

"Just in case they were looking," he explained as he continued to follow the pair, very, very carefully.

Eventually, Fallon and her accomplice drove into a subdivision and turned onto a long street with mainly ranch-style, brick houses. Most of the yards were nicely manicured—with one exception. And the yard of that house stood out like a sore thumb. It was full of weeds and dead grass and trash. A place that was obviously unkempt and unloved. So different from the places that Caleb built and sold. Unfortunately, it was also the place that Fallon turned into and raced up the driveway, hitting the brakes when she got close to the garage and the walkway that led to the weathered front door. She was followed by the black car that pulled in directly behind her.

Matt anticipated their movements and slipped his truck close to the curb down the street, in front of another home.

All the while, Caleb gulped hard and kept the binoculars trained on the two vehicles. He watched as Fallon jumped out of her car, and the man in the black car opened his door and took his time before he slid out.

That's when Caleb got his first real look at the guy. And he could hardly believe his eyes.

"I recognize him . . . that's Logan Smith," Caleb said with astonishment. "He's the one I told you about. The guy who was in our office, asking all kinds of questions about me."

"The man who pretended to be interested in building a custom home, right?" Matt clarified.

"One and the same," Caleb told him, as he watched Logan pull a cigarette from a pack and light it, just as Fallon reached up for a kiss.

But the guy didn't respond to her right away. Instead, he dropped the empty cigarette pack onto the driveway and scratched his armpit first, tugging at his stained and ripped T-shirt. He blew out a huge ring of smoke before he wrapped an arm around Fallon's waist. Then he finally kissed her back, hard, while she leaned into him. Without looking behind them, the two strolled up to the front door, arm in arm.

Caleb's chin nearly dropped to his chest. So this was the real man in Fallon's life? Her . . . boyfriend? Her significant other? Not to mention, her partner in crime?

For a few seconds, Caleb was too shocked to speak.

"You okay?" Matt asked him.

But all Caleb could do was stammer and hyperventilate in shock. Here he had fretted and worried over this woman, afraid she might attempt suicide since she was so upset. And because she was always crying, crying, crying. He had rescued her, thinking he was doing the right thing. Thinking he was being a good guy. An honorable man.

Yet all the while, she had been playing him like a sap.

And he had fallen for the whole thing. Hook, line, and sinking heart.

"Even the darkness will not be dark to you; the night will shine like the day, for darkness is as light to you."
(Psalms 139:12, NIV)

Chapter Ten

The funeral was a fine affair, as the saying goes. A big church event with poinsettias and holly, decorations left over from Christmas. But that was hardly as important as all the friends and relatives and work associates who crowded in, all there to pay their respects to Devin. And to support Libby.

Devin's old college buddies had shown up, too, along with his distant cousins and more. His parents and sister were there, of course, and even Mr. Ritchie was sweet enough to slip into a pew near the back and give Libby a supportive nod.

Though to be honest, it all felt like a big blur to her, and she felt strangely detached. Probably since it seemed like she had lost Devin days before he took his final breath. And now, as she heard the pastor talk with heartfelt compassion, it felt like time was standing still, and she sat there frozen, like she wasn't really there at all. Like she was only watching some movie.

Later, there was a reception at her house, one that her mother had arranged, thankfully. Her parents had driven down a few days earlier, and they had taken the reins when

Libby couldn't. Amazingly, plenty of food had materialized around her kitchen, with everyone standing and eating on plastic plates.

The people who were there couldn't have been nicer, offering hugs and words of condolence. Of course, she was well aware that most of the people were struggling to find the right words to say to her. To be honest, she found the awkward expressions of the tongue-tied to be even more endearing, and maybe this was one of those times when the thought really and truly did count the most. Plus, it was nice to see Jessica and Bert and Candace again, and she knew Candace had probably been responsible for plenty of the food. That's when Libby realized how blessed she was to know these people.

Especially when Jessica handed her a plate filled with Candace's specialties. "Eat," Jessica insisted. "You're withering away. I know this is a rough day, which is all the more reason for you to keep your strength up."

Knowing better than to argue, Libby took a few bites of a fried wonton.

"I noticed you had a whole bunch of lamps on your dresser in your bedroom," Jessica said as she devoured a cookie. "They're beautiful! I've never seen anything like them. Are you trying to decide on a replacement for the lamp that wasn't working?"

Bert came to stand with them. "Oh, so you decided to replace your lamp instead of fixing it? Did you have trouble finding a lamp kit?"

"No, not at all," Libby told them. "But I used my first lamp kit to make a whole new lamp. I sold that one and a second one for three hundred dollars apiece. Then I just kept on making lamps. And making them and making them. I have absolutely no idea what I'm going to do with all those lamps. I only stuck them in my bedroom so they'd be out of the way for the reception. I can't explain it . . . but creating these lamps just seems to help me deal with everything."

"I've heard of this before," Jessica said with a nod. "That trauma and grief can spawn creativity. I've heard of people locking themselves away and writing entire novels while they're grieving."

"And poets write poetry," Bert put in as Candace came to stand beside him.

"Plus, musicians pour their grief into their songs," Jessica went on. "So for you, Libby, maybe it's making lamps. Whatever works. But either way, your artistry is incredible."

"I agree," Candace told them. "Of course, I always cook and bake when I'm upset. It helps a lot. And by the way, I'd like to buy one of your lamps, Libby. Maybe two."

Jessica's eyebrows shot up. "I want to buy one, too!"

That's when Libby let out a little laugh. "You don't have to do this because you feel sorry for me."

Jessica rolled her eyes and waved everyone toward Libby's bedroom. "We just want one of your lamps because they're so stunning," she said, leading the charge. "And they're one of a kind. So we'd better get one now, before you become so famous that we can't even begin to afford your work."

That made Libby smile as she entered her bedroom with the small crowd that rushed in alongside her. And before she could say a word, people started grabbing up the lamps she'd already made.

Jessica pointed to one of Libby's creations. "I call dibs on this one. I love all the old spoons that are arched out side-by-side around that spindle. As well as all the vintage jewelry you've added. That is so cool."

"And I want those two with the velvet backing and vintage necklaces woven around them," Candace said excitedly as she grabbed her own choices.

Bert laughed and Libby shook her head. Then before she knew it, she had checks in her hand and lamps going out the door. Plus, all the lamps she'd made so far were now officially sold.

"Are you going to make more?" Jessica asked after she returned to the kitchen, having safely stowed her purchase in her car.

Libby tilted her head. "I guess so. I won't be going back to work for a little while, so I might as well fill my days with something. Now that I'm no longer spending every day at the hospital."

"Don't forget to make a lamp for yourself," Jessica added.

"To replace the one that wasn't working."

"Oh . . . I don't know," Libby said, hesitating. "I think I'm going to keep that light."

"But it's so plain compared to the ones you're creating," Candace pointed out. "Your art lamps."

"I know," Libby said with a shrug. "But you might say, it has sentimental value to me."

Bert nodded. "I'd keep it, too. Because you're going to need all the lamps you make for inventory. And you'll need plenty of inventory to start your business."

Libby choked. "Business?"

"Yes, you just raked in a bunch of cash from a bunch of sales," Bert pointed out matter-of-factly. "Like it or not, Lib, you're in business. Best to make it legal. So you're going to need a business license and a tax I.D. I can get that all set up for you. You might even want to become an LLC. That's usually a good way to go."

Just then, Mr. Ritchie's ears perked up, and he wandered over from the group of people he'd been chatting with. "I couldn't help but overhear, Libby, and I wholeheartedly agree with your friend. It's a good idea to make your business official. Because I would like to add more of your lamps to my own store inventory, since I sold the first two so quickly. Meaning, I have no doubt I can sell more. Plus, with a tax idea number, I can sell your supplies to you at a wholesale price."

That's when Libby laughed and threw her hands in the air. "But I have no idea how long I'm going to be doing this. It's probably just a temporary hobby. Something to help me deal with Devin's death."

Jessica shook her head. "You say that now, but I've seen how plenty of artists work. Once they get started, they can't stop."

Bert's eyes went wide. "And for Heaven's sake, don't ever refer to your work as a hobby."

"So what are you going to call your company?" Jessica went on.

Libby felt the room start to spin. "I have no idea. I wasn't even planning on *starting* a company."

"I think she should call it 'Lamps with Panache,'" Candace

suggested, her dark eyes shining brightly.

"Nice," Bert agreed. "It does have a ring to it. But better to use an alliteration. Or a play on words. To help people remember it."

"I think she should call it 'Lovely Luminations,'" Jessica put in. "Since you never know, she might want to expand her repertoire and make other light fixtures. Of course, she'll need business cards and we'll have to set up a website."

Bert nodded. "Lovely Luminations. Catchy. That could work."

"Which brings up another point," Mr. Ritchie said, turning to Libby. "We're going to be hosting a class on electricity and wiring this week at the store. I think it'd be a good idea for you to attend."

Libby nodded. "Umm . . . okay . . . sounds good. I'll be there."

And at that exact moment, she didn't know whether to laugh or cry. Here she was, barely a widow for two days, and the lovable, well-meaning people around her were practically hijacking her life. Not to mention, her new . . . ahem . . . business venture. Though one thing was quickly becoming crystal clear—if she wanted to have any say in her new company, she had better jump in now.

"How about Libby's Lights?" she suggested, addressing the group.

"I like it," Bert said. "Simple. Memorable."

"Sounds bright, joyful," Candace put in.

"Easy to remember," Mr. Ritchie agreed.

"It's perfect," Jessica announced. "You always have the best ideas, Lib."

"Libby's Lights," Mr. Ritchie repeated. "Who knows where a venture like this might lead you?"

"So true," Jessica agreed. "Something like this could take you down a path you never even imagined. Though I sure hope you'll still come back to work one of these days. I miss you there."

"I will," Libby told her. "Once I've recovered a little more. Because I miss all of you, too."

Jessica gave her a quick hug. "Call if you need anything. In the meantime, I think you'll have lots to keep you busy."

But the next day, after Libby said goodbye to her in-laws and her parents before they left town, she shut her front door, fully aware that her life *with* Devin had officially ended. And her life *without him* had officially started. She was all alone now, with her grief and with her memories.

Memories of some of the happiest days of her life.

Suddenly her house felt much too big and empty and quiet.

Despite herself, she started to tremble just a little, especially when she realized that the day she had dreaded the most had arrived.

All at once, tears formed in her eyes and threatened to roll down her cheeks. But frankly, she was so tired of crying.

Crying, crying, crying.

"Not today," she said to the empty room. "And not at this moment. I'm not giving in to this right now."

Then she quickly wiped away her tears and went straight to her kitchen. She spread her drop cloth across Devin's huge kitchen table, grabbed her lamp-making supplies, and set them out around the table.

Without thinking, she just let her creativity take over, and she started working on her next lamp project. For some reason, it simply made the grief more bearable. Though she wasn't kidding herself. She knew full well that it wasn't going to be easy to navigate her world without Devin.

Even so, she knew she had to.

One day at a time.

One lamp at a time.

"Libby's Lights," she repeated, sniffling and wiping away her tears. "In that case, let there be light."

*Wait for the LORD; be strong and take heart and wait
for the LORD. (Psalms 27:14, NIV)*

Chapter Eleven

Caleb was mostly functioning on autopilot as he ran his rounds and checked on his job sites. Because today, no matter what, his heart just wasn't in it. Not even when he stopped at his favorite house in progress, the one that was his project alone. And not even when he walked around and admired the beauty of the coffered ceiling that had just been added to the living room. A stunning and elegant feature that normally would have cheered him right up. Especially since the light from the recessed fixtures that had already been installed in the corners and over the fireplace now bounced along the dropped beams and sunken panels of the ceiling, alternately casting light and shadow around the room.

Something that created both depth and warmth.

Thankfully, the Van Sant's had taken Caleb's advice when it came to lighting, and he had to say, it was really paying off. Caleb had learned long ago that lighting was an extremely important aspect of any home, and while a builder could install all kinds of interesting architectural features, if they didn't have the right kind of light at the perfect angles, those fancy features always fell flat. Meaning, lighting and light fixtures could really make or break a room.

And over the past few months, Caleb and the Van Sants had managed to pick out the perfect light fixtures for the whole house, with the exception of the area above the large, curved kitchen island. And that fixture needed to be something special. Very special. A real showstopper. After all, the kitchen was the focal point of the home, and the island was the place where everyone would gather.

But so far, they hadn't had any luck in finding the right piece.

Though today definitely was not the day to go hunting for that final fixture. Not when his mind just wasn't in the right place, and he couldn't stop thinking about what had happened a couple of days ago. In fact, it seemed like his brain was stuck on instant replay ever since he'd seen Fallon in front of her run-down home, kissing the guy who was clearly her "significant other." That's when it finally sunk in for Caleb that Fallon had really and truly scammed him. And that he'd probably been a very easy mark, since he'd never suspected a thing. Yet all her charm and smiles and compliments, and later, her tears and hints of suicide, were nothing but a well-crafted manipulation. An utter deception. And until that moment, Caleb hadn't fully believed it.

Naturally, his kneejerk reaction at the time had been to bounce out of Matt's truck and race right over to confront Fallon. And the guy she was with. More than anything in the world, he wanted to tell them off. Honestly, he couldn't remember ever being so angry in his entire life. Not to mention, he felt like such an idiot for falling for their scheme. He had been blind, all right, but at that exact moment, he was blind with rage.

Thankfully, Matt was an absolute rock in the storm when he grabbed Caleb's arm and ordered him to stay put. For some reason, Caleb instantly obeyed, probably thanks to his Army training, where taking orders had been drilled into him.

"I told you to brace yourself," Matt said firmly. "Now take some deep breaths and try to calm down. We're going to take care of this." He let go of Caleb's arm and then snapped off a round of pictures, using a high-dollar, digital camera with a telephoto lens.

Caleb grabbed onto the armrest and tried to get his breathing under control. "Take care of this? But how? She's going to destroy my family's business reputation. And everything we worked for."

Matt shook his head. "Not if we outsmart her. And do this the *right* way. The legal way. She and her partner need to be put behind bars."

Caleb ran his hand over his face, like he was wiping away the misery of the moment. "So you think we should call the police?"

"Not just yet. At this point, we don't have much proof of a crime. It'll be your word against hers. They'll say you're a jilted lover bent on revenge."

Caleb watched as Fallon and the other guy went in through the weathered front door of the house. Then he stared at the front yard where the grass had pretty much been strangled out by the weeds, weeds that seemed to be multiplying before their very eyes. Almost as fast as the paint seemed to be peeling from the front porch. Obviously, the house needed a lot of love and work, and it wasn't going to get it from Fallon and her cohort. Even though he guessed the place was a rental, plenty of people rented homes and took good care of them. This pair had no respect for the property, and no respect for how their neighbors probably felt living next door to such a mess.

Funny, but Caleb couldn't help but compare the life Fallon had with her guy to the life Caleb had to offer a woman. One with a nice home that he built himself. And a beautiful yard. With a happy, hardworking family.

Instead, this was the life Fallon had chosen for herself.

A life of crime.

Which clearly did not pay.

Caleb took a very deep breath. "Okay, Matt. So what do we do? I'm all ears."

Matt put his camera down. "First, let's string her along. Let's give her the impression that she's going to get the money, without actually *saying* she's going to get the money. Since that's all she really wants anyway."

"Okay. How do we do that?"

Cindy Vincent

Matt squinted his eyes and stared down the street. "Let's beat her at her own game. Start by opening up one of the selfies you took at the restaurant. Then do some minor edits, any edits at all. And save it as a copy. So it won't show an earlier time stamp."

Caleb nodded and did as Matt instructed.

"Now send it to her with another text," Matt went on. "Say something like, 'Why didn't you wait for me? Why did you leave? Just because I messed up and got the wrong restaurant? I thought you wanted your money. I thought you wanted me.'"

"Got it," Caleb said as his thumbs typed away.

"Then drive the deal home," Matt went on. "Ask her if she even loves you."

Caleb blinked. "But there were no 'I love yous' while we were going out. Sure, I found her incredibly attractive when we first started dating. But I backed off when I felt something wasn't quite right."

"Which is when she probably started her crying routine," Matt explained. "Either way, it doesn't matter. Because we're just using it to reel her in. So add in a 'Did you *ever* love me?' while you're at it. For effect."

"Okay," Caleb answered with a wry chuckle as he sent the text. "But I think we all know the answer to that."

"Yup, we do," Matt agreed. "But she doesn't *know* that you know. My guess is, she still thinks she's got you fooled."

Something that didn't help matters when Caleb got a text back in a matter of seconds. He even felt a little sick to his stomach when he read it.

"Wow, the girl is a world-class liar," Caleb said, chomping on his words. "She just told me that, yes, of course, she loves me. And that something came up and she couldn't wait for me today."

"Uh-huh," Matt said with a chuckle of his own. "In that case, let's really get her to go out on a limb. And let's cause a little rift between her and her partner. Because even the strongest of them get annoyed when their woman is texting another man that she loves him."

"Sounds like a plan to me," Caleb said. "Should I repeat my question to her and make her text it again?"

Matt smiled a sly smile. "Better yet, ask her to prove that she loves you. Tell her that you want assurance that she's not just in it for the money. Let's really toy with her. Use all that anger you're feeling to play the role of the jilted boyfriend."

"Got it," Caleb said before he quickly penned another text.

She immediately replied with a lengthy, rambling message where she declared her undying love for him. A message filled with so many platitudes, Caleb wondered if she'd ever worked for a greeting card company.

Matt read the message over Caleb's shoulder. "That was fast. She must have had those phrases in her phone already. To send them out so quick. They're probably the same load of trash she's used with all her marks. Words meant to manipulate."

"And the sad thing is," Caleb said, "she did manipulate me before. Very, very well."

"As you can see, she's obviously had a lot of practice. But now it seems like she's pulling out all the stops. So let's do some manipulating of our own. Tell her you can't meet her until after New Year's Day, that you've gotta go out of town for business. Then tell her you've been giving your relationship a lot of thought, and you've realized your true feelings. Say you'd like to go out for a very romantic dinner when you get back. Something fancy. Tell her you've got something really important you want to talk about. And ask what her ring size is."

Caleb just shook his head and did as he'd been told. "Wow, we're really taking this to the limit."

"Just a little insurance policy," Matt said with a smile. "A girl like her wouldn't miss out on a nice diamond ring. Not when she could hawk it for even more money."

Caleb crinkled his brow. "But doesn't this all seem a little bit fishy? I mean, if a couple had really reached the stage of getting engaged, wouldn't they be calling and texting each other several times a day?"

Matt nodded. "That's right, kid! You've nailed it. Another sign that it's a fake relationship. Otherwise, she'd be back and forth with you far more than this. But she thinks she's stringing you along perfectly. In the meantime, she's free to spend the holidays with her real guy."

Caleb rolled his eyes. "Wow, she's really got this down pat, doesn't she?"

"Yup, and I'll bet she's got her response down pat, too."

And Matt's prediction proved to be correct, when Fallon texted back with, "*Ooooh*! I can hardly wait! And you'll bring my money then, too, right? I want us to be fair and square, with everything settled and behind us. So there will be nothing between us as we step into our new life together."

"I'll take care of everything," Caleb wrote in return, following Matt's instructions.

It was hard to believe that he was even talking about giving her an engagement ring, especially when the thought had actually crossed his mind after their first couple of dates.

But that was when he'd thought she was a wonderful woman. Someone very different from who she *really* was.

And to think, it had all been nothing but a big, gigantic con.

So why hadn't he picked up on it?

While he still didn't know the answer, one message had come through loud and clear for Caleb—he couldn't trust his own instincts. Apparently, he didn't have the right stuff when it came to making good judgment calls about women.

Matt started his truck and headed down the street. As they passed the house where Fallon and "her guy" lived, Caleb grabbed a couple of quick photos.

"Quite a dump," Matt muttered. "For someone who doled out remodeling tips. Ones she wants to get paid for."

"You can say that again," Caleb replied as they left the neighborhood.

He remained quiet the whole way back to Matt's office. Yet his brain couldn't stop racing as he recalled practically every moment he'd spent with Fallon. Only now, he looked at it through different eyes, and from the perspective of knowing that Fallon had been scamming him the entire time.

"Chin up," the older man insisted as he pulled the truck into a parking space in front of his office building. "I'm going upstairs to get to work. This could take a while. I'll call you as soon as I've got the info I'm looking for. Then we'll come up with the next part of our plan. In the meantime, try not to think about it. Let it go for a while."

Something Caleb couldn't have done if he tried.

Not even now as he walked through his favorite home under construction with Ginger tucked into his shirt. He plopped down onto the staircase, wondering what he'd done to deserve all this. He couldn't remember ever feeling so low in his entire life. What was the point of it all anyway? Working so hard, chasing his dream, and trying to be the best person he could be?

"Why, God? Why?" he said as he looked up into the open expanse of the twenty-five-foot entryway. "Would you please send me the woman of my dreams?"

Just then Ginger stirred and meowed up to him.

For some reason, he couldn't help but laugh. He cuddled the little cat for a moment or two, and much as he hated to admit it, he found her presence to be oddly comforting.

But that didn't last long, not after his phone buzzed, and his heart immediately caught in his throat. Was it Fallon calling? The last thing in the world he wanted to do was talk to her.

Thankfully, after he glanced at the screen, he saw it was Matt.

"Well, kid, I uncovered some very interesting stuff," the P.I.'s deep voice said through the phone. "And I wanted to pass it on. I hope you're sitting down."

"Must be pretty bad," Caleb responded. "If I need to be sitting."

Matt's silence spoke volumes.

"Okay, I'm sitting," Caleb said. "So shoot. What did you find out?"

"You probably already guessed it," Matt started, "but Fallon O'Malley is not her real name."

"So what is?"

"Her name is Kinley Karnowski, and she's from Chicago."

"I guess that explains her odd 'Texas' accent."

"Yup, but you can bet she studied it fairly well," Matt replied. "So she could play the role. The man we saw her with is Arnie Lynch, and he's about five years older than she is. They have never officially been married, but they've lived together for about eight years."

"Wow," was all Caleb could manage to say.

"And here's the clincher," Matt went on. "They have a number of aliases that I could find, and they've operated in several states. They both have records. Minor stuff, really. But they've had arrests for bigger stuff in Michigan, Ohio, and Illinois. Unfortunately, nothing ever stuck. Probably since the victims didn't really want to push it, and most of them were probably too embarrassed to go the distance when it came to court. Anyway, from what I could gather, this pair started working their way south, most likely scamming people along the way."

"Wow, sounds like somebody needs to stop them," came Caleb's instant reply.

That's when Matt's voice suddenly perked up. "Yes, Caleb, you're exactly right. *Somebody* does need to stop them. And you could be just the man for the job."

Caleb felt his heart start to pound. "Me? What can I do? I'm just another sucker who fell for their scam."

Matt chuckled from the other end of the line. "Believe it or not, Caleb, you're probably one of the few who had the backbone to step back and get help. And unlike a lot of her victims, you never paid her a dime."

"Well . . . okay, I guess that's true."

"Do you remember me talking about going after them the legal way, so we can put them in jail? Well, we now have the chance to set something up to get the kind of evidence we need to get the local police involved. Something that will demonstrate that it's not just your word against hers."

Caleb's mouth fell open. "We do?"

"Oh, yeah. And we'll do it during that so-called romantic dinner I had you text her about."

"What do you mean?"

"I've got an idea . . . We can set things up so the ball is in our court. And we could use some help from your brothers, too. Just in case Fallon's friend shows up and things get ugly. He wouldn't pull anything if he's got three more big guys staring him down."

"I don't know . . ." Caleb muttered. "I've put my family through enough already. I really hate to involve them. And to tell you the truth, I never, ever want to see Fallon again."

"I understand where you're coming from," Matt told him. "But she's not gonna go away. She thinks she's latched onto a pretty good money source, and she wants to tap into it. So we've got to finish what we started here."

Caleb groaned. After all, he knew Matt was right. Fallon's threat was still out there, hanging over him like a dark, swirling cloud. Much as he hated to face that fact right at the moment. Because, more than anything, he just wanted to let the memory of Fallon fade off into history. And if he never heard her name again, it would be too soon.

But clearly Matt wasn't going to let it go. "Just think about this, Caleb. Not only will you be protecting your family and their reputation, but this is your chance to put a stop to the woman and her accomplice. So they can never do this to another guy again. You could be the hero here, Caleb. You could save lots of other poor, unsuspecting 'saps' from her scams."

Caleb closed his eyes and cringed. Here Matt was talking about him being a hero and saving others from crimes that Fallon hadn't even committed yet. Future scams against other guys just like him.

But if he agreed to do what Matt had wanted him to do, did that make him a "rescuer" again?

A role that had proven to do more harm than good.

Way more harm.

Yet if he didn't put a stop to Fallon and her partner, who would? And how many other people would they hurt?

Caleb sighed and rolled his eyes. "Fine, Matt, I'll do it."

But when he listened as the P.I. laid out his plan, Caleb truly wondered if he'd left the real world behind and stepped straight into a hard-boiled detective movie.

Of course, there were a few common denominators with most of those movies. Namely, that things never went according to the P.I.'s plans. And when those plans went awry, they went awry spectacularly. And usually in a way that involved a whole lot of trouble.

And a whole lot of danger.

Chapter Twelve

The night of the class at Mr. Ritchie's store, the one on wiring and electricity, rolled around a lot quicker than Libby had imagined. And now as she got ready to go, she felt oddly anxious, and for a moment or two, she thought about cancelling. But she didn't want to let Mr. Ritchie down. Not after he'd personally invited her and even phoned a few times during the week to make sure she would be there.

Of course, she had a pretty good idea the class wasn't the only reason he'd been calling. She knew he'd also been checking up on her, just to make sure she was okay. And while plenty of other people had so thoughtfully touched base with her, too, somehow, she found Mr. Ritchie's words to be the most comforting of all.

Probably because he had been there.

"I know you might not feel like going out much and being around people right now," he'd told her. "But a person in grief can spiral downward in a hurry, and believe me, it's easy to fall into a big, black hole. So it's important that you do get out of the house some. Even if you don't feel totally comfortable, you'll be surprised at how much better you'll feel overall. And a class like this is perfect. You don't have to chat with people if you don't feel like it. But technically, you'll still be out and around others."

And sure, Libby knew that Mr. Ritchie was right, but it was still tough to make herself go anywhere. Mostly because she had such horrible crying episodes that could come on at the mere mention of Devin's death. And frankly, she wasn't crazy about the idea of having a meltdown in the middle of a class. Or at the grocery store, for that matter. Which was why she'd been sticking with curbside pickup whenever she needed food.

But it was more than just the uncontrollable crying that held her back. To be honest, she felt like she was a different person now, having watched her husband die of cancer. It had given her a completely different perspective on life. Yet oddly enough, it was death that had taught her how precious life really is. So the idea of trivial, talk-about-the-weather kind of small talk seemed so meaningless to her these days. And the only subjects she wanted to talk about were deep and intense, and probably not too socially appropriate with a group of strangers.

Of course, she could always talk about her newfound, nonstop obsession with creating lamps, which would probably be a real snooze-fest of a subject to most people.

Amazingly, she actually missed her days of going to the hospital. Even though Devin barely knew she was there most of the time, she still saw people every day. Nurses and aides and doctors. Family members. There was always somebody around. People who didn't expect her to be witty or well-versed on current affairs. People who understood what she was going through.

But now she spent her days by herself, and she probably would until she went back to work. Though it was strange, she hardly noticed the hours ticking by, and she certainly didn't keep regular hours. She just grabbed some sleep whenever she felt tired enough, lying down for a long nap on the couch or on top of her already made bed. She didn't even bother to turn off any lights, including her bedside lamp.

No, her main focus at the moment was to create more and more lamps. In fact, she was pretty sure she couldn't stop making them, even if she wanted to. Not only did she want to build up an "inventory" like Bert had suggested, but creating her lamps seemed to be the only thing that really and truly eased her grief right now. She had even started to experiment with different styles. Some ornate like her first lamps, and others more sleek and modern. She ordered a book on art deco styles, and she tried to figure out how she might incorporate some of those styles into her art lamps as well.

Of course, for the purposes of expanding her "light" business, she also knew it would be good for her to learn about electricity and wiring at tonight's class. The first in a series of two. But as she pulled on her best pair of jeans, she was surprised to find they were huge. When and how had she lost so much weight?

Then again, she hadn't exactly been eating regular meals.

Though apparently, she'd been eating a lot less than she realized. And normally, she would've been excited to lose a few pounds. But not when she'd had different plans. A year ago, she'd been hoping she would need maternity clothes by Christmas.

Just thinking about it caused tears to prick at the back of her eyes.

"Don't go there, Libby," she commanded her image in the mirror. "You don't need another crying spell right before you leave the house. So don't think about it and just try on another pair of jeans. Until you find something that fits."

Which was another thing she'd been doing a lot of lately— talking to herself. And sometimes she even talked to Devin, wondering if he could hear her somewhere. Other times she talked to God, wondering if He could hear her, too.

"I'm sure I've got some old jeans crammed in here somewhere," she said to the pants hanging in her closet.

That's when it suddenly occurred to her that she no longer needed to share a closet. And maybe it was time for her to box up Devin's clothes and give them to a thrift store.

"It makes it seem so final . . ." she murmured with a sigh. "But it has to be done," she said with as much resolve as she could muster. "In the meantime, I still need to find something to wear."

Then she dug deeper into her closet and found an old pair of smaller-sized jeans that hadn't fit her for years. Why she'd kept them, she didn't know. But tonight, they were a perfect fit.

Once she was dressed, she pulled her hair into a ponytail and swiped on some mascara and lip gloss. Then she grabbed her keys and purse and took off.

A few minutes later, she pulled into the parking lot of Mr. Ritchie's store. That's when panic overtook her. Who else would be at this class? Probably people whose everyday conversations included words like "amps" and "watts." Things she'd barely even heard of. If it weren't for the instructions on the lamp kits she'd been buying, she wouldn't have heard of them at all. She also wondered if she would be the only woman in the class.

"That's enough," she told herself. "You're going in and that's that. It doesn't matter who is in this class. You're here to learn, and that's all there is to it. You don't even have to speak to anyone else. Except for Mr. Ritchie, of course. And you don't want to let him down by not showing up."

So she got out of her car, squared her shoulders and took a very deep breath. Then she practically marched herself right up to the front door. She took another deep breath and stepped inside.

Only to be greeted right away by Mr. Ritchie. "I'm so glad you're here, young lady. I know it probably took some gumption on your part to come tonight. And I've got a spot reserved just for you." He put his arm around her shoulders and led her to a section of the store that had been cleared out for rows of banquet-sized tables, set on either side of an aisle. Folding chairs had been placed behind the tables, so they faced the front of the room. There, a computer had already been set out on a podium, with a big screen just to the side of it.

"I've got you seated right here," Mr. Ritchie told her, pointing to a chair in the middle of a row at a table closer to the back.

And sure enough, she spotted a place card with her name on it. Funny, but as a grown-up, she'd never attended a class with assigned seating. But who was she to argue with Mr. Ritchie? So she took her seat and pulled out her computer, ready to start taking notes. Then she perused the little handout booklet that had been left before all the chairs.

Right away, her heart sank. Because the subject matter

looked way too complicated for her to understand. Why on earth had she agreed to take this class?

She glanced over to the name card at the seat to her left. *Kayla MacKnight.* And then she looked at the card on the other side. *Gabby Guerraro.* Well, if nothing else, at least Libby wasn't going to be the only woman in the class.

And she soon realized there were even more women attending when a middle-aged woman wandered in with her husband, and then another woman who looked to be in her forties came rushing in, too. The rest of the students were men of various ages.

Gabby Guerraro, a petite young woman who looked like she was barely out of high school, arrived a few seconds later and took her seat. "I'm so glad I made it," she said with a smile to Libby. "The traffic was terrible."

"I can imagine," Libby said with a smile in return. "I'm lucky I live close by."

"You are," Gabby agreed as she pulled out her own computer. "I'm Gabby. As you can see from my place card," she added with a giggle, her dark eyes flashing with joy.

"And my name is close to yours. Two *b*'s and a *y*," Libby told her. "I'm Libby."

"Nice to meet you," Gabby said, tucking her long, dark hair behind her ears.

Just as Kayla breezed in and grabbed her chair. "Hi, ladies. So glad to see there are other women in this class! I was afraid I was going to be the only one." Her bright blue eyes showed her nervousness as she flipped her strawberry blonde bob out of her eyes. She was a tall, thin woman, about the same age as Libby, and she had the friendliest smile Libby had ever seen.

"Me, too," Libby agreed with a laugh.

"Make that three," Gabby added.

They made quick and quiet introductions as the instructor moved to the front of the room and put the first of his slides up on the screen.

The tall, gray-haired man with a military-style haircut looked to be a little younger than Libby's dad, and he was dressed much like her father would have been. Plaid, button-down shirt and relaxed fitting jeans. No belt.

He smiled and pointed to the screen. "Good evening, everyone. My name's Tony Dirkus and I'm going to be your instructor. I know tonight's topic can be a little intimidating for some, so I thought I'd start with something funny. To break the ice, you might say."

Then he proceeded to read aloud what was on his screen. "I bought a blanket that was picking up static electricity, so I returned it to the store. They gave me another one, free of charge."

Words that were received with groans and laughter.

But Tony continued to smile, undaunted. "I heard about a man who opened his water bill and his electric bill at the same time. He was shocked."

Libby rolled her eyes and laughed, looking first at Kayla and then to Gabby, who did the same.

The instructor went on. "Someone tried to explain electricity to me, but I had no idea *Watt* he was talking about."

And that was all it took for the crowd to relax. And start to learn, as the instructor went through things step-by-step, with excellent explanations on each point. Then once he'd gone over several pages of material, he repeated and summed up what he had taught so far.

Libby quickly found herself taken in by the entire topic. Probably since she'd already been working with the lamp kits that she'd been buying at Mr. Ritchie's store. And oddly enough, as her brain focused on amps and watts and voltage, she forgot all about the grief that had been weighing her down for so long.

And by the time they reached a break, she even joined Kayla and Gabby for the cookies and coffee that Mr. Ritchie had set out for the class.

"I'm having a hard time keeping up," Kayla admitted. "But I've gotta say, this stuff is really interesting. How about you two?"

Gabby beamed a bright smile. "I'm really into it. My grandfather was an electrician, so I'm not completely new to all this. What made both of you decide to take this class?"

Kayla laughed. "To be honest, it wasn't exactly my idea. Mr. Ritchie is a friend of my husband's family. I married the youngest of four brothers, and they all run a construction business. Along with their father. They build custom homes. But Mr. Ritchie pulled me aside one day and suggested that I take some of these classes, so I'll know what my husband and his family are talking about."

Libby nodded. "Good plan. Mr. Ritchie is a real sweetheart. And he gives great advice."

"He really does," Gabby went on. "He and my grandfather were friends. He suggested this class for me, too. As part of my long-term game plan."

"Plan?" Libby repeated.

"Yup," Gabby told her. "There's a company in town who will provide on-the-job training for people who want to become electricians. They pay you as you learn. It's a great deal, really. And as soon as I become a full-fledged electrician, I want to pay my way through college. And become an electrical engineer."

"That sounds like a lot of work," Kayla told her, wide-eyed. "But what a great way to get your degree!"

"I think so, too," Libby said before she took a sip of her coffee. "Because you won't have any school loans hanging over you when you graduate."

"Especially since I still live at home," Gabby went on. "It's going to take some extra years, but that's okay. It'll be worth it in the end. How about you, Libby? What brought you here tonight?"

And that's when Libby froze. Tongue-tied. Because she didn't want to ruin these happy moments by telling them about Devin's death and all that went with it. And she definitely did not want one of her crying episodes to hit right at that moment.

But with these women, she quickly realized she could talk about her latest endeavor. And they probably wouldn't find it boring at all.

So she told them, "I create lamps. Art lamps. So far, I've only ever used lamp kits when it comes to the wiring and switches and plugs. But Mr. Ritchie thought this class would be a good idea for me, to learn more about wiring." Then she quickly scrolled through her phone and showed Gabby and

Kayla some of her work, since she had taken photos of every lamp she had made thus far.

The other women responded with "*Oooohs*" and "*Aaaahs.*"

As they did, one of the men in the group nosed in and glanced at her pictures. "Did you make those?" he asked Libby.

"I did," she said with a nod.

"Are they for sale? My wife would love a couple of those."

Mr. Ritchie joined the group and smiled. "Libby makes fantastic lamps. And she's already sold several through my store."

Libby glanced at him hopefully. "Could we do that again, Mr. Ritchie? My official business isn't completely set up just yet."

"Of course we can," he agreed. "I will sell your lamps here for as long as you like. I would be happy to. Even after you're officially in business."

And with that, Libby agreed to bring plenty of lamps to Mr. Ritchie's store on the night of the next class. So the other people who were attending could pick out which ones they wanted and officially buy them there.

"Your work is absolutely beautiful," Kayla said to her when they headed back to their seats after the break was over. "I know lots of people who would love those. Even the people in my husband's family."

"That's very sweet of you," Libby told her.

And much to her amazement, she left the class that night with a smile on her face. She'd managed to make it through without any tears, and without having to tell anyone that she was a grieving widow. So she'd avoided the inevitable reaction and those awful looks of sympathy that always seemed to come whenever someone learned the truth. Yet tonight, instead of being the grieving widow, she'd simply been Libby. A creative person who loved to make lamps. It had been such a relief to escape her world of constant grief and just be a regular person again. And not focus on the way her life had turned out. Or rather, the way it *hadn't* turned out.

On top of all that, she'd even sold a bunch more of her lamps.

And while it had all been wonderful, in her heart, she knew

it probably wouldn't stay that way. At some point, people would likely find out the truth. And then she would no longer be just Libby Dawson. No, people would immediately see her as that "poor, sad woman who lost her husband when she was so young."

A person to be pitied.

Instead of the fun, interesting, and outgoing person she'd once been.

Would she ever be that person again? In her eyes and in the eyes of others?

Chapter Thirteen

Caleb tugged on his shirt collar and glanced around the upscale restaurant. Right then and there, he was thankful the place was so dimly lit, because he truly hoped it might help hide his nervousness. Meaning, there would be less of a chance that Fallon, or rather, Kinley, would pick up on his true feelings and suspect something was going on. Sure, *she* was obviously an expert when it came to lying and deception and, for that matter, pretending to be someone else. But Caleb had never been any good when it came to acting. He'd been lousy in school plays, and his kindhearted teachers had carefully steered him toward building backdrops and stage props instead.

Something he excelled at.

Then as a grown-up, he'd been a what-you-see-is-what-you-get kind of guy. In fact, everyone always said so. But knowing that only made him more nervous that Fallon might see right through him and his act. And the role he was supposed to be playing.

Needless to say, he didn't exactly like all the subterfuge and deception, even if it was for a good reason. It just wasn't him. But as Matt had insisted, sometimes you had to fight fire with fire.

Caleb scooted his chair closer to the table where he'd been

waiting. Then he stretched his long legs underneath the nearly floor-length, white tablecloth, as though it were a fort that would provide some protection from his so-called date. His nemesis. Not a wolf in *sheep's* clothing, but a monster who had the outer appearance of a perfectly beautiful woman.

He glanced at his phone again, before looking around the restaurant one more time. Fallon was late. Very late. And now he wondered if she was going to show up at all. It was strange—while a part of him was anxious for her to get there, another part of him never wanted to lay eyes on her again.

"She's playing you," came Matt's voice, thanks to the tiny communication bud Caleb had hidden in his ear.

The kind of wireless earbud that he'd only ever seen on TV shows or in the movies. But never in real life.

Until now.

"And she's trying to make you anxious," Matt went on. "By making you wait."

"Well, it's working," Caleb muttered in return, trying to keep his voice low so he didn't look like he was talking to himself.

"Let's hope she's not planning to stand you up," the P.I. added.

"Yeah, since I stood her up," Caleb responded. "Maybe she wants to get even."

"Maybe . . ." came Matt's reply. "But I doubt that's her real motivation. She's probably just trying to get the upper hand. She's used to taking advantage of her marks, so I doubt she can handle someone who doesn't comply with her manipulations. Like when you didn't show up last time."

"Either way, I wish we could get this show on the road," Caleb said under his breath.

Because that was exactly what this was—a show. A very big show. And mentally, Caleb kept rehearsing the part he was meant to play. He was supposed to get her to spell out her terms, without specifically asking her to do just that. And without him using those exact words. After all, this wasn't simply some business deal. No, he couldn't merely request a contract that they both needed to sign and notarize. Instead, he had to be cool and calm and maneuver her into more or less admitting to her scheme. And her threats.

While Matt recorded the whole thing.

Of course, that recording wasn't something that would stand up in court. But it would be enough to get the police interested, and law enforcement could take it from there.

"Remember, kid, nerves of steel," Matt told him. "Take deep breaths and keep your eye on the prize. Do this for you and your family. And so no other guys out there will become her future victims."

"Speaking of family," Caleb said under his breath. "How are my brothers holding up?"

"They're all good," Matt told him. "I've got them positioned in different areas of the parking lot. Keeping their eyes peeled for her arrival. And the arrival of her boyfriend."

The thought of his brothers being involved in some surveillance activity made Caleb smile. While he was in here sweating bullets, he guessed they were out there enjoying themselves right about now.

"You sure she won't recognize them?" Caleb asked.

"Not with their new short haircuts and clean-shaven faces. I didn't even recognize them myself. Not without their beards."

Caleb chuckled. "I think my sisters-in-law are pretty happy about it."

"I'll bet. You got the ring ready?"

Caleb patted the pocket of his suit jacket. "Got it right here."

"Now remember," Matt said in Caleb's ear. "Only flash the ring once you've gotten her to admit to the rest. Or unless you're losing her."

"Got it," Caleb murmured. "How much did this ring set you back anyway?"

"It's the best cubic zirconia that twenty-five dollars could buy. And it's also the best looking fake I've ever seen," Matt deadpanned. "But it's time to put your game face on, kid. Luke just spotted the boyfriend's car. He's parking in the back row."

"But no Fallon?"

"Not yet."

All of a sudden, Caleb became acutely aware of how much his palms were sweating. He'd never be able to think straight and pull this off if he was so hyped up. Like it or not, he had to force himself to calm down.

But all this waiting only made his anxiety level grow by the second.

"Maybe we should abort this," Caleb whispered, taking a sip of his ice water. He tugged at his collar again, which was starting to feel more like a noose, especially since he was wearing a tie.

The waiter showed up and refilled his water glass. "Are you feeling all right, sir? Can I get you something from the bar? A glass of wine to go with dinner, perhaps?"

"We'll probably order wine when my date gets here," Caleb said with all the calmness he could muster. "She's just running late, that's all."

The sandy-haired man gave him a look of pure pity. "I'm sure that's it, sir. But I'd be happy to show you a menu in the meantime."

Caleb did his best to smile. "Thanks, but I'll wait," he mumbled before the man walked away.

"Incoming," Matt's voice suddenly announced in his ear. "And she's dressed to kill."

"Hopefully, not literally," Caleb murmured.

And that's when he wondered just how far Fallon might go when it came to crime. After all, she'd already crossed one major line when she became a con artist. Was it possible she might cross another?

"We're all right here," Matt assured him. "If she pulls any funny stuff."

"Like poisoning my wine?"

Matt chuckled in his ear. "Remember, you're worth more to her alive than dead. Unless, of course, she's afraid you might testify against her in court . . ."

"Oh, great!" Matt said louder than he'd intended, just as Fallon appeared before him.

"Great to see you, too," she practically purred.

Right then, Matt's words echoed through his head. Because he had nailed it—Fallon *was* dressed to kill. Caleb even wondered if she'd just spent a week at a spa. Her hair color was a shade or two lighter, and it was so shiny that it looked like it had been coated with polyurethane, much like her perfectly polished nails. And her makeup had been applied pretty thick, bringing to mind the way his drywall contractor expertly applied mud with a trowel, before smoothing it down to hide any divots or bumps. Then there was her dress, a black one-shoulder number that was short in the front and dipped down to the floor in the back.

While she had the eye of every man in the room, the mere sight of her made Caleb's stomach turn. If only she was as pretty on the inside as she was on the outside.

He stood and kissed her cheek. "You look stunning," he told her.

"And you look nervous," she said, taking a step back and giving him the once over. "What's going on?"

Right away, Caleb heard Matt's voice in his ear. "Play up the big night. Any guy would be nervous if he was about to propose."

Caleb gulped. "Well, big steps can be a little scary."

She smiled and looked adoringly into his eyes, without wavering or revealing even a hint of deception. And that's when Caleb finally realized what a professional criminal she truly was. In fact, he also fully understood the word "artist" in the term "con artist." Because Fallon was an expert, and her expertise probably came at the expense of so many men before him.

Then all of a sudden, Caleb wasn't so nervous anymore. Instead, he felt anger rising in his chest, which, oddly enough, gave him the strength he needed to go through with his role.

"Let me get your chair for you," he said as he stood and raced to her side of the table.

He had barely gotten her settled when the waiter appeared with menus. "Would you care to see a wine list?"

Fallon twinkled up to the man. "I think I'd prefer iced tea tonight. One of my New Year's resolutions is to give up alcohol."

If only she'd given up crime instead, Caleb thought to himself.

Though he had a pretty idea why she didn't want any wine. She probably wanted to keep her wits about her tonight. Which was fine by him. He wanted to do the same.

Cindy Vincent

She flashed Caleb her high beam smile. "But you go ahead and order some for yourself, honey. It looks like you could use a drink."

"I think I'll pass on the wine tonight, too," Caleb told the waiter.

"Very good, sir," the man said with a polite smile. "I'll give you a few moments to peruse the menu, and then I'll be back to take your orders."

Fallon crinkled her brow as the waiter walked away. "It's all right with me, honey, if you feel like you need a drink or two. You just look so tense. And nervous."

"Notice how she keeps reminding you that you're nervous?" Matt's voice said quietly in Caleb's ear. "She's working overtime to rattle you. Time to repay the favor. Start using words like 'fake' and 'phony.'"

"It's okay," Caleb said smoothly to Fallon. "After all, if you're quitting, then I'd better quit, too. You know, Fallon, that's something I really love about you. You're so sincere. There's nothing phony about you."

And that's when he saw it, but for a second. A momentary flinch in her eyes.

"Of course I'm not phony," she said with a hollow laugh. "I'm as real as they get."

"I can tell," Caleb replied, pouring on the charm. "So many women today are so fake. I'm glad you're not."

Now she frowned at him. "Why would such a thought even cross your mind?"

"Got her," came Matt's comment. "Now, take her hands."

So Caleb did. "Wow, you seem kind of jumpy yourself tonight. I guess a girl would be when she's about to hear those words she's always longed to hear."

"Why, Caleb . . ." she uttered just as the waiter showed up again.

"Are you ready to order?" the man asked.

"Yes," Caleb told him. "But on second thought, I think we'll need some champagne after all. Because we're going to be celebrating."

By now, Fallon's lovely façade was starting to show a few cracks.

96

And right after the waiter left to get the champagne, Caleb continued to stare straight into her eyes, without blinking. "I've got something very important to ask you," he said, pulling the ring box from his pocket and setting it on the table. "But before I do, I think we'd better clear up one or two things. Minor details, really. Because I don't want anything to come between us. I want us to start our new life with all our cards on the table. Complete honesty."

Her eyelashes flew up for a second before she stared at the ring box. "Why, yes, Caleb. I've always been honest with you."

He squeezed her hands. "Good. Then let's clear up that little matter of the money first. Such an ugly subject should never tear us apart. Lots of couples fight about money, and I don't want that to be us."

"Money . . ." she repeated quietly.

"Yes, you know, the money you wanted me to pay you. I'm still a little unclear on why you wanted it."

"Well," she said, looking a little flustered for the first time since she'd arrived. "Honey, it's pretty simple. I did work for your company, and I should get paid for it."

"Umm . . . but *honey*, I never actually hired you."

Tears formed in her eyes. "But I worked for your company."

"What work did you do exactly?"

A lone tear rolled down her cheek. "How can you ask me that? I helped you decorate and stage houses. And I worked with customers, and I helped you with designs . . . I went to all your job sites, just like you did. I have videos of it all, to prove it. But hey, wait a minute . . . you are going to pay me, right?" She dabbed at her eyes.

"Okay, Caleb, just like we rehearsed," came Matt's voice through the earbud. "Make it long-winded."

So Caleb did just that, starting with an exaggerated sigh. "Well, to be honest, I'm a little short on cash at the moment. Because, let's face it, a ring costs a lot of money these days. And I thought it was more important to spend money on a ring. My sister-in-law, Kayla, helped me pick it out. She's got really good taste, and all the other sisters-in-law couldn't agree more. Along with my mom. I told them all what a classy girl you are, and they said you would need a ring that was very classy, too. So, Kayla immediately saw one she thought you would like. But these things cost an arm and a leg. Then again, you're buying it for a lifetime, not just for a day, so it's worth the money. But as a result, I'm kind of strapped for cash at the moment. Anyway, what happens if I can't pay you right away?"

"Then I will have no choice but to . . ." she started to say, like she was simply repeating a line she'd said a hundred times before, to a hundred other guys.

But then she caught herself. "Wait a minute . . . What are you trying to pull?"

Caleb immediately feigned shock. "I'm not trying to pull anything. I'm just trying to do this right. This is the most important night of my life! And I'm hoping it's the most important night of your life, too."

Fallon's face fell into a deep pout. "Then . . . are you saying you're not going to pay me? I thought you were an honorable man. I thought you were going to give me the money you owe me."

"Lean in toward her," came Matt's instructions in Caleb's ear. "Close the gap and catch her off guard."

Caleb smiled. "But what would happen if I can't? I don't understand."

Fallon leaned back and stared at him. "What's going on, Caleb? You're different tonight. . ."

"Okay, we're losing her," Matt said with urgency in his voice. "Time to go for the ring."

Caleb took a deep breath. "Fallon, honey, I can't help it if I'm nervous tonight. Because I've figured out a perfect solution to our problem."

"Better hurry," Matt instructed.

So Caleb grabbed the ring box just as the waiter arrived with two flutes of champagne. Caleb took a quick sip from his glass and then got down on one knee.

Fallon looked a little startled with all that was happening. Probably since it was clear that she was no longer in control of the situation.

But before she could react, Caleb said loudly, very loudly, "Fallon O'Malley, would you do me the honor of becoming my one and only? And marry me?"

Suddenly, the whole room seemed to be paying attention to them. Gasps arose from the other diners as Caleb popped open the ring box. Then all eyes went from Caleb to Fallon, while it seemed like everyone collectively held their breath. Waiting for her response. Some of those sitting nearby even pulled out their phones and started recording the moment.

Sparks flashed in Fallon's eyes for a second or two, but she quickly recovered with a perfectly polished smile. "Yes, yes, of course I'll marry you!"

Caleb grinned as applause rose from the room. Then he slipped the huge, phony diamond ring on her finger.

After that, he toasted her with his glass of champagne.

She clinked her glass to his and took a dainty, little sip. The waiter immediately offered his congratulations.

Caleb handed his phone to the man. "Could you please take our picture?"

And before Fallon could protest, Caleb ran around behind her. He leaned over her head and held her hand up, so the ring would be front and center in the picture, too. Then the waiter snapped off a dozen or so photos, and there was a flurry of activity in the room, with other diners offering their congratulations.

After things died down, the waiter took their orders and Fallon spent the next few minutes admiring her ring. From what Caleb could tell, it had passed muster. Matt had been right—it really did look like a genuine diamond. Even a con artist like Fallon seemed to be a little dazzled by it.

At last, she turned to him with a saccharine-sweet smile. "Honey, I'm afraid I'm still going to need some money. To tide me over until the wedding."

Caleb pretended to be shocked again. "Wait a minute . . . why do you need money if we're planning on getting married? I mean, my money will be your money then. And I'm perfectly happy to be the sole breadwinner. You'll have access to everything I make."

"I know . . . but . . ." She took a few ragged breaths, and then, like someone had flipped on a switch, tears immediately started to flow from her eyes. "But I'm really broke at the moment. After I lost my job and all. I'm about to be evicted. I don't have any money to get me through . . ."

That's when Caleb took her hand. "Oh, that's no problem. We can get married tomorrow. We can go to the justice of the peace. You can meet me downtown to get the marriage license. And as soon as we're married, you can move in with me. It'll be wonderful."

"But . . . but . . . but . . ." she stammered. "Wouldn't you rather have a nice, big wedding? And invite your whole family?"

Caleb shook his head. "Naw, stuff like that doesn't matter to me. We can have a big ceremony later if you want. And a big reception. But I'm not the kind of guy who likes to wait around. Now that I've made up my mind, I just want to marry you. The sooner the better. So say you'll meet me at city hall tomorrow. You can even wear that dress you've got on now. It's beautiful, and you look beautiful in it!"

A vein popped out on her forehead, and just like that, her tears stopped just as quickly as they'd started. "But . . . I want to wear a white wedding dress. I only got this dress for our date tonight."

"Oh, but it looks like it cost you a pretty penny. And if you spent so much on it, you really should get your money's worth by wearing it again."

Without responding, Fallon clenched her jaw and simply stared at Caleb for a moment. "Okay, then. I'll meet you there tomorrow."

He flashed her his biggest smile. "You've made me the happiest man in the world."

"Could you excuse me for a few minutes?" she told him smoothly. "I need to go powder my nose."

He stood and helped her with her chair. For effect, he even kissed her on the cheek before she left.

A kiss goodbye, he was well aware.

"Out the door?" he murmured to Matt once she was gone.

"Making a beeline for it," Matt said with a chuckle. "You may not have gotten her to admit to the extortion, but I think you and your family are in the clear now. She can't very well trash a man whom she abandoned on the night of their engagement. Not when she took off with that big honker of a diamond ring."

"A ring as phony as she is," Caleb added.

Then as soon as he'd gotten the "all clear," he finally relaxed, just as his brother, Joshua, showed up and took Fallon's chair.

"You did good," Joshua said with a grin. "You handled that well, little bro."

"Thanks," Caleb said.

And before he could say more, Jacob, Luke and Matt all waltzed in, too, and pulled up chairs to join Caleb and Joshua.

"The boyfriend left right after she did," Matt informed Caleb. "Followed her straight out of the parking lot."

"Not surprising," Caleb said. "At least they didn't give us any trouble."

"We were there for you, bro, in case things got ugly," Luke said as he grabbed Fallon's glass of champagne and took a swig.

Matt helped himself to a dinner roll. "Just for effect, send her a few texts and ask her where she is."

So Caleb did just that. "No response," he murmured. "Number no longer in service."

"Wow, that was fast," Jacob said, wide-eyed.

Matt grinned. "That's a very good sign. She thinks she's disappeared from your life."

"And she has no idea that we know who she is and where she is," Caleb added.

Now the waiter appeared before them all, as they sat cramped at the table for two. "Umm . . . shall I find your party a bigger table?" he asked with a look of pure confusion etched across his face.

"That would be good," Luke said with a nod.

And while they were being led to another table, a lady a few tables over waved to get Caleb's attention. "What happened to your fiancée?" she asked, loud enough for the whole place to hear.

"It's a 'no-go,'" Luke explained.

Which provoked "*oooohs*" from the other diners and sparked lots of conversation around them.

Once they'd all taken their seats, Jacob turned to Matt. "So you don't think she'll make good on her threat to slander our family online?"

Matt shook his head. "I doubt it. By proposing and getting her to accept, I think we've neutralized any leverage she had for extortion. After all, she can't very well go after a guy who not only wanted to marry her, but also gave her a gigantic ring. One that she took off with."

Joshua nodded. "Yup, it would be pretty hard to believe a sob story from a woman who abandoned her new fiancé at the restaurant. And immediately deactivated her phone number."

"Exactly," Matt said. "But just in case, I'll keep my eyes open to see if anything pops up online. If it does, we'll counteract it with engagement photos and her taking off with the ring. Plus, it'll be more fuel for the fire to go after her."

"And will we keep going after her?" Caleb asked.

"I'm game if you're game," Matt told him. "I think we should. Once I figure out a new plan."

With that, all four of the brothers nodded and agreed.

"Wait till she finds out that ring is a fake," Joshua said with a laugh.

Matt grinned. "She'll just think Caleb is a real sap for buying it. I think that's basically how she sees men anyway."

"Maybe the next time you do this, it'll be for real," Jacob put in. "With a real ring."

"Yeah," Luke added. "You'll find the right woman. All your sisters-in-law are on a mission now. They're scouring the county for your soulmate."

Caleb sighed and rolled his eyes. "Believe me, dating is not on my docket these days."

Their food arrived just as lots of the other diners started to clear out. They each made a point of walking by Caleb and patting him on the shoulder. He heard choruses of, "Don't worry, there are plenty of fish in the sea," as well as, "The right woman is out there. Don't give up." And best of all, "That one wasn't good enough for you."

Still, while he knew people meant well, Caleb cringed at the condolences. In a matter of days, he'd gone from "rescuing" to "being rescued," in a sense. And to be honest, that didn't exactly sound like progress to him.

If only he could have gotten Fallon to admit to her extortion scheme. Then this night would be having a very different ending for him. And he would be one step closer to putting this fiasco with Fallon behind him. Not only that, but he couldn't forget that she was still out there and probably in search of her next victim by now. And frankly, until she was securely behind bars and not putting another guy through the same kind of agony that she'd put him through, Caleb wasn't sure this entire episode with Fallon would ever really be over.

Chapter Fourteen

"Mom, I'm going to be late for my class," Libby said as she put her phone on "speaker" and set it on her kitchen counter. So she had her hands free to finish wrapping plastic bubble-sheets around her lamps that she was packing.

"Well then, dear, just say yes and I'll let you go," her mother replied in her usual cheerful but not-going-to-take-no-for-an-answer tone.

Libby rolled her eyes. "Thanks, Mom, for asking, but I really don't want to go on a cruise. I'm not ready for that kind of social setting yet. All those people asking questions about my life. Where are you from and what do you do and are you married? And me having to use the '*W*' word to explain it all to them."

"The word is 'widow', dear. And I think it's time you started saying it."

"I'm perfectly capable of saying it, Mom. I just hate the reaction whenever I do. Not only do people feel sorry for me, but they give me the most horrible look of pity. I've seen it at the grocery store and the drugstore and the post office."

"I think it's nice that people care so much."

Libby sighed with frustration. "Yes, but those same people quickly turn into experts on how I should be acting right now. They're always full of advice like 'You should be at home, crying your eyes out.' Or 'You should go right out and find yourself another husband.' You know, to replace the one I lost, like he was nothing more than a puppy who ran away. It's mind-boggling. As if any of those people have ever gone through what I'm going through. It just makes me feel worse, like I've suddenly become a child. All because I lost my husband."

Though Mr. Ritchie had never treated her like that, and the advice she got from him was beyond valuable. Probably because he *had* been there, and his advice came from experience.

"I know, dear," her mother sympathized. "But people are only human. And most of the time, they have no idea what to say to someone who recently lost a loved one. Sure, they can give the usual niceties at the funeral, and all that support is wonderful. But as time goes on, and a person goes through all the stages of grieving, it gets harder and harder to figure out what to say to them. For the most part, people don't want to see someone suffering, so they just do their best. That's probably one of the reasons why grief is such a lonely road."

"But how would *you* know, Mom? You've still got Daddy."

That's when Libby heard a gigantic intake of air from the other end of the line, a sound she was all too familiar with. And she knew full well what was coming next. She could picture her mom's cornflower blue eyes turning a dark navy while she shook her shoulder-length, caramel-colored hair.

"*Excuuusse me*, young lady," her mom said breathlessly. "I don't believe I raised you to show such disrespect to your mother. And may I remind you that I lost my brother when I was your age? And that he was killed while he was serving overseas in the Army, and that I still miss him every single day? And that I also suffered several miscarriages, which was an unimaginable loss, one that didn't come with the luxury of a funeral back then? So I've lost plenty of people over the years, and I've grieved each and every one of them. I know you're suffering, my dear, but never get the idea that you have a corner on the market when it comes to grief."

Libby closed her eyes for a moment. "Yes, ma'am. That was a rotten thing for me to say. I know you've gone through plenty of stuff in your life."

"I most certainly have. Though I am well aware that it's different when you lose a husband," her mother added more gently. "And I realize this is a very delicate and complicated time for you. I know what an emotional roller coaster grief can be."

Libby sighed again. "Roller coaster is right."

"Just be careful, though, because it's very easy to let your mourning completely consume you. A person can become so focused on their own misery that they forget about everyone else and the rest of the world. So I'm going to say this with the utmost of love, my dear, that with everyone jumping in with extra care and kindness these days, it's easy to start feeling like you're the center of the universe. Especially since everything seems to revolve around you and your grief right now."

Libby glanced up at the ceiling, not sure if she was more annoyed or enlightened. "Okay . . ."

"And don't forget, dear, that even though you're suffering, you're not the only person in the world who's dealing with a major loss. There are other people out there who have lost loved ones or pets or jobs and all kinds of things."

"Point taken . . ." Libby murmured.

Like it or not, she had to admit, her mother's words hit home. And now Libby couldn't help but wonder if they were true. Had she become completely self-centered, making everything all about her? In fact, when she thought about it, it seemed like she probably *was* the center of attention whenever she was around Jessica or Bert or Candace, because the conversation always turned to Devin's death. And how Libby was handling it.

Yet Libby did nothing to steer the conversation to any other topic, including what was going on in *their* lives. Not even after Bert and Jessica had been so gracious to set up her limited liability company as Libby's Lights and do some free marketing work on the side. Thanks to their help, she was now officially in business.

But did she show them how much she appreciated all that they'd done? Because the truth was, she was beyond blessed to have friends like them. She couldn't have gotten her business started without them, and her "light" business was definitely something that was helping her to move on.

Yet, was she "giving" as well as taking when it came to her friendships?

On top of it all, people were always calling to check on her. But did she call anyone else to see how they were doing? Frankly, she didn't even know what was going on in Jessica's or Bert's lives these days. Plus, she'd met plenty of people at the hospital who were losing husbands and wives and mothers and fathers and brothers and sisters and children. She hadn't bothered to check on a one of them. For that matter, she hadn't even gotten their contact information.

Libby closed her eyes. "Mom, I'm sorry. I haven't been myself lately. At all. And you're right, I've probably been living in my own little world. It's all so . . . so . . ."

"Painful?" her mother supplied.

"Yeah, Mom. It's very painful."

"I know, dear. I know. And that's why I think it would do you a world of good to go on a cruise. It might give you a little break from all that misery. In fact, there may be other people on board this cruise who are in grief, too. Maybe that's why they're going. But you don't have to socialize if you don't feel like it. I'll just explain to people that you only speak Ookanawabowbeen and that you don't know any English. Or Spanish. Or French."

Despite herself, Libby couldn't help but laugh. "Ookana what?"

"Don't worry, dear, I just made that up. To cheer you up. Anyway, if you go, we'll find a way for you to keep to yourself if that's what you want. You can simply sit on the deck and stare out at the ocean. You know how you always love the water. And boats."

"And cruise ships . . ." Libby added.

"Plus, it's only a five-day cruise," her mom went on. "It's sailing out of Galveston, so I'll drive down and pick you up and we'll have an easy drive to the port."

"I don't know, Mom . . . Maybe Daddy could go with you instead."

"Nope, he's got a golf tournament. And he agreed that a

girl's trip would be good for you."

By now, Libby knew there was no use fighting it. She loved her mother dearly, but she also knew the woman was like a dog with a bone. Once she latched onto an idea, she would never let it go. Ever.

Besides, Libby was blatantly aware that her mom was doing this just for her. Tough love, no doubt. But love, nonetheless.

And her mother certainly had that "tough love" routine down to a fine art. She'd been the quintessential homemaker since the day she'd gotten married—a role that many in Libby's generation often ridiculed—but Libby and her brothers had grown up respecting that role at their house. Her father had been the breadwinner, but when it came to the household, her mother ran the show, like a drill sergeant with perfectly coiffed hair who softened her commands with a little "sugar."

"All right, Mom," Libby finally agreed with a laugh. "I'll go. I'm still off work for a while anyway."

"Wonderful!" her mother exclaimed. "I knew you'd come around! Now, don't forget you'll need a nice dress to wear for formal night. And dresses to wear to dinner."

"But I don't have . . . I mean, nothing fits me anymore. I've lost so much weight over the past few months."

"I know you have, dear. Grief will do that to a person. So I suggest you get shopping. You don't have much time."

"I don't even know what size I wear these days," Libby muttered aloud after they'd said their goodbyes. "I guess I'll just have to go to the store and try things on," she added as she finished packing the boxes with her lamps.

She'd spent the whole week working on those lamps. Since so many people in her class wanted one, or even two, she knew she needed to bring a nice supply with her tonight. Plus, Mr. Ritchie had clearly been excited about the idea of carrying her lamps in his store on a regular basis, since he'd sold everything she'd already brought him within a matter of days.

In other words, much to her amazement, her products had become a hot commodity. And hopefully, the number of lamps she was bringing tonight would tide him over for a while.

Of course, once she'd completed the whole collection, she'd set them up in her dining room to test them out, using several power strips to plug them in. Then she turned all the lamps on and the overhead lights off, before sitting back and admiring her work. And for the first time in a long time, she smiled. Really smiled. Amazed at the joy all those beautiful lights could bring.

Right away, she couldn't help but think about the lamp she had in her bedroom. The one that seemed to have a mind of its own. Funny, but she'd been keeping such erratic hours these days, and she rarely slept in her bed, so she'd practically forgotten about that lamp. Yet just thinking about it brought her a strange sense of comfort.

And now, as she loaded her boxes into her car, she hoped other people might find that same comfort or joy from the lamps she'd created. Though she was pretty sure these lamps would go on and off according to the switch position.

She laughed at her own private joke as she placed the boxes on the back seat and in the trunk. And that's when she became acutely aware of how small her car was compared to the amount of merchandise she was trying to haul.

"I think I'm going to need a bigger vehicle," she announced before she glanced at Devin's little sports car that had been parked in the garage since the day she'd taken him to the hospital. If she traded in her car and his old car, she could probably afford a very nice SUV. One that she could use to cart all her stuff around.

But the thought of getting rid of Devin's car sent pangs of sadness through her heart. He had loved that red car with black racing stripes, and it was one of the last vestiges she had of him. Sure, she had gotten the courage to cart all his old clothes to Goodwill, but letting go of his car was a different story. Would she ever be able to sell it, even if she needed to?

A decision for another day, she told herself as she backed out of her garage. Still, she couldn't help but imagine driving a nice, roomy SUV. One with plenty of space for more and more boxes of lamps that she could sell.

She glanced at her car's clock as she pulled into the parking lot of Mr. Ritchie's store. Thankfully, she'd arrived a full hour before tonight's class—the second and final one on wiring and electricity. She wanted to give herself plenty of time to get everything unpacked and set on display. Not to mention, give Mr. Ritchie time to enter it all into inventory before the rest of the class arrived. Of course, the older gentleman happily helped her carry everything inside.

She glanced up at him as they walked to the door. "Mr. Ritchie, I want to thank you for everything you've done for me. And I do mean *everything*. You've helped me so much. I really appreciate it."

He smiled at her like her grandfather would have smiled at her. "Thank you, young lady. That's very nice to hear."

"And I've never asked how you are doing. How is business?"

Mr. Ritchie leaned against the door to hold it open while she went through, carrying a box. "That's very sweet of you to ask. And yes, I'm doing well, and the business is doing well. But now that you mention it, I do have one little problem . . . and maybe it's something you could help me with."

Funny, but Libby had been so busy being "helped out" lately that she hadn't even thought of helping someone else out.

"Just let me know what I can do," she responded without hesitation, deciding it was time that she stepped up to the plate.

"Well, there's this tiny, calico kitten that's wandered over to my place," he said. "And I can't keep it because my grandson is allergic. Would you mind giving her a home?"

Libby gulped, and for a split second, she was sorry she'd asked. *A kitten?* One that grew into a full-size cat? Before, she hadn't thought about getting a cat since Devin was a dog person. But the truth was, she actually liked cats. She simply hadn't pushed the idea since she knew Devin would've hated it. But now that she was on her own, there was no reason why she couldn't take in a little kitten.

"Sure, Mr. Ritchie. I'll be going on a cruise with my mother in a couple of weeks. Could I get the kitten from you after that? I'm sure I could figure out how to take care of her."

He smiled as he started to take inventory of her lamps. "I have no doubt that you could figure out how to do *anything* you put your mind to. As for the kitten, she's such a joyful little thing, and she was born around Christmastime. So I call her Merry Anne, spelled *M-e-r-r-y*, and Anne with an 'e' at the end. After my late sister, Anne. But you can name the kitten whatever you want."

Libby couldn't help but chuckle. "Anne was my grandmother's name. So I think I'll keep it. Especially if that's what you've already been calling her."

"Perfect," Mr. Ritchie said with a laugh as he put price tags on her lamps and directed her to arrange them on a display table.

Ready to sell.

All the while, Libby was in a daze. A kitten? What was she getting herself into?

Once she had all the lamps nicely arranged, she took her seat for the class. After practically living like a recluse lately, she was surprised by how happy she was to see both Kayla and Gabby. She immediately told them about the kitten that she would be getting from Mr. Ritchie, and they jumped in with stories about their own pets. Libby couldn't help but notice how easily the conversation flowed. And none of it revolved around Devin's death. Especially since the other women had no idea that Libby was a widow.

Not yet anyway.

During their break, as she stood with Gabby and Kayla near their table, one of the guys in the class made his way over to Libby.

A movie-star handsome guy who filled out his plaid shirt and blue jeans quite nicely.

"You've done a fantastic job with your lamps," he told her. "And since you like lighting so much, I'd like to invite you to a conference that we're having in a few months. It's a Christmas lights conference. There will be all kinds of classes on setting up pixels and programming them on your computer. I even helped write some of the software."

"Sounds interesting," Libby told him, suddenly feeling shy. "Though I have to admit, I'm not sure what pixels are."

"They're a kind of RGB LED lights," he told her.

"LED," Gabby repeated, jumping in. "Light emitting diode. They're so popular they've practically replaced all the old, incandescent lights. When it comes to Christmas lights anyway."

111

"Right," the thirtysomething man answered. "And RGB stands for red, green, and blue. Each pixel light can turn any of those colors, depending on what the computer directs them to do. And they can also turn any combination of those colors."

Something that clicked in Libby's brain. "Which means you could basically make a pixel turn any color you want."

The man flashed her a smile that was probably as bright as the LED lights he worked with. "Exactly. Any color of the rainbow. You can choose or create your own colors. You can make beautiful designs, and you can make all those lights run, dance, and spin. The sky is the limit when it comes to pixels. From an artistic perspective, at least."

Libby's eyes went wide. "Okay, now I'm definitely interested."

"Then here's my card," he told her, pulling his wallet from his pocket and handing her a surprisingly wrinkle-free card. "It's got the website for the conference, and if you'd like to go, you can sign up there. I'm Chase Adams, by the way."

"I'm Libby. I don't have a business card with me, but . . . here," she said as she leaned down and grabbed the place card in front of her spot. "Take my place card. I won't be needing it after this class anyway."

He laughed. "That works. If you'd like to give me an email address, I can send you the class schedule for the conference."

"Sounds good," Libby told him, scribbling down her information. "And by the way, this is Kayla and Gabby."

"Nice to meet you all," he responded, though his eyes never wavered from Libby.

"*Ooooh*," Gabby whispered after he'd walked away. "That guy is so hot, and he was totally hitting on you."

"I don't think so," Libby replied with a laugh. "I think he was only trying to sell me on his conference."

But Kayla was already shaking her head. "Oh, no, he was *definitely* hitting on you. Because he didn't invite me or Gabby to that conference. But before you look at him, you really should meet my brother-in-law. In fact, he shops here a lot. He might even be around here somewhere." She crinkled her brow and glanced behind them and past the back row.

Libby felt her heart start to pound. Had the moment finally

come? When she would have to reveal the truth about her life? Oh, how she hated to ruin the fun with such a sad subject.

Thankfully, before they could talk more, the instructor returned to the front of the room and called for everyone to take their seats again.

So Libby simply held up her hands and looked from Kayla to Gabby. "Umm . . . my last relationship just . . . umm . . . ended. It was very painful and I'm not ready to talk about it yet. So dating isn't even on my radar right now."

"For the right guy," Kayla said with a wink, "I think you should get a new radar."

That made Libby smile. "Not yet. But I think I will go to this Christmas lights conference."

Kayla and Gabby both laughed, before the three of them sat down again.

Libby chuckled along with them, while she secretly hoped she could sneak out after class before her two new friends pressed her for details about her last "relationship." Namely Devin. Which would lead to talk about his untimely death. Because, more than anything, she didn't want something to ruin the happiness, and well, the normalcy, that she was feeling.

Funny, but Libby had simply come tonight with the goal of getting through the class and selling more lamps. Yet not only had she learned a lot when it came to wiring and electricity, but here she was, about to leave with money in her pocket and the possibility of signing up for a Christmas lights conference. Not to mention, she would be adopting a kitten named Merry Anne in a few weeks.

What a U-turn her life had suddenly taken, all thanks to Mr. Ritchie insisting that she sign up for a simple class at a hardware store. Amazing how one simple step could lead to so much.

Yet something inside told her she had barely gotten started on this journey she seemed to be on. And something also told her there was more to come.

Much more.

Chapter Fifteen

Caleb did his best to act casual as he walked past the class that was being held at Mr. Ritchie's store. Unfortunately, he'd arrived a whole lot later than he had planned, thanks to Ginger, who'd put up such a fuss when he was leaving his house that he ended up taking a detour to drop her off at Jacob's place instead. Along with all the stuff she had to have with her wherever she went. Litter box, food dish, water dish, scratching post, toys and more. The orange kitten traveled like a movie star, bringing a whole new meaning to the phrase "high maintenance." But at least she seemed pretty happy when he left her to play with Jacob's kids, especially nine-year-old Jackson. In fact, she probably had a kindred spirit in Caleb's nephew, since the kid was every bit as curious and mischievous as Ginger was.

And Caleb had a feeling they would end up in time-out together before long. Since Jacob and his wife, Daphne, didn't put up with fits and tantrums and bad behavior from their children.

But they had certainly met their match with Jackson.

Much like Caleb had met his match with Ginger. Her conniption tonight meant that Caleb was late, and he'd completely missed the class break, the time when his sister-in-law, Kayla, had wanted him to show up. And now, from what he could tell, the class was well into the second half.

Not that he was exactly keen on being there anyway. To be honest, he was only showing up because Kayla had insisted that he come tonight, claiming she'd found the *perfect* woman for him. Major emphasis on the word "*perfect.*" And since Kayla and his other sisters-in-law were on an absolute mission to find him a match, well, he didn't have the heart to say no. Though he was well aware that any possible introductions tonight would probably end up as nothing but a dead end. Mostly because he wasn't even sure he wanted to start dating again, not with his history of unhappily ever after endings.

Though if nothing else, at least he already had another supply order for Mr. Ritchie, so the trip wasn't a total loss. And as he stood behind the class and listened to the instructor for a minute or two, he had to admit, he was impressed. It was great to hear the guy teaching all about wiring and light fixtures and electrical components. Especially since Caleb had dealt with lots of new homeowners over the years who didn't know a single thing about such basics as GFCI outlets or circuit breakers. And those were important things to know about if a person ever tripped a breaker and lost power. Which immediately made Caleb think about Christmas decorating, when plenty of people plugged in *way* more outdoor lights than their systems could handle. Of course, that overload was a perfect example of something that could trip a breaker and make an entire Christmas display go dark.

Not that he hadn't been there a time or two himself, with all the Christmas lights he liked to put out.

But thankfully, Caleb had solved the problem by simply installing a dedicated Christmas light circuit and a series of outlets in all the new homes he built. Something his customers absolutely appreciated.

The thought of it made him smile as he listened to the instructor for a few more minutes. But since he wasn't here for a refresher course on a subject that he could just as easily teach, Caleb strolled ever-so-nonchalantly on, staying behind the class. Yet as he went, he tried to recall the name of the woman Kayla had wanted him to meet. But all he could remember was that her name had two consecutive *b*'s in it.

Was it Abby? Debbie? He glanced to where Kayla was seated, since she'd told him this "perfect" woman was sitting in her row.

And that's when he noticed the place cards for each person attending. Mr. Ritchie's idea, no doubt, and something he'd picked up from his late wife. He often talked about how she liked to make people feel comfortable in social settings, and putting out place cards was just one of the ways she did it. It was better than a name tag, which usually meant staring at someone's chest, something that could cause a whole lot of awkwardness for everyone. But tonight, those place cards ended up being a big help for Caleb, too, since it made it easy for him to spot the woman Kayla had wanted him to meet.

And when he did, his jaw nearly hit the floor. Sure, the girl was very pretty, exotic looking even, with her dark hair and eyes. But wow, oh wow, was she ever young! Barely out of high school, from what he could guess. And way, way, *way* too young for him.

Just to be sure, he glanced at her place card once more. "Gabby," it read. A name with two *b's, side by side*. She *had* to be the one that Kayla had been talking about. If only Kayla had been talking about the woman who was sitting *between* her and Gabby. That woman was every bit as pretty—beautiful, even, in a wholesome sort of way. And oddly enough, Caleb had a strange, instantaneous reaction the minute he saw her.

A reaction he couldn't explain, and one that didn't exactly make sense.

He looked for her place card, but this other woman didn't have one. Which must have meant she wasn't actually part of the class, since Caleb knew Mr. Ritchie would never leave someone out. That meant she was probably one of Kayla's friends who had stopped by to chat during the break and just hadn't left yet. And that friend must have been married or in a committed relationship or something, otherwise he was sure Kayla would have introduced her to him long ago.

Whatever the case, dating Gabby was *definitely* not an option, and Caleb decided to get out of there before Kayla spotted him and tried to push the issue. So he vamoosed to the other side of the store, to chat with Mr. Ritchie instead. Yet all the while, he couldn't help but wonder, what had Kayla been thinking? Trying to line him up with a girl who looked like she was still in her teens? Was the search to find him the right woman so desperate that they couldn't even stick to women of his generation? And now they'd started going down a generation or two to find him a match?

Mr. Ritchie crinkled his brows when he saw Caleb. "You okay, son? You look like you've seen a ghost."

"Too young to be a ghost, and too young for me," Caleb replied, shaking his head.

"Oh, all right . . . maybe you could clarify that?"

Which was precisely what Caleb did *not* want to do. Not today anyway.

So he quickly changed the subject by pointing to a display of art lamps on a table. "Those are nice. I love all the details and small pieces, and the way they fit together. They're very artistic."

"That's what I thought, too," Mr. Ritchie agreed. "The young woman who makes these has quite a natural gift."

"You know . . ." Caleb started to say, putting a finger to his chin. "Since my mom is a decorator and she likes unique things, I'll bet she would *love* one of these."

Mr. Ritchie smiled. "I think she would, too. But if you see something you think she'd like, you'd better get it now. Each lamp is one of a kind, and they sell just as fast as I get them in."

"In that case, I'll take this one," Caleb said as he picked out a lamp with an obvious 1940s flare. "My mom collects vintage jewelry, and this one looks like it's been decorated with a bunch of it. I wish I could find something so unique for one of my housing projects. I'm still searching for a fixture to go over the kitchen island."

"Hmmm . . . what do you have in mind? I could check all my catalogues if you like," Mr. Ritchie told him.

Caleb shook his head. "That's part of the problem. I really don't know what I'm looking for. So I'll probably put up a basic fixture for now, just to have something in place while I keep on searching. I guess I'll know the right one when I see it."

Mr. Ritchie gave him a knowing smile and grabbed a large

box and put a layer of packing paper on the bottom. "Well, that's something that could apply to a lot of situations. Because your heart will tell you when it's right, and it's best not to settle for anything less."

"Ummm . . . I guess that's true . . ."

"Someday, the right one will come along," Mr. Ritchie went on as he removed the maroon brocade lampshade from the lamp so he could pack it properly. "And just remember that, when it does, your heart has to be open and ready for it."

Caleb raised an eyebrow, becoming fully aware that the older man wasn't just talking about light fixtures anymore. And while he always appreciated Mr. Ritchie's advice, tonight he preferred to keep the conversation on a less sensitive subject.

So he pointed to the specialty light bulb that was screwed into the lamp's socket, one that had facets on it, like a gemstone. "I've never seen a bulb like this one before."

"Neither had I, until recently," Mr. Ritchie responded as he unscrewed the bulb and tucked it safely away in the bottom corner of the box. "But that little bulb diffuses the light and sends shadows and light rays across the entire shade. It's one of the things that makes this lamp stand out."

"Wow," Caleb murmured. "The lamp would be beautiful on its own, but the bulb gives it an added touch. The details matter, don't they?"

"They certainly do, son. Like they say, 'God is in the details.'"

"And that bulb is a very nice detail," Caleb agreed.

In fact, it was something that took the lamp from being "very good" to being "outstanding." A concept that Caleb kept in mind with his own work.

Mr. Ritchie nodded as he started to wrap the lamp with plastic bubble sheets. "If you don't mind my asking, did you contact Matt?"

"Yup, I did," Caleb told him. "And I'm really glad you recommended him. In a nutshell, we think the threat against my family is basically neutralized. But we're still going after Fallon, so she can't harm anyone else. I don't know the specifics on how we're going to do that, or what Matt has in mind, but I'm meeting him for a beer in a few minutes. So I guess I'll find out then."

"Sometime when we have more time, I'd love to hear all about it," Mr. Ritchie told him, as he carefully placed the wrapped lamp in the box and set the shade on top.

"Deal," Caleb agreed. "And here's my latest supply order."

That brought a big smile to Mr. Ritchie's face. "I'm happy to see business is so good."

"Thanks. And for you, too. It looks like you've been expanding."

Mr. Ritchie nodded. "Yes, I have been blessed beyond measure. Especially with all the young people who've been coming in lately."

Right away, his words lifted Caleb's spirits. Sure, in comparison to Mr. Ritchie, he was still a young guy. But after what he'd been through with Fallon, Caleb had been feeling old beyond his years lately. Yet here he was, talking to a man who was decades and decades older than him. If only he could have the kind of life and marriage and success that Mr. Ritchie had had over the years. Then Caleb would have a life well lived, too, beyond a doubt.

He left Mr. Ritchie's store with a smile on his face and the lamp he'd bought nestled safely in the box. Yet on the way out, he couldn't help but take one last look at the woman sitting next to Kayla. At least, as much of her as he could see anyway.

And just like before, there was something about her that seemed to draw him in. Some force of nature. Something he couldn't explain, even if he wanted to.

Though he was pretty sure it only meant that he hadn't learned his lesson when it came to relationships. And he was the same old sap that he'd always been. So if he were smart, he would do well to avoid those "supernatural" moments of getting drawn in by a woman. Any woman. Not until he got himself straightened out. Because, at this point in his life, he still couldn't trust his own instincts when it came to being attracted to someone.

Something he repeated to himself as he drove to the sports bar to meet Matt. He arrived fifteen minutes late, thanks to traffic, and he was surprised to find the P.I. sitting at a round, wooden table with five other guys.

Matt motioned him over to the only empty chair. "Hey, Caleb, I've got some friends I'd like you to meet."

Though these "friends" didn't exactly seem like a chatty bunch. They barely even looked up and acknowledged him before they went back to staring into their beers.

Caleb took his seat, wondering what Matt was getting him into. He did his best to size up the group and try to figure out some kind of common denominator among the men. Did they all work together? Were they part of a club? A few of the guys looked like they were slightly older than Caleb—one with blonde hair that went to his shoulders, and another with short, red hair. Then there was a balding man who was much, much older. Probably close to the age of Caleb's father. Next to him was a guy with medium-brown hair and dark-rimmed glasses, who looked to be about a decade older. And sitting beside him was another guy with close-cropped, dark hair and jet-black eyes who looked like he was quite a bit younger than Caleb.

Matt caught Caleb's eye and nodded to him, almost like he was reading his mind. "I'll bet you want to know why I called you to this meeting tonight. Just like I'm sure all of you men want to know why I invited you here."

Naturally, those words got everyone's attention, and all eyes were now on Matt.

"But first, let's start with introductions," Matt went on. "Our newcomer is Caleb, and on the other side of the table is Finn," he said, pointing to the older man. "Then we have Reggie . . ."

And the younger man with the dark-rimmed glasses raised his hand. "Present. I'm Reggie."

"Next we have Armando," Matt continued, which brought a wave from the dark-haired, younger guy.

"And I'm C.J.," said the red-haired man.

"So . . . that makes me the last to be picked for the team," the blonde man added, eliciting laughter from the whole group. "I'm Richard."

Matt grinned. "So . . . now that we've gotten past the 'who,' let's go for the 'why.' My investigations have shown that you all have something in common. It turns out, you've all been scammed by the same woman. And her partner."

And that was the moment when the otherwise laid-back bunch suddenly became animated. Gasps and groans rose to the ceiling, while mouths dropped open.

Caleb was the first to speak. "Fallon."

"Do you mean Crystal?" the older man added.

"Or Lily?" C. J. put in.

"Anna?" Armando asked.

"Tiffany!" Reggie blurted out.

Richard seemed to have trouble even forming words at all. "Do you mean . . . do you mean Sunny?"

"Yes, yes, and yes," Matt told the men. "All yesses. Except, as Caleb already knows, her real name is Kinley Karnowski."

More groans and murmurs rose from the bunch, and the men all looked at each other.

"She was a busy girl," said Finn. "I'm a widower, and let me tell you, she did a world-class job of getting her talons into me."

Richard shook his head. "I'm a widower, too. I lost my wife to cancer a year ago. Turbo cancer, someone called it. She went quick. And this woman, Sunny, showed up around the same time as the life insurance check did. I was so lost I was barely able to run my business. And let me tell you, she took full advantage of my grieving."

"Rotten," Caleb responded. "Super rotten. Sounds like something she'd do."

Armando nodded. "Well, she took full advantage of me, period. I've never been married, but I was so blinded by her beauty that I couldn't see straight. Plus, people in my family all get married young and have big families. And I thought that would be me and Anna, too. So I didn't see what was coming until it was too late. She sort of inserted herself into my father's house-building company when we started dating. And that's how she managed to get money out of me. She claimed she'd done work for us, and we owed her. She said if I didn't pay up, she'd ruin my family online."

"Me, too," Caleb added. "So what did you do?"

Armando shrugged. "At first I ignored her. I thought she was bluffing. But when customers suddenly started telling me about bad reviews and negative posts about our company online, I found out she meant it. In the end, I paid up. And she took down all those posts, including the pictures she had taken and distorted. Still, the damage was done, and I can't say our company has fully recovered yet."

"Lousy," Reggie said. "She pulled the same number on me. Let's face it, I'm not exactly what you'd call a movie star in the looks department, and I thought I'd hit the mother lode when Tiffany was suddenly interested in me. In fact, I couldn't believe my luck. Especially since I have a software company, and I don't even get out much. But then she started telling me how I should market my products. Her advice was all bogus, of course, since she didn't know squat about marketing. Or software, for that matter. But then she claimed I'd hired her, and that I owed her for her work. Which wasn't true."

"How did you handle it?" Armando asked.

"I just wanted her to go away. So I paid her," Reggie said, cringing. "Thankfully, I've never heard from her since."

And so the conversation went. Caleb quickly learned that all the men owned their own businesses or were part of a family business. Among the group, there were a handful of home-building contractors, a software engineer, a restaurant owner, and a man who owned a small oil company.

After everyone else had told their story, all eyes turned to Caleb.

"How about you?" Richard asked. "Did you pay her off, too, Caleb?"

That's when a sly smile crossed Caleb's face. "Nope," he said before he took a sip of his beer. "Instead of paying her, I made a fake marriage proposal. And I insisted that we get married the next morning, saying that my money would be her money once we were married. So there was no need for me to pay her at that moment."

"Brilliant!" Richard exclaimed with a laugh.

"If only I'd thought of that," Armando put in.

Caleb shook his head. "But it wasn't my idea. It was Matt's idea. And you should see the fake ring I gave her."

"She took the ring and ran," Matt said with a grin.

Reggie's dark eyes went wide. "But what if she'd gone through with it?"

Matt's grin never dipped. "Her partner never would've allowed it. There's no way he would have agreed to let his girlfriend marry Caleb here."

Richard raised his beer. "So we're all in the same boat. Birds of a feather."

"Sorry saps," C.J. added, raising his own beer.

"Here's to the first meeting of the Sorry Saps Society," Finn said formally as he raised his own mug.

This brought forth more laughter from the rest of the men as they raised their glasses and "clinked" with the others. "To the Sorry Saps," they said in unison.

After that, the conversation flowed, with more talk about Kinley.

Eventually, Matt waved to get everyone's attention. "Okay, there is one more thing I'd like to discuss. I still have hopes of catching Kinley in the act and recording her extortion attempts. Direct from the horse's mouth, so to speak. Then we can go straight to the police. The recording probably won't be admissible in court, but it should be enough to get the police interested and involved. Because I want to see her and her partner rot in jail."

Words that brought another toast from the entire bunch.

"Sounds good to me," Finn said. "I'm all ears. What do we need to do?"

"We'll have to set up a sting," Matt explained. "But first we need to find a man who's willing to help us. A single guy with his own business. Someone who will play along and lead her on. To get her to pull her usual tricks while we record it. Anyone have any ideas of someone who might be willing to help us out?"

And that's when the group went silent, and no one seemed to have an answer.

"Well, that will be our next step," Matt told them all. "So let's keep our eyes open for someone who could fit the bill."

"That could be a real challenge," Richard put in.

"Yup," Matt agreed. "It sure could. But that doesn't mean it can't be done. And I have confidence that we'll find the right guy."

Caleb nodded along with the others, before he took another

sip of his beer. More than anything, he hoped the P.I. was on the right track with this idea. Sure, his plan seemed a little farfetched. But even so, Caleb had to admit, Matt hadn't steered him wrong yet.

So from that moment on, Caleb decided to be on the lookout for a guy who would be willing to help.

The lives of plenty of other guys depended on it.

Chapter Sixteen

Libby took one more glance in the wall mirror of the cruise ship suite and hardly recognized herself. She had lost at least twenty pounds—a side effect, she'd been told, of grieving. Plus, she'd gone to her hairdresser for the first time in six months, where she not only had ten inches cut from her long tresses, but she also had the whole works lightened to a golden blonde. The desire to change one's hair, apparently, was also a side effect of grieving.

And though the reflection staring back at her was unfamiliar, she had to admit, this new version of herself was, well . . . kind of elegant. Glamorous, even. In fact, the young woman she saw before her could have walked the red carpet, with her hair parted to the side and falling in soft, loopy curls, and her midnight blue gown with its off-the-shoulder sleeves, accented with sequins. The dress had been a last-minute purchase, something she'd found just two days ago, and something she'd paid way too much money for. Yet thanks to all her lamp sales, she was able to afford the dress without breaking the bank. Though it didn't help matters that she'd also had to buy a whole new wardrobe—dresses, shorts, tops and shoes—since she had next to nothing in her closet that fit anymore.

Strange, but Devin's old clothes weren't the only ones she'd donated to thrift stores. She'd actually ended up clearing out plenty of her own stuff, too.

Changes, changes, changes. So many changes.

Which included the image she now saw in the mirror. And while it was going to take some getting used to, she still had to admit—the new evening gown was certainly working its magic. Plus, with her new red lipstick and one of the vintage necklaces she'd bought at the antique store, she wondered if she might be the belle of the ball. Or, at least, the belle of the formal night here on the cruise ship, *Freedom Queen*.

So much for keeping to herself and avoiding social situations. With this outfit, she wouldn't exactly be coming in under the radar.

Her mom emerged from the suite's bathroom and snapped on a pair of dangly earrings. "That dress was a great find, dear. You look stunning!"

Libby nodded to her. "So do you, Mom."

"Want to borrow my sapphire bracelet? It would look gorgeous with your gown."

"I don't know . . . I'd be afraid I might lose it."

Her mom waved her off. "Nonsense. Beautiful jewelry is meant to be worn. Besides, it's got a safety chain."

And before Libby could say another word, her mom reached over and fastened the blue-jeweled bracelet to her left wrist.

"Wow, thanks, Mom. But don't you want to wear a bracelet or two yourself?"

Her mom flashed her a wide smile. "Of course, dear. But tonight, I'm going with diamonds. And only diamonds." And so she did, when she snapped a couple of diamond bracelets onto her own wrist.

All the while, Libby couldn't help but notice how spectacular her mother looked in her one-shoulder, dark purple gown with a cascading ruffle down the side of the skirt. Even as a middle-aged woman, her mother was still a fashion plate. And just like any self-respecting Texan who was proud of her heritage, she was not the kind of woman to simply grow old gracefully, and she wasn't about to go "gentle into that good night," as the famous poem said. No, her mother was the kind of person who took life by the longhorns, jumped on

126

board, and went for a wild ride. Maybe it was because she had experienced some losses over the years that she fully understood the value of being alive. And maybe that was enough to make her want to live life to the fullest and enjoy every moment she had in this world.

A mindset that Libby considered adopting for herself. Someday, when she was ready. And when her grief had subsided.

The idea of it made Libby smile, and for the first time since she'd been young, Libby realized just how much she admired her mother. Sure, they'd had their sparring matches over the years. But her mother had been a rock when Libby needed her. And besides that, she'd always been one heck of a role model.

Her mother grabbed her rhinestone clutch and handed Libby's evening bag to her. "Ready, dear daughter? Shall we go out and show 'em how it's done?"

Libby couldn't help but laugh. "Yes, Mom. Let's do it. We're definitely a force to be reckoned with."

The appreciative glances started the minute they emerged from the elevator and stepped into the long hallway of the Promenade. Funny, but she almost felt like she and her mom should be wearing tiaras, the way people were staring at them. Especially when they paused at one of the photographer stations and got their picture taken.

But she also noticed how stunning the rest of the passengers looked, too. And she quickly paid as many compliments as she received. It was like going to prom all over again. Only this time, it was an elegant, grown-up kind of prom.

For a while, Libby even forgot she was a grieving widow. Until they were led to their seats at a large, round table set with nine places. And that's when she felt her heart start to sink. What would happen if the others found out the truth about her? Would she droop into a puddle of tears, something that, no doubt, would put a real damper on an otherwise enjoyable evening?

Her mother touched Libby's arm. "Chin up, dear. You've got this. And don't forget, I'll run interference, so you don't have to talk about anything you don't want to talk about. And I can still tell people that you only speak Ookanawabowbeen."

Despite herself, Libby couldn't help but laugh. "Thanks, Mom," she murmured as she slid gracefully onto her chair while the waiter held it for her.

A few minutes later, the rest of the passengers who were assigned to their table joined them. First there were a couple of women about ten years older than Libby. One with sandy hair and a wide smile, and the other with auburn hair and teary, blue eyes. Then came a thin, older, gray-haired man. After that, a stylish, silver-haired woman who was probably in her forties showed up, along with her two, dark-haired teenage daughters. Seconds after they arrived, another woman joined them, and judging by the obvious familial resemblance, Libby guessed this woman was probably a sister to the silver-haired lady. Though the second woman sported hair that had been expertly dyed, with highlights and lowlights that ranged from golden brown to pale blonde.

Always the quintessential hostess, Libby's mom started the introductions. Or, at least, she tried to.

The silver-haired woman immediately shot Libby's mom a sharp look. "I'm sorry, but we requested a table for four. So if you don't mind, we would appreciate it if you pretended like we're not even here."

Then the woman turned to her sister and the two teens, and they proceeded to start up their own, private conversation, basically ignoring the rest of the group. And though Libby was—quite frankly—perfectly fine with not having to converse with the four of them, she couldn't help but notice the sudden tension it created at the table.

"As you wish," Libby's mom replied, not letting her smile dip one little bit.

And though she wasn't outwardly fazed by their discourtesy, Libby knew her mother would be inwardly seething over such horrendous rudeness. After all, her mother could write volumes and volumes on the importance of good manners, and she believed in being courteous above all else.

And to prove it, she turned to the only man at the table, and found out his name was Nash. "It's interesting that you were put at a table with all women," her mother went on.

"It's my good fortune," he told her with a smile. "Sitting at a table with such beautiful women. I've been traveling alone since I lost my dear wife ten years ago. So I always enjoy the opportunity to converse with new people."

"Well, it's lovely to meet you," Libby's mom said sincerely.

Then she and Nash both turned to the auburn-haired woman, sitting between them. "I'm Bridget," the woman barely managed to squeak out. Panic instantly flared in her eyes, and she looked as though she might start to cry.

That's when the sandy-haired woman, who introduced herself as Ella, sort of hijacked the conversation and ran with it. "My husband wouldn't go with me, even though he promised he would, but he doesn't like to go to the spa on board and I do. Plus, he says the Caribbean is way too hot, and he doesn't want to go ashore and do fun things. But me, I love to go snorkeling and swimming and all that stuff. Plus, I've got to have my margaritas in Mexico. They just make the best ones ever down there, don't you think? Anyway, he backed out last minute, and I remembered that Bridget might like to go. So I called her up to see if she was free. Thankfully she was. We've been having the best time. This ship is so spectacular, don't you think?"

Beside her, Bridget bit her lip, and Libby couldn't help but think of what her mom had said about running interference. Was that what Ella was doing now? For her friend? Because something was clearly bothering Bridget.

Libby offered up her best smile, in hopes of making Bridget feel more comfortable. "Are you from the Houston area?" she asked.

Bridget nodded. "I am. But Ella flew in from South Carolina. We went to high school together. How about you? Are you from Houston?"

"Just outside of Houston," Libby went on while her mother chatted with Ella. "I live in Destiny. But my mom here lives a few hours north and west."

Bridget nodded. "Oh, yes, I've heard of Destiny. In fact, my husband once told me . . ." she started to say, and then hesitated. "That is . . ."

And right away, Libby knew what was going on. "I think I

understand," she said with a nod. "I'm guessing you're . . ."

"Yes," Bridget responded as tears gathered in her eyes. "I'm a widow. For just a few months now. I wasn't sure if I was ready for a trip like this, but Ella insisted that I come with her. Now I'm wondering if I should have stayed home."

Libby took a deep breath and mustered every ounce of courage she could find. For some reason, she had the desire to make this other woman feel more at ease. Maybe she was more of her mother's daughter than she realized. And maybe by helping Bridget, she was actually helping herself, oddly enough.

"My mom insisted that I come, too," Libby told Bridget. "Because I'm also a . . ."

And that's when Bridget gave her a knowing smile. "The 'W' word. That's what I usually say. It's just easier."

"Agreed," Nash added, jumping in. "It's much easier than saying 'widower.' Maybe because people have to stop and think about it for a second or two, while they try to figure out what the 'W' stands for. Then you don't get the instant sad faces. Or the pity."

Now the woman with the perfectly highlighted and lowlighted hair on the other side of the table suddenly piped up and joined the conversation. "I agree, as well. I say the same thing."

"So . . . you are . . . too?" Libby asked.

"Yup, I am. And my name is Caroline," she said with a nod. "Four months now."

Her sister sighed. "I'm Kate, and I'm sorry for being so rude earlier. But it was hard for Caroline to come on this trip. And I was just trying to protect her from any conversation that might trigger her grief."

That's when Libby's mom smiled. "Apology accepted, because I planned to do the same thing for my daughter. Run interference, you might say."

"Me, too," Ella added.

And from there, the conversation flowed like they were all old friends, with everyone joining in. Both those who had lost a spouse, and those who were there to support them. Right away, Libby felt oddly relieved that everyone knew her big secret, and much to her surprise, it turned out it wasn't such a big secret after all. Not only that, but she soon learned firsthand that the rest of the widows and the one widower were going through so many of the same things that she'd been going through herself.

She wasn't sure when the conversation turned, but at some point, it most definitely did. And it went away from the topic of grief, and soon the whole bunch started to talk about their planned shore excursions and other activities they were looking forward to around the ship. And they talked about clothes and shoes and all kinds of things. The only ones who didn't really join in were the dark-haired teens. And once the meal was over, they simply turned to each other, rolled their eyes, and left without saying goodbye.

Not that Libby cared. Because she quickly started to relax in a way that she hadn't relaxed in a long time. Then before she knew it, she actually found herself laughing every now and then.

"Should we continue this party at the jazz bar upstairs in a little while?" Bridget finally suggested.

"Sounds good to me," Libby agreed. "Mom and I are going to the comedy show first, but after that would be great."

Her mom smiled and shook her head. "I think I'll probably turn in after the show. So you go ahead and join the others, dear daughter."

"That's past my bedtime," Nash told them. "So I'll see everyone tomorrow night at dinner."

"You go without me, Caroline," Kate told her sister.

And so it was decided. An hour and a half later, Libby said goodnight to her mom and took the elevator to the lounge at the top of the ship. Bridget spotted her the minute she entered the huge room that had floor-to-ceiling windows overlooking the open decks below. She waved her over, and Libby joined her and Caroline. A woman with dark hair and green eyes that was about the same age as Libby was with them.

"This is Tessa," Bridget told her.

"Nice to meet you," Libby responded, barely able to hear her own voice.

Bridget scanned the crowd. "This place is so packed and so

loud that we won't be able to hear each other talk. Maybe we should get a glass of wine and go sit out on the deck."

Without hesitation, Libby and the other two nodded. And a few minutes later, she was more than glad that they'd gone outside. Because the stars were so bright, and the full moon was so brilliant that it was absolutely breathtaking. The lamps that Libby created at home couldn't even begin to compare to what God could do.

"This is heavenly," Caroline said as they sat at a little table. Then she pointed to some of the stars in the night sky. "Do you think they're up there? Our husbands?"

For a moment or two, they all looked upward, each lost in their own thoughts while a slight, salt breeze ruffled their hair.

"Maybe we should tell each other about our husbands," Caroline suggested. "And what they were like."

"Good idea," Bridget agreed as she nodded to Tessa. "But first let me tell you how I ran into Tessa, who is in a stateroom just a few doors down from mine. She's also one of the 'W' words, just like us."

Tessa nodded. "Bridget rescued me when I was going down the hallway," she said with tears in her eyes. "I guess I looked a little upset. I lost my husband four months ago, and I wasn't sure this trip would be a good idea. I'm on board with my aunt, and she practically forced me to come."

The other women responded with knowing nods.

"Thank God we have those people in our lives, who convinced us to take this trip," Libby murmured. "An aunt, an old friend, a sister, and in my case, my mom. Where would we be without their support?"

"Maybe we should buy them gifts at the jewelry store downstairs," Bridget suggested. "To say thank-you."

To which they all immediately agreed.

"Let's meet tomorrow afternoon and go shopping together," Libby said, adding to the idea. "Then we can give them their gifts at dinner tomorrow night."

"Sounds perfect," Tessa put in. She smiled, yet despite her best efforts, tears started to fall. "I sure wish I'd bought stock in tissue companies, because I've gone through a gazillion of them." She held up a handful of tissues for the rest of the women to see.

"Join the club," Libby assured her. "I don't go anywhere without a good supply."

The other two women simply laughed, fully understanding what it was like.

"Hey, wait a minute," Libby said. "Maybe that's what we are. Maybe we're kind of a club. A widow's club."

Caroline nodded. "Make that a 'Merry Widows Club' and I'm in. Because, even through our grieving, I think we should still be able to live life. And find some kind of happiness. Our late husbands would've wanted it."

Bridget nodded. "So true. Sometimes, we have to be able to smile through our tears."

Libby held up her glass. "To the first ever get-together of the Merry Widows Club of the *Freedom Queen*."

Without waiting a single second, they all raised their glasses and clinked with one another's.

Much to Libby's amazement, she couldn't help but notice how much she felt like herself again. A new version of herself anyway. Especially in the days that followed, when her new club made it a point to meet for more activities. And before they disembarked, they made sure they had each other's information, with plans to get-together again before long.

Her mom was all smiles as she drove Libby home and pulled into her driveway. "What a fun trip. Aren't you glad you went?"

"I am, Mom. This was a fantastic idea. Thank you so much for suggesting this."

"And thank you again for the beautiful butterfly necklace," her mom said as she helped Libby bring her luggage into her house. "I will cherish it always. And speaking of cherish, I'd better get home to your daddy. Love you, daughter," she added with a hug.

"Love you, too, Mom."

But her mom had barely been gone five minutes when Libby felt it. The silence. The quiet. Closing in on her. After the camaraderie of her new friends and the nonstop activity of the cruise ship, the silence felt stifling. Oppressive. And for the first time since she'd lost Devin, Libby suddenly felt panic rising in her chest.

"Okay, okay," she murmured out loud. "Libby, girl, you can handle this. You'll be all right. You're going back to work pretty soon anyway."

Yet no matter how many times she repeated those very words to herself, she quickly realized it wasn't working. Funny how having so much fun for a few days had only pointed out how lonely her life had been since she'd lost Devin.

Thankfully, her phone rang. And she grabbed it with a newfound desperateness. Maybe it was one of the other widows calling. Or maybe her mom had decided to turn around and stay the night. She would take anything over the smothering silence of her house.

Much to her surprise, it was Mr. Ritchie. "Welcome back, young one. I'm sorry to bother you so soon after your vacation, but I was hoping you could stop by and pick up Merry Anne."

"Merry Anne . . ." Libby repeated.

She'd forgotten all about the calico kitten she'd promised to take from Mr. Ritchie.

But maybe a kitten was just what she needed right now.

"I'll be right over," she told him.

Half an hour later, she arrived back home, with an adorable longhaired kitten in a pet carrier. A kitten who continued to meow and meow and meow. Not in a terrified, upset, discombobulated way. No, this kitten seemed to be carrying on a running commentary. And when Libby brought the kitten into her house, Merry Anne made direct eye contact with her and just kept on talking . . . no, *insisting* . . . that Libby let her out of the pet carrier so she could make herself at home.

Which was exactly what the little cat did after Libby unzipped the soft-sided carrier. And as Merry Anne explored the house and became familiar with her new surroundings, she just kept on talking and talking and talking. It wasn't long before Libby realized this cat was practically meowing in full sentences. She even made kind of a *"num-num-num"* sound when she ate the food that Libby put in her dish.

While Libby wasn't sure what to think just yet, one thing she did know beyond a doubt—any silence that had been hanging around inside the house was now gone, banished by this nonstop, noisy kitten.

Talk about filling the void.

The realization made Libby laugh. Funny, but she'd gone from Merry Widows to Merry Anne in one short day. And with this kitten who climbed on her lap and meowed and purred up at her, Libby now wondered if a little silence might actually be a good thing.

Plus, she couldn't help but wonder—what had she gotten herself into?

"Let your light shine before others, that they may see your good deeds and glorify your Father in heaven."
(Matthew 5:16, NIV)

Chapter Seventeen

Spring leaves were budding out around Destiny as Caleb drove to his parents' house with his ever-present kitten in tow. By now, Ginger had grown so much that she didn't fit inside his shirt anymore. And since she still refused to travel in her pet carrier, Caleb allowed her to ride on the dashboard, where she made herself at home in the warm sunshine.

And much as he hated to admit it, the two had fallen into even more of a routine. Whenever she saw him heading for work in the morning, she made sure she was right there and ready to zoom through the door the second he opened it. Then she would race to his truck and jump in when he opened the driver's side door, making a beeline for her spot on the dashboard. As always, she went with him daily to check out his housing projects, and she rode on his shoulder as he walked through the construction sites. Thankfully, his customers and contractors alike absolutely loved her. And he couldn't believe how much she had become a part of his life.

But this morning, he wasn't crazy about the way she was

eyeballing the box he'd put on the passenger seat. The one that held the carefully wrapped lamp that he'd gotten for his mom at Mr. Ritchie's store. Ginger had a hard time resisting the urge to leap full force into any box, but if she jumped into this one, she would crush the brocade lampshade that was just inside. And that maroon shade was the perfect touch for the piece. The artist who made the lamp had even decorated the shade, too, with beautifully balanced details.

"God is in the details," Caleb murmured aloud.

Of course, he should have taken the lamp to his mom weeks and weeks ago when he first bought it. But the truth was, he was seriously dragging his feet when it came to visiting her. Mostly because he'd never actually talked to her one-on-one about his fiasco with Fallon. And just thinking about it made him feel like he was back in high school again, coming home brokenhearted after the head cheerleader had dumped him. But how could he have known that she was simply using him to make her old boyfriend jealous—a guy who'd graduated a few years ahead of them? And *the* guy she really wanted to be with.

Who also happened to be the guy she was miserably married to even to this day, and the father of her three children who were probably just as miserable.

Regardless, his mom had been there to pick up the pieces back then. Just like she always did after his failed relationships. And now, here he was again, a grown man who still hadn't gotten his act together when it came to women. Which wasn't exactly something he wanted to admit to his mom.

Not only that, but he truly wondered if he was making any progress. Or was he simply repeating the same old, same old pattern? Over and over? Unfortunately, the stakes were getting higher each time he messed up. And this latest mistake with Fallon could have been the most costly of all.

"When are you going to get it together?" he asked himself out loud as he parked his truck in the driveway of his parents' custom home. A home with all the bells and whistles—and a few other things as well.

Ginger gave him a terse meow.

"No, I don't mean you," he said with a laugh as he got out of the truck. "Nobody could *ever* accuse you of not having it together." He patted his shoulder, and she quickly jumped over and up, taking her spot.

Then he grabbed the box with the lamp and headed up the front walkway. His mom opened the hardwood door before he'd even made it onto the front porch. Tall and slim, she was but a few inches shorter than he was, with her long, dark blonde hair in a high ponytail.

She smiled when she glanced up at Ginger riding on Caleb's shoulder. "How is my little grandcat today?" she cooed as she held the door wide and let the pair into the extra tall foyer. "You're such a pretty girl, Ginger. And so sweet. Has your daddy been taking good care of you?"

Caleb groaned and rolled his eyes. "Trust me, Mom, that cat has *the* best of everything, and I've got the pet store receipts to prove it. Not to mention, the vet bill for her shots and checkup, which wasn't cheap, either. I'm not sure real kids cost this much."

That's when his mom laughed and took Ginger from his shoulder. "Oh, Son . . . I'm afraid I've got bad news for you. Believe it or not, you're getting off cheap with little Ginger here." She cuddled the orange kitten, who immediately looked up at her with great adoration, all the while purring as loud as a lawnmower.

Caleb shook his head. "You know, maybe being a bachelor my whole life isn't so bad. I've got nieces and nephews, and maybe that's enough."

"I don't think you're the bachelor type, Caleb. When you were eight, and you went to work with your dad one day, you came home and told me you could hardly wait to have kids so you could take them all to work with you. As I recall, you informed me that you'd be having all four of your kids at once. So they wouldn't have to put up with an older brother like Jacob." She motioned for him to follow her through the living room and into the kitchen.

This made Caleb chuckle as he followed behind. "I think Jacob was born bossy. And judgy."

"Don't forget," Caleb's mom went on. "He had to put up

with three younger brothers who were always plotting against him. And you boys were pretty sneaky, too. For some reason, your great plans always seemed to involve bugs and spiders and snakes."

"Garter snakes, Mom. Garter snakes. Completely harmless." Caleb set his box on the granite countertop of the huge kitchen island.

"Uh-huh. But the point is, you gave as good as you got." Still cuddling Ginger with one arm, his mom reached into a glass-front cupboard for a coffee cup.

Caleb laughed. "I guess that does sort of account for why Jacob is so bossy."

"Call it self-preservation," his mom informed him as she poured him a cup of coffee and passed it to him.

Then she poured a little cream into a saucer for Ginger and put it and the orange kitten on the floor. Ginger started lapping up the cream like it was the greatest thing she'd ever tasted.

In the meantime, Caleb poured cream into his own coffee and then took a nice, long sip. As always, he couldn't help but admire the way his mom had successfully pulled red accents into the sunny kitchen with white cabinets, Kashmir black granite countertops, and brass drawer pulls. A look that brought both joy and energy into the room.

Much like the rest of the house had been so expertly decorated. His mom, who had a degree in interior design, had outdone herself with this house, putting her knowledge and experience to the test. It wasn't just a show home; it was a dream home. In fact, they sometimes brought new customers inside, just to give them ideas of what could be built into their own custom homes. Of course, his mom always worked with those people when it came to interior decorating, as her part in the family business.

For some reason, just looking around his mom's perfectly designed and decorated kitchen made Caleb think of Fallon and her phony advice that she doled out without being asked, and then later tried to pass off as actual work. When it came to decorating, she really had no clue, especially if her own front yard was any indication.

But when it came to being a con artist, well, in that case, she was an expert.

Caleb's mom topped off her own cup with more coffee and cream and turned her attention back to Caleb. "You know, Son, they always say your own kids are payback for all the things you did in your childhood. In that case, you and your other brothers had better watch out." She grinned at him.

"I don't think it's going to be a problem," Caleb muttered as he slid onto one of the island barstools. "Ginger will probably be about the closest thing that I'll ever have when it comes to kids."

"Hmmm . . . I doubt that's true. And it sounds like there's something you need to talk about."

"Nope, Mom. Nothing to talk about."

She took a sip of her coffee and raised an eyebrow. "Gee, that's funny. Because that's not what I heard."

Caleb's jaw dropped. "Oh, really . . . what have you heard? And who told you?"

His mother laughed. "Seriously, Son. You don't think you can keep things secret in this family, do you?"

Caleb sighed and closed his eyes. Evidently, the moment of truth had come, when he was going to have to tell his mom what had happened with Fallon.

And that's when it suddenly occurred to him that *now* was the *perfect* time to give her the lamp he'd brought her.

"Here," he said, pushing the box toward her like he was five years old and showing her the frog that he'd just caught and stuck in a box. "I brought you something. Consider it an early Mother's Day present."

Both of her eyebrows shot up this time. "Wow, Caleb . . . a present? I wondered what was in the box. That was so thoughtful of you. What is it?"

"Something I think you'll really love, Mom."

She took another quick sip of her coffee and set the cup on the counter. Then she glanced into the box and carefully pulled out the lampshade. She let out sort of an "*ooooh*" sound when she saw it. She set the shade to the side and reached into the box again, this time pulling out the lamp itself. Then she slowly started to unwrap it, and gasped as more and more of the lamp was revealed. Finally, she found the specialty light bulb that had been nestled safely in the corner of the box. One with facets like a gemstone. Without hesitation, she screwed the bulb into the lamp's socket and attached the lampshade. Then she plugged the lamp in and turned on the switch.

That's when her eyes went wide. "Oh, my goodness, Caleb! Wow! I've never seen an art lamp like this before . . . This is . . . this is . . . absolutely stunning!"

"Glad you like it, Mom," he said, beaming and feeling like he was five once more, and his mom had just approved of the flowers he'd picked for her.

"Thank you so much!" she gushed, giving him a quick hug before she went back to admiring her new lamp. "Where in the world did you find this?"

"At Mr. Ritchie's store. He's selling stuff from some new artist, and as far as I know, she only makes lamps. Mr. Ritchie sells them out just as quick as she makes them."

"Well, whoever she is, she is extremely talented. I'd like to meet her sometime, and maybe get her to sign this piece. In any case, I will cherish this always. And yes, I think you're good to go for this Mother's Day and probably several more after that."

Caleb grinned a sheepish grin. "That's why I'm your favorite, right?"

To which she laughed again. "You're all my favorites. Would you like some banana bread? I baked it last night."

"Thanks, Mom. Sounds great."

Yet as she pulled a loaf from the pantry and preceded to slice it, he could tell she was having a hard time taking her eyes off the lamp. "There are so many wonderful details to this work. I could look at it all day," she finally admitted.

"Cool."

She put a plate with several slices of banana bread before him. "And just so you know, I know all about your situation with Fallon," she murmured as she grabbed a tub of butter and a knife and set them next to the plate.

That's when he started to choke. "Dad didn't want us to tell you about it before Christmas. He didn't want to upset you and ruin the holidays."

She chuckled and refilled his coffee cup. "Upset me? He was probably more worried that I'd go after the girl myself. You may be a grown man, Caleb, but I'm still your mother. And I don't take kindly to some con artist going after my baby. Or rather, my son."

"Geez, Mom. That's another reason why I didn't want to tell you. The idea of having my mom bail me out at this age doesn't exactly boost the ego." He gave her a cross-eyed look before he poured more cream into his coffee.

She took a sip of her own coffee. "Someday when you have kids of your own, you'll understand," she told him, though her eyes kept wandering back to her new lamp. "Maybe you could marry an artist like the woman who makes these lights. We could certainly use a lamp and light fixture artist in the family."

Now he laughed. "I'd be happy with a marriage like grandma and grandpa had. Dad's folks."

She nodded. "I know how much you admired your grandfather."

He buttered a slice of banana bread. "I still miss him. He was such a hero, serving in the war. I've always tried to be just like him, a regular nineteen-forties kind of guy. The only problem is, I'm finding out that 'Nineteen-forties Guy' doesn't fit into the modern world. Or modern relationships. Because whenever I act like he did, like a hero, and I rescue a woman, I end up getting 'used' instead."

Now it was her turn to choke. "Rescue?"

He stared into his coffee. "Yup, I do it all the time. Sometimes I don't mean to, but it seems like I do it out of habit. That seems to be my downfall. Because the women I rescue always turn out to be snakes."

"Whatever gave you the idea that you need to 'rescue' a woman? In a relationship?"

He looked at her sideways. "Huh? Aren't men supposed to be chivalrous? Like old-fashioned white knights who jumped in to rescue a woman?"

She laughed. "Maybe if a woman was in serious danger, like being trapped in a burning building or being physically attacked. Or drowning. And then that concept applies to pretty much *anyone* who might need to be rescued from something bad. But day-to-day, as a general rule, women aren't helpless femme fatales who can't make it through the day without being rescued."

"But Grandpa . . ." Caleb started to say. "He earned a good living and provided a nice house for his family. And everything they could want."

His mom nodded. "Sure, men will often take on the role of being the main provider in the family, but that's different."

Caleb glanced down at Ginger, who had licked every last drop of cream from her plate. "But Grandpa helped save the country and the free world, during World War Two. That's what inspired me to serve my time in the Army. Because thanks to men like him who stepped up to the plate and risked their own lives, the whole world was 'rescued.'"

"All very true. Your grandfather was incredibly brave and self-sacrificing, and yes, he truly was a hero. But I think you may be missing part of the equation."

He looked at her sideways. "I am?"

She nodded and took another sip of her coffee. "Yup. Because your grandmother was a hero, too. In fact, she was one of the strongest people I've ever met."

"Grandma? I thought grandma was just a . . ." he started to say, but he had the good sense to hold his tongue before he let the words slip out.

"Just a . . . homemaker?" his mother supplied. "A housewife?"

"Well . . ." He quickly took another bite of his banana bread.

She shook her head. "Did you know your grandmother also served in the military during the war? She was a World War Two hero, too."

Caleb wasn't sure he'd heard her right. "Wait a minute . . . Grandma?"

"Most definitely. But she was much quieter about it. Your grandfather was the one who got most of the attention, probably since being a pilot during the war was much more glamorous, in a sense."

"And more dangerous," Caleb added.

"True, but don't forget—everyone in that generation played

a role. One way or another. Your grandmother was a WAC. Meaning, she served with the Women's Army Corps. She was an air traffic controller, and she took her job very seriously. Her country needed her, and she stepped up to the plate during a time when women didn't do much of that kind of work. It took a lot of courage on her part. But she excelled at it. And without her, plenty of planes wouldn't have landed safely. So, in a sense, she saved lives, too."

Caleb took a sip of his coffee and buttered another slice of banana bread. "I guess I never heard about what she did during the war."

"Well, let me tell you, she knew her stuff. Then after the war, when she and your grandfather got married, she stayed home and raised your dad and his brothers. And believe me, she had her hands full, especially with your Uncle Chad."

"While Grandpa went to work."

That's when his mom laughed. "Your grandma worked, too, running the household. Which isn't nearly as easy as you seem to think. It takes tremendous mental strength and patience and stamina. Once you become a parent, you never get a break."

"I guess so . . . still . . ."

His mom leveled him with a steely gaze. "I think I know how to settle this. Why don't you give it a try for a weekend? Jacob and Daphne have to go out of town next month and they wanted me to babysit for them. But I think it would be a good idea if you babysat instead. It would give you a better idea of what 'homemakers' go through. Because Daphne runs a pretty tight ship over there. She probably has to, since little Jackson is a real handful."

"Okay, okay, Mom. There's no need to push it. Yeah, I'm sure raising kids is hard work. But I don't need to take care of my nephew and nieces to prove it. Especially not Jackson. The kid's probably a genius, but he's like Ginger, in a way. He's got to check out everything and figure out how things work."

"Yes, his curiosity definitely gets the best of him," she added with a laugh.

"Which is why he's always in trouble," Caleb quickly agreed.

"Which is also why I think it would be perfect for you to

watch him and his two little sisters for a weekend. Frankly, Caleb, it might just show you the other side of the equation. And for you, maybe that's the missing piece of the puzzle. Women aren't as helpless and in need of rescue as you seem to think. And a good marriage, a true relationship, is one where both partners are pulling their weight. Even when one partner stays home and does most of the child-rearing and the other one brings home the bacon. In a sense, you might say their roles are equal but different."

For some reason, her statement left Caleb speechless. And the gears in his head started to turn. Could it be that he'd gotten it all wrong? Maybe he'd been so zeroed in on his grandfather being a hero that he'd missed an important part of the whole picture?

Before he could say another word, his mom already had Daphne on the phone. And the two of them were busy making arrangements for Caleb to babysit. While he could overhear Daphne putting up a few token protests, frankly, she didn't seem to be fighting the idea all *that* much. Like he would have expected someone who "ran a tight ship" would do.

Was it possible his mom had already talked to her about this? And she practically had the whole arrangement set up already?

"There," she said with a smile after she got off the phone. "It's all set."

"Why do I have the feeling I'm being railroaded here?" he asked as Ginger chose that exact moment to climb up his jeans and onto his lap.

His mom grinned. "Looks like Ginger's in. So . . . how about you? Are you in?"

Caleb rolled his eyes. "All right, fine, Mom. I'll do it."

Of course, he couldn't say he was exactly excited about the prospect. Still, it was only for a weekend.

And honestly, how hard could it be?

Chapter Eighteen

"You are such a little chatterbox," Libby said to her new kitten. "But an awfully sweet and adorable little chatterbox." Looking into Merry Anne's big, green eyes, Libby laughed, something she'd been doing a lot of since the kitten had come to live with her.

The little cat responded with meows and chirrups and the full range of cute noises that she was capable of making. And for that matter, usually did make. Nonstop. And while Libby mostly shortened the cat's name to "Merry," the tiny feline herself never had a shortage of things to say in her own little cat language. Thankfully, Libby had learned to decipher most of her squeaks and trills and other sounds, so she had a pretty good idea what Merry wanted at that moment. Which meant she knew to scoop the kitten up into her arms and cuddle her close. As always, Merry leaned up on Libby's shoulder and stared directly into her eyes, as though she needed to be up close and personal for the conversation they were—no doubt—about to have.

Funny, but now that Merry had been with Libby for almost a month and had settled into her new home, Libby thought the high-energy calico would be a little less . . . well, verbal. Outspoken. Whatever the word was that described the super happy and very chatty kitten. But that hadn't happened. Not even close. If anything, Merry seemed to have even more to say as the days went on.

On top of that, Merry went wherever Libby went. Or, at least, wherever Libby allowed the kitten to go, which was around the house or in the garage. Plus, she slept with Libby on the couch at night, and she even went so far as to jump in the shower with Libby a few times, though she was careful to stay out of the spray. Naturally, Merry was also right there when Libby worked on her lamps. Though at least Libby had learned to corral the kitten's behavior somewhat while she worked. As long as Merry had some toys of her own to play with, she pretty much kept her paws off Libby's works in progress. Even so, having Merry in the house was almost like having a small child around. And except for the times when Merry took a nap, Libby didn't have a moment to herself.

Something that was a complete surprise to Libby.

After all, weren't cats supposed to be independent? And so much different from dogs who needed nonstop attention? Libby even wondered if there might be some health issue with her stunningly beautiful kitten. One whose face was half orange and half black, with a spotted pink nose. And one orange front leg and one black front leg, with white paws. And a white belly. Frankly, the little cat looked like one of Libby's collage lamps, with different colors and pieces being fit in here and there. Yet all well-balanced to create a perfectly imperfect work of art.

Art in motion, Libby decided with a laugh. *Art that is always in motion. And art that doesn't quit talking.*

Finally, Libby asked her vet about Merry when she took her in for kitten shots. "She is so talkative," Libby explained. "And she's into everything. Not to mention, she wants to be in on *everything* I do. I had no idea that cats hung out with their humans so much. Do you think she's okay?"

But the vet just laughed and shook her head. "Your kitten is very healthy, Libby. Lots of people are surprised by how sociable cats can be. And Merry Anne is an especially outgoing girl. To top it off, she's very intelligent and needs a great deal of mental stimulation."

Libby's mouth dropped open. "Mental stimulation? A cat

needs mental stimulation?"

"They most definitely do. In fact, I'd suggest getting her a playmate. Another kitten about her age so she has someone to pal around with. Though if you decide to do that, just make sure you have a nice block of time where you can properly introduce them. So they'll have a good, lifelong relationship. In the meantime, I'd suggest getting Merry Anne some automated toys that either roll around or move across the floor. Or just keep spinning. Cats like her often appreciate robot vacuums. Anything to keep her mind occupied. Especially while you're at work."

"Rolling and moving," Libby repeated as she carried Merry back to the car in her soft-sided pet carrier. "And spinning . . . Spinning, spinning, spinning."

Which was exactly what her brain seemed to be doing when she drove Merry back home. Especially with Merry meowing and chirping and trilling from the passenger seat. Clearly, the little kitten had an opinion about her vet visit, and she happily voiced it—loudly—as she rode home.

"We'll be there soon," Libby assured the colorful kitten, who immediately responded with more chatter.

That's when Libby rolled her eyes. "Well, at least I'm not talking to *myself* as much as I used to . . . I'm just talking to a cat now . . ."

She immediately chuckled when she realized how much this tiny, furry creature had become the center of her attention these days. And now her vet suggested that she get a second one? She hadn't even gotten used to the first one.

Yet it seemed par for the course, considering the way her life had been going lately. She'd gone through so many big changes over the last several months that she couldn't even list them all. And every one of those changes also required a major adjustment on her part. Then it seemed like the minute she did adjust, there'd be another big change, which would require more adjusting. Change, adjust, change, adjust. Change. Rinse and repeat. Exactly how much more change could she adjust to in her life?

Even so, if Merry was bored and lonely, it was Libby's job to fix that. As a pet parent. Because Libby certainly understood what it was like to be lonely. Especially at night, when she missed Devin the most, and she was painfully reminded that he was no longer there, and he would *never* sleep next to her again.

A change that she still hadn't adjusted to.

Which was why she completely avoided sleeping in her bed, and why she wasn't sleeping regular hours. Instead, it just seemed easier to work on her lamps at night and take naps on her couch whenever she felt like sleeping.

She had hoped that going back to work might help, and make her life feel more normal again. But oddly enough, it didn't. Not with everyone there treating her with kid gloves. She no longer felt like "Libby in the marketing department." Instead, it now seemed like she was "Libby in the marketing department whose husband died and isn't that so sad?"

Regardless, she didn't want to seem ungrateful to her friends. Especially when they were only reacting like she probably would've reacted if she were in their shoes. And they were trying so hard to be thoughtful to her.

"You have a cat?" Jessica said one morning when they took a coffee break. "I didn't think you even liked cats."

"That was Devin who didn't like cats," Libby told her. "He was strictly a dog person. But I've always liked cats, even though I've never had one before. And you should see how cute my little Merry is," Libby said as she used her phone to log into the app for the camera she'd set up at home.

Right away, Jessica laughed as the image of Libby's family room, strewn with automated cat toys, showed up on the screen. "Wow, that's a lot of stuff for one kitten. And you're right, she is adorable."

For a minute or two, they watched as Merry wandered from one toy to the next and to the next. Playing and attacking along the way. They even had a good view of the DVD that Libby had left playing on her big screen TV. A program specifically made for cats, with segments featuring birds and mice and fish.

Jessica couldn't help but smile. "Gee, it's not like this cat is spoiled or anything . . ."

"Watch this." Libby grinned and touched the "Talk" icon on the app. Then she called out Merry's name and the little cat immediately came running to the camera, purring like a motorboat.

"That's amazing," Jessica said, shaking her head. "I thought cats were supposed to be so aloof. This kitten seems to hang on your every word. Literally."

"Oh, yeah, I'm pretty sure she'd like us to be attached at the hip," Libby admitted as they watched Merry head to the robot vacuum and jump on board, before riding it around like a carnival ride.

Jessica laughed again. "Maybe you need to get her another cat to play with."

"That's what the vet suggested, too," Libby told her. "So I'm on the lookout for another kitten."

"You could name the other cat Ginger," Bert put in, rubbing his bald head. "Get it? Ginger and Mary Ann?"

Libby rolled her eyes and laughed. "Cute, Bert."

"Gilligan's Island," Jessica murmured.

"Gotta love the classics," he said with a sly grin. "Now that Candace and I are expecting, I've been noticing names like never before."

"Hopefully you won't be picking a name from Gilligan's Island," Jessica teased him.

Bert shrugged. "Who knows? Maybe Gilly Anne? Or Thurston?"

"I'm glad Candace is in on this," Libby said with a smile. "Otherwise, who knows what your baby might be named."

Bert grinned. "Maybe I can practice by coming up with a name for your new kitten."

Libby finished the last of her coffee. "We'll see. But I won't be able to get her a friend right away, since the vet said to make sure I had enough time set aside to introduce the kittens properly."

"How hard is it to introduce two kittens?" Bert asked, raising an eyebrow.

"The vet told me it takes time," Libby explained. "And this weekend won't work, since I'm going to be out most of the weekend."

Jessica's mouth fell open wide. "Are you going on a date? If you're ready to start dating, I know a great guy. The guy I'm going out with has a terrific friend."

Libby shook her head. "No, nothing like that. I'm going to a Christmas lights conference. And I really hate leaving little Merry all alone."

Now Bert jumped in. "There's a group of senior volunteers who'll come in and pet sit lonely pets during the day. They mostly just keep the animals company, but it goes both ways."

Jessica was already nodding. "The animals keep the seniors company, too."

Bert put a pod in the coffee maker and started to brew a cup. "You got it. And you pay them whatever you think it's worth. I'll get you the number."

And shortly after that, Libby made arrangements for Merry to have a visitor throughout the upcoming weekend. Mrs. Carstairs even came over to Libby's house that evening, to meet Merry and learn about her schedule.

Not surprisingly, Merry took to the older, gray-haired lady in a matter of seconds. She meowed and chattered like she was telling Mrs. Carstairs her entire life story. And for that matter, she probably was.

Mrs. Carstairs chuckled, and then she picked up Merry and held her close, without an ounce of hesitation. "My, but this one is a real talker. I guess we'll be having quite the conversation while you're out."

Libby smiled at Merry. "I think you're right. Merry is like a black hole when it comes to attention. She just can't seem to get enough. That's why I didn't want her to be all by herself all weekend. I'll be home at night, of course, but it'll be late. And then I'll be leaving again early the next morning. So I really appreciate your sitting with her while I'm at my conference."

Mrs. Carstairs nodded sympathetically. "I understand completely, dear, and please call me Evelyn. I look after lots of animals here in Destiny. Once in a while, I take care of the most beautiful, orange kitten that belongs to a very nice young man who builds houses. That cat throws an absolute conniption whenever he leaves her alone. And though he takes her with him most days, there are times when he just can't. So I go over to keep her company."

"How long have you been pet sitting?" Libby asked as she

pointed out Merry's food and water dish.

"Ever since I lost my husband several years ago," Evelyn explained. "We were married fifty years, and I went through a pretty rough time when he passed. I just found it easier to be around animals instead of people at the time. And since my condo association frowns on the residents having pets, I go out and take care of everyone else's pets."

"Maybe you'd like to be part of our club," Libby suggested. "We call ourselves the Merry Widows."

Evelyn's eyes went wide, and she stared at Libby, searching her face. "Oh, I didn't realize, dear . . . But yes, it sounds interesting. I would love an invitation."

So Libby gave her the details while she showed her around the house.

"My, but you're such a creative young woman," Evelyn gushed when she saw that Libby had turned her dining room into a work area for building lamps. "These are beautiful. But it looks like you're going to need your own shop. Or maybe you could use your garage."

"I think you're right," Libby agreed. "I am running out of space. Especially since I'm going to be taking welding and lampworking classes, so I can start making light fixtures that hang from the ceiling, too. And all that welding equipment and those lampworking supplies are going to take up lots of room. Plus, I guess I'm going to need good ventilation for that kind of work."

"Sounds like quite an undertaking!" Evelyn said with wide eyes. "How did you decide to take classes like that?"

"The man who runs the local hardware store, Mr. Ritchie, suggested that I take them. He even directed me to the community college where they're held."

"That was kind. I've heard of Mr. Ritchie, though I've never met him personally. But I gather he's practically a legend in our community," Evelyn added as she glanced down at Merry, who had fallen fast asleep in her arms.

Libby stared in amazement at her usually overactive kitten. "He is, and with good reason. I'd be happy to introduce you sometime."

Right away, she couldn't help but think that Evelyn and Mr.

Ritchie would become fast friends. They were about the same age and two of the nicest people a girl could ever meet.

"I'd like that," Evelyn said. "And the lampworking sounds interesting. That's where the artist uses a blowtorch to shape glass into objects, right?"

"Yes, that's it," Libby told her as she led them back to the kitchen. "I'll be using it to make embellishments for my lamps, and hopefully I'll even create some small chandeliers."

"Wow! I can hardly wait to see them," Evelyn said.

For that matter, Libby could hardly wait to see them herself. And her imagination began to swim with ideas of what she could create.

Though her focus quickly shifted as she drove into Houston for the Christmas lights conference a few mornings later. She barely managed to find a seat for the opening presentation, held in a hotel ballroom that was absolutely packed full of people. From there, she had a hard time picking which classes she wanted to take, mostly because there were a surprising number to choose from. And frankly, all the course descriptions sounded good to her.

She enjoyed her first two classes, and then, right after lunch, she headed to the vendor hall. From the minute she set foot inside the wide-open space, she was dazzled by the brilliance of all the lights. Everywhere. From booth to booth to booth. And she was amazed by the joy she suddenly felt.

Apparently, the other conference attendees must have felt the same way, and it wasn't long before Libby found herself absolutely engulfed in a whole community of happy people who loved Christmas lights. To be honest, she wasn't sure if she'd ever met such a joyful bunch before. Lots of people had flown in from around the country, and others had driven in from all across Texas. But no matter where they were from, everyone had stories and videos to share of their own decorating experiences. And even though Libby was a novice compared to most everyone there, people were happy to show her the ropes.

Including actual rope lights.

Along with plenty of other types of lights. Yet as Libby wandered around, she couldn't help but fall in love with the pixel lights that could be used to create any color imaginable, with colors that were true and vivid. Colors that were mesmerizing.

Plus, she was also surprised to find the classes were much more technical than she'd realized. While there were plenty of instructions on actually setting up and connecting the strands of pixels and other lights, most of the classes focused on how to use the software for designing light shows. Much to her amazement, the lights could be sequenced to run and dance and move in ways that she had never imagined lights could move. It was like painting a picture, but instead of using paint, the artist used lights. Moving lights.

Of course, it wasn't long before her mind was absolutely swirling with possibilities. For her front yard and the front yards of other people. Potential customers.

"Customers?" she murmured to herself in the hallway between classes.

As in, adding a new facet to her Libby's Lights business? What was she thinking? She already had a full-time job, and she created lamps in her free time. Yet here she was, considering the prospect of expanding her business to include Christmas light decorating.

Had she completely lost her mind?

Honestly, she *really* didn't need more things to do. Yet somehow, the idea stayed with her and would not let go. No matter how many times she tried to steer her focus elsewhere. It didn't help that the people around her were egging her on with what was rapidly becoming a whole new obsession for her.

On the last day, after the farewell presentation had ended, she ran into Chase Adams again, the incredibly good-looking guy who'd invited her to the conference in the first place.

"Libby," he said breathlessly. "I can't believe I haven't bumped into you before now! Did you enjoy the conference?"

"Yes, I absolutely loved it! I can't believe how much I learned this weekend, and I can hardly wait to start using those pixel lights. They are dazzling," she found herself gushing.

"Pixels are pretty incredible, and creating Christmas light

displays can be pretty addicting," he said with a nod as he flashed a smile that was almost as bright as the lights she had seen throughout the weekend. "I'm really glad you liked the conference. And I'm even more glad that I found you again. Because I had something I wanted to ask you."

"Sure, ask away," she said, returning his smile.

All the while, she couldn't help but wonder what his question might be. Maybe he wanted her to join a light decorating crew. Working with a seasoned professional for a while could be a dream come true.

His smile never dipped. "I was wondering if you'd like to go out to dinner sometime."

And that's when Libby froze.

Completely froze.

Sure, she was well aware that a moment like this would probably happen at some time or another. But now that it had, she was at a loss. Totally caught off guard. Her mind went blank, and for the life of her, she couldn't think of a single thing to say.

"Chase . . ." was the most she could manage to squeak out.

Probably because she knew what would be coming next. She would have to explain that she was a widow and on and on and on. And after all the fun and excitement of the weekend, the last thing she wanted to do was return to such a sad subject.

But was it really necessary? Did she even have to bring it up? After all, she was a grown-up, and for that matter, she was also single. She wouldn't be doing anything wrong if she accepted a date with this attractive guy.

So why did it feel like she was cheating on Devin? And why were tears suddenly pricking at the back of her eyes? What a rotten time for one of her crying episodes.

Chase blushed. "Okay . . . well, that's not exactly the reaction I was hoping for. But I get it, you're not interested. And I mean, *definitely* not interested."

Libby bit her lip and shook her head. "No, I'm afraid you don't understand. It's not you. It's me . . ."

He laughed nervously and glanced down the hallway, ready to make his escape. "Yikes! The 'it's not you it's me' speech already? That didn't take long. Usually people say that when they're trying to get out of a relationship. But I guess you're just being efficient. And saving us both some time."

"No, it *really* isn't you! I'm . . ."

"Involved? Just out of a bad relationship? About to join a convent?"

"No, none of those. I'm . . . the '*W*' word."

He crinkled his brow. "The '*W*' word? Which '*W*' word exactly? Witty? Wise? Wealthy?"

"Maybe a couple of those," Libby added with a laugh. "But I'm referring to the word . . . 'widow.'"

"Oh . . ." Chase said with a nod. "*Ooooh*," he repeated, as though it finally registered. "I'm sorry, I never would've guessed. You're so young for that. And you really seem like you've got it all together. Anyway, you're basically telling me that you're not . . ."

"Not ready," she said with a sigh. "But someday . . ."

"Got it."

"I mean," Libby went on, "it's not that you're not attractive. Because you really are."

"Good to know. I hate to think it had something to do with my new haircut. Or my flannel shirt."

To which Libby laughed. "No, you're terrific. Ruggedly handsome, as they say, and interesting and all that. But it's going to take me some time before I'm really ready to date again."

"That's a shame. Because I think it would have been fun. You've got my card if you ever change your mind."

"Yes, I do. And you'll be the first to know."

With that, he touched two fingers to his head like he was tipping a hat. Then he smiled and headed down the hallway.

Libby practically ran to her car and drove home with her head in a whirlwind. There was a time when she couldn't even imagine moving on. Because she'd always believed that Devin was the love of her life. The *one and only* love of her life.

But was it possible . . . Could love really happen a second time? And should she start thinking of . . . well, moving on?

"Baby steps," she told herself. "*Baaaaby* steps!"

Maybe she needed to start by moving back into her bedroom. And sleeping in her own bed again.

The Light

So later that night, when Merry made a beeline for the couch—all ready to cuddle up and fall asleep with Libby like she did every night—Libby shook her head. "Not this time, little one," she said as she scooped up the kitten. "Tonight, we're going to sleep where we're supposed to sleep."

She kissed Merry on her forehead and walked back to the bedroom. Then as she stood at the end of the bed, she realized how foreign this space suddenly felt. Sure, she passed through it every day, several times a day even. Whenever she showered or got dressed. But she usually went through on autopilot, not really paying attention to the room.

But tonight, that was going to change.

So she set Merry on the bed and took a deep breath. Then she pulled the covers back and climbed on in, letting her head fall back onto the pillows. At once, she noticed how cool and comfortable the sheets felt against her skin. And how nice it felt to be back in her bed again.

That was, until she pulled the comforter over her and picked up on the faint scent of Devin's cologne.

It was almost more than she could stand.

Even so, she knew she couldn't back down. Not tonight. Because like it or not, she had to take this step. Hard as it may be. If she didn't, she would never be able to get on with her life.

Merry tiptoed to the head of the bed and made her way to Libby's shoulder, clearly unsure of what they were doing in this strange room. For once, the little cat wasn't her usual chatty self as she curled up and settled in, tucking her head under Libby's chin.

As soon as Merry was in place, Libby reached over and turned off the bedside lamp. Right away, she remembered the times when the lamp had gone on again by itself. Would that happen tonight?

But to her surprise, the lamp stayed off. Even as Libby felt a rush of emotions well up inside her, and images of Devin and their time together flashed through her mind. Tears immediately started to fall, and she reached for the box of tissues that were still by her bedside. Yet before she could grab them, Merry started to lick the salty tears from Libby's cheeks.

And that's when Libby laughed. Despite her tears.

157

She cuddled the kitten close. "We're going to make it, aren't we, little one?"

Merry's only response was to purr. And before long, Libby and her kitten both fell fast asleep.

Chapter Nineteen

With his brother and sister-in-law due home in a couple of hours, Caleb grabbed the wireless controller and sat back on the family room couch to play a video game. A well-deserved reward after an entire weekend of babysitting his nieces and nephew. A job, he decided, that turned out to be much, much easier than everyone said it would be. In fact, he wondered why his family had acted like babysitting for the weekend was such a big deal. Sure, it kept him incredibly busy, and he didn't have any time to himself. What with all the cooking and washing dishes and making sure the kids brushed their teeth.

And yes, as predicted, his nephew Jackson had been his usual handful, and he most definitely kept Caleb hopping.

The *entire* weekend.

Of course, Caleb caught on quickly that Jackson's favorite word was "how," since the child demanded to know how everything worked around the house. And that meant *everything!* Nothing was off-limits when it came to that kid's curiosity. And with Ginger practically glued to the little boy's side throughout the whole weekend, they were like two peas in a pod. Or more accurately, two partners in crime, going from room to room as Jackson searched for more things to ask Caleb about. Though Caleb had a pretty good idea that this wasn't the first time Jackson had asked some of his questions.

Cindy Vincent

No doubt, he was taking full advantage of having his contractor uncle at his beck and call.

On the first day, Caleb found Jackson investigating a window in the family room with Ginger at his feet. "*How* does this stay open, Uncle Caleb?" Jackson wanted to know as he pushed the window up. "Why doesn't it fall down?"

"Let me show you, buddy," Caleb said as he proceeded to demonstrate how a window could be dismantled. Then he explained the "track" that held things in place. All the while, Jackson stared up at Caleb with wide, blue eyes, completely entranced as his uncle spoke.

Once the little boy had his answer, he went on to his next question. "*How* do the blinds work? Are they like the windows? *How* come they don't fall back down after I pull on the strings?"

So Caleb explained how the blinds worked, after taking one down and showing Jackson the mechanism inside the headrail. He pointed out the drum and the cord locks and named all the different parts, giving him a complete rundown of the inner workings. Jackson nodded, clearly impressed, but he had a few more questions before he was completely satisfied with the subject.

Then Caleb put the blinds back on the window while Jackson went on to his next question. And to his next question, and to his next. Eventually, Caleb answered a "how" question of his own as he figured out *how* to distract his nephew by planting him in front of the TV and scheduling a whole series of "how to" construction videos to play. One right after the other. Something that was going to take hours. But instead of sitting on the family room couch and watching, Jackson preferred to stand right next to the TV, so he could catch every nuance and detail of whatever was being worked on in each episode. Meanwhile, Ginger grabbed a couple of her toy mice and played with them at the little boy's feet.

"He is definitely the son of a builder," Caleb muttered, chuckling to himself.

From what he could tell, Jackson was way more interested in construction matters than most kids his age. Probably since his dad took him to building sites a lot.

160

"I've gotta go upstairs and check on your sisters," Caleb said to Jackson. "Holler if you need anything, okay, buddy?"

"Okay, Uncle Caleb."

Caleb tousled the little boy's blonde hair and then took off for the upstairs playroom. As it turned out, taking care of his nieces was much less complicated than taking care of Jackson, since the two younger girls were simply content to play dress up and have perpetual fashion shows. Of course, they insisted that Uncle Caleb walk the catwalk, too, wearing a feather boa and a floppy hat.

By Sunday night, with the kids full of pizza and tucked into bed, Caleb even grinned and congratulated himself on a job well done. Sure, his mom had suggested, or rather, *coerced* him into babysitting this weekend. Apparently, so he could learn something. Though at the moment, he had no idea what it was that he was supposed to learn. Because from what he could tell, he had this job down pat. And with everything taken care of and Jacob and Daphne due home soon, he relaxed and simply enjoyed his video game. Blasting alien jet fighters and bumping off extraterrestrial bad guys.

He was even smiling when the first drop of water hit his nose. In fact, he barely noticed it at all. He brushed it away, along with the second and third drops.

But when the fourth drop of cold water hit his forehead— with a loud *"splaaaat!"*—he woke up from his video game stupor.

"Huh? Where in the world did that come from?" he wondered aloud as another drop hit him on the head.

That's when he looked up.

And he immediately knew the source of that water. It was coming from the room directly above him. Jackson's bathroom, to be precise.

"What the . . .? A leak!"

Then in one fluid movement, he was up and off the couch and racing for the stairs. He took them three at a time, knowing full well the kind of damage water could do to a home. Had a pipe burst? Or had the connection to a tap broken off? Honestly, the house was too new to have any real plumbing issues already.

Caleb reached the upper floor and practically flew around the corner. He raced down the hallway, keeping his eyes peeled for any signs of a water leak. He finally found it when he reached the open door to the bathroom. Despite having turned off the lights an hour ago, the lights were now blazing brightly, and the floor was covered with at least an inch of water. Maybe two or more. And there stood Jackson, flushing the toilet for all he was worth, while water gushed up and over the top of the bowl. An assortment of toy cars and rubber ducks swirled in the water of the toilet, along with some other items that Caleb couldn't identify right off the bat.

All the while, Ginger sat on top of the tank, absolutely enthralled and entertained, as she stared wide-eyed at the toys floating around and around. For a moment, Caleb thought she might even jump into the water.

He practically shrieked when he saw the pair. "Jackson, what happened? What's going on here?"

His nephew looked up at him with wide, innocent eyes. "I was just trying to fix the P-trap. Or maybe it was the S-trap. On my toilet. I thought it was clogged. So I was trying to dislodge what was in there."

Caleb gasped in disbelief. "You thought what?"

"It was on the video. The one about plumbing. And the guy had a clogged P-trap. Or an S-trap. I don't know for sure. So I was trying to fix mine."

"By flushing stuff down the toilet?" With his heart pounding, Caleb reached down and turned the football-shaped knob of the water supply valve. Thus stopping the flow of water from the toilet once and for all.

"I thought it would push it out," Jackson explained. "The guy in the video used a long metal thing to unplug it. He called it a snake. But I didn't have one of those, so I used my rubber snake instead. And now I can't get it out. It's stuck. So I thought I'd put some cars and stuff in there to push that out."

"It only clogged it up worse," Caleb hollered as he picked up Jackson and set him in the ironically dry bathtub. "Now don't move!"

Then Caleb splashed through the water and grabbed all the towels he could find in the linen cupboard. He tossed them willy-nilly around the huge puddle on the tile floor.

"But Uncle Caleb . . . I don't understand . . ." Jackson said as he started to climb out of the tub and back into the water.

Caleb let out a loud "*gaaaawk!*" sound. "Seriously, Jackson, do not move! *Stay* in that tub. Why aren't you in bed? You're supposed to be in bed. That's where I left you!"

Caleb searched another cupboard for more towels and added them to the wet mess on the floor.

Right before he realized the water was receding.

But receding to *where* exactly?

"Downstairs!" he hollered as he splashed through the water and raced for the staircase again.

Then he half-ran and half-slipped down the stairs, sliding down the last few on his rear. But he was up and running the second his feet hit the floor. He got to the family room just in time to see two things happen at almost the exact same moment.

First, Jacob and Daphne walked in through the garage door to the family room.

And second, a huge chunk of the ceiling came crashing down. Along with a waterfall of water.

Right onto the very spot where Caleb had been sitting and playing video games.

Daphne screamed and Jacob shrieked.

And Caleb nearly passed out.

Then Jacob started to sputter, apparently so shocked he could barely manage to get the words out. "What the . . .? What the . . .? Why is my ceiling on my couch? Why, why, why?"

"Are the kids okay?" Daphne hollered. "What's going on?"

That's when Jackson suddenly appeared at the bottom of the stairs. He glanced up at the huge gap in the ceiling and then at his parents and finally to Caleb.

"Wow, I guess I should've worked on that P-trap a long time ago," the little boy announced. "Or maybe it was an S-trap."

"Worked on what?" Jacob sputtered some more. "Did you have something to do with this?"

Jackson nodded. "I was only trying to fix the toilet upstairs. Like in the videos that Uncle Caleb showed me."

"Videos?" Jacob repeated, clearly becoming angry. "What

videos did Uncle Caleb show you?"

But before Jackson could say more, Caleb jumped in and did his best to explain. Though it seemed like the more he *explained*, the worse it sounded and the more upset his brother got. To the point where he thought Jacob might hyperventilate as he stared at the mess.

"Am I in trouble, Dad?" Jackson finally asked, as he hid behind Caleb's leg.

"You'd better believe you're in trouble!" Jacob spit out. "And then some. Now go upstairs and we'll talk about your punishment later."

Jackson picked up Ginger. "Is Uncle Caleb in trouble, too?"

A vein popped out on Jacob's forehead. "Oh, yeah. He's in trouble, all right. That's the understatement of the century."

"I am so sorry," Caleb said after Jackson went up to bed. "I don't understand what happened. Everything was going so well. I put the kids to bed a while ago. Then I sat back to play a video game and . . ."

Jacob choked. "You were playing a video game? While Jackson was upstairs clogging up the toilet and flooding the house? We left you in charge . . ."

Caleb groaned. "Again, I am *soooo* sorry. I will get this all fixed. I promise."

"Oh, yeah, you'd better believe you'll fix this mess," Jacob said through clenched teeth.

And so Caleb did. In the following weeks, he and his crew replaced the drywall of the ceiling in the family room. Along with all new light fixtures. And new tile, and baseboards, and a new toilet in the upstairs bathroom. He also bought a new couch to replace the one that was ruined.

Still, he could hardly believe what had happened, and that a weekend that had gone so well could take such an unexpected turn. Here he thought he'd done such a great job of babysitting. And yet he'd only turned his back on his nephew for a few minutes.

But apparently, that was all it took.

Even so, despite the turmoil, Caleb did manage to find one silver lining in the whole catastrophe. Because, if nothing else, at least Jackson took a very active role in helping with the

164

restoration.

"I'm really sorry, Uncle Caleb," Jackson said one Saturday while he helped Caleb install the new toilet. "Did you get grounded, too?"

"In a way," Caleb replied. "How about you?"

"Oh, I got grounded, all right," Jackson told him. "And I got my allowance taken away for a whole year, since my mom and dad said I had to help pay for what I broke."

"You mean, like the old toilet and the floor and the ceiling?"

"Uh-huh," Jackson said with a moan.

Caleb raised an eyebrow. "So what do you think about that? Does that seem fair?"

"No, it's not fair at all!" Jackson insisted. "This sure didn't happen in the videos I watched. And I didn't know the ceiling was going to fall down."

"Maybe not, buddy. But you could have called me when the toilet started overflowing. Before it did all that damage."

Jackson bit his lip. "Well . . . okay. I guess so."

Caleb pointed to the silver valve alongside the newly installed toilet. "And I'll bet you also knew where the shutoff valve was. You could have turned it off."

"Well, yeah . . . My dad showed me that a long time ago."

Caleb nodded. "Plus, you shouldn't have been working on it at night in the first place. Not without asking a grown-up for permission."

Jackson frowned. "Umm . . . I guess not."

Caleb went to the sink to wash his hands. "On top of that, you got me in big trouble, too. And this mess is costing a lot to fix."

"Boy, you got that right."

"So I need you to promise me something," he said as he dried his hands and hung the towel back on the rack.

"What?" Jackson asked as he washed his hands, too.

"That you'll never work on the house again without a grown-up's permission. Deal?"

"Deal, Uncle Caleb."

"Fist bump?"

To which his nephew grinned and practically smashed his little fist into Caleb's.

"Now, would you like to ask your dad if you can go with me to Mr. Ritchie's store? They've got a working model of a toilet set up. With clear, plastic pipes. So you can see how a toilet really works. And so you can understand what went wrong that night."

"Cool!" Jackson shouted. "But my dad's still pretty mad at me."

"He's pretty mad at me, too," Caleb added with a sigh.

"Can you blame me?" Jacob murmured as he stepped into the bathroom and glanced around at the progress.

"No," Caleb told him. "I'd probably feel the same way if I were in your shoes. And once again, I want you to know how sorry I am." That's when he nudged the little boy. "Don't you have something to say, too, Jackson?"

"Huh?" the little boy asked. "What do I have to say?"

"Don't you think you should tell your dad that you're sorry? For making such a mess?"

Jackson hung his head. "Oh . . . that." Then he took a deep breath and looked up at his father. "I'm sorry, Dad. I made a big mistake."

Caleb sighed. "We both did, Jacob. And we're both really sorry. So now, I have to ask, can you ever forgive us?"

Jacob let out a little chuckle. "Yes, I forgive you, Caleb. I've been doing it my whole life. And yes, I forgive you, too, Jackson. I'm your father, and it's my job."

"That's good," Jackson said with great seriousness. "Because I don't want you to be mad at me forever."

"And that goes double for me," Caleb added, before he turned his attention back to Jackson. "Do you have something else you'd like to ask your dad?"

Jackson's eyes lit up. "Yes! Can I go with Uncle Caleb to Mr. Ritchie's store, Dad? Please? I promise I'll be good."

"Okay. But be home in time for dinner," Jacob told his son.

Jackson let out a "Woo-hoo!" and picked up Ginger, his constant sidekick. Then he raced for the stairs.

Jacob laughed while he and Caleb followed. "Thanks for taking him down there. That boy is so smart, and he always needs to understand things. It's like his brain needs information like most of us just need food. So Daphne and I found a STEM school for him. He'll be starting in September."

"STEM school?" Caleb asked as they reached the first floor.

"It stands for Science, Technology, Engineering and Mathematics," Jacob explained, watching as Jackson ran to Caleb's truck with Ginger in his arms.

Caleb stood by the open front door and kept his eyes on his nephew. "That'll be perfect for him. Is it expensive?"

Jacob nodded. "Oh, yeah. It's private school. Believe me, it won't be cheap."

"I'm happy to help out in any way that I can."

"Thanks, bro. I appreciate it. We could use some help with transportation, because it's quite a way from here."

"Add me to the rotation," Caleb offered with a smile before he said goodbye and headed to his truck.

He found Jackson all buckled in and ready to go. Not surprisingly, the little boy was full of questions as they drove to Mr. Ritchie's store.

Caleb chuckled and answered everything the best he could. Funny, but he'd been wondering what his mom thought he might learn after babysitting Jacob and Daphne's kids. And right at that moment, he realized he had actually learned plenty. First, he could never turn his back on a kid as smart as Jackson. Because the minute he did, the boy would get into trouble. A kid like Jackson needed a lot of supervision and direction. No doubt, he could be a real challenge for anyone.

But Caleb had also learned that being the main caretaker for a bunch of kids was not an easy job at all. Especially for someone who did it full-time. Which meant his grandmother had been just as strong and every bit as much of a hero as his grandfather. Not only that, but Caleb had to hand it to his own mom—she had wanted to teach him a valuable lesson, and she'd found the perfect way to do it.

Even though Caleb wasn't exactly a kid anymore.

For some reason, thoughts of Fallon came to his mind. When he'd been dating her, he'd mistakenly believed that women needed to be rescued, and it was his job, as a man, to do just that. And of course, Fallon had certainly played the part of the ultimate victim. With her constant crying, she'd manipulated him with her tears, and maneuvered him right into her clutches. For her own selfish purposes.

Yet now, when he thought about it, he couldn't imagine her having the strength and selflessness it took to raise children. Not with the kind of love and direction that kids needed. And it also made him realize that she was absolutely not the type of woman he wanted in his life.

Was that what could be called a revelation? Was he making progress and moving away from his old patterns into something that was more healthy? Stable, even?

He had barely parked his truck in the lot of Mr. Ritchie's store when Jackson grabbed Ginger and pushed his door open.

"Wait!" Caleb hollered at him. "Don't go running off without me. Have you even looked for any moving cars in the parking lot?"

"Geesh, Uncle Caleb. You're starting to sound just like my dad."

Something that made Caleb smile. "Thank you. Because you have a really great dad. Don't you think?"

Jackson thought this over for a minute. "Well . . . um, yeah. I love my dad."

Then together the trio walked into Mr. Ritchie's store. Right away, Jackson squealed at the sight of everything, and he was so excited about all the tools and building products and more. But he was especially elated when they headed to the plumbing department. Mr. Ritchie joined them, and he and Jackson shook hands before Mr. Ritchie explained the toilet and pipe display. One that was made from clear plexiglass pipes and demonstrated precisely how the plumbing worked. Of course, it wasn't long before Mr. Ritchie also heard about the "Great Ceiling Drop" incident.

And naturally, Mr. Ritchie had some very good advice for Jackson. "There's an old saying in the building world that might apply here. Measure twice but cut once."

"Huh?" came Jackson's immediate response.

"That's right, young man. It's a good idea to double-check things and make sure you've got it right. Before you do something that can't be undone."

Jackson crinkled his eyebrows. "I don't understand, Mr. Ritchie."

"Well, it's like this," the elderly man explained. "Before you put something down that toilet, maybe it would have been a good idea to make sure it was the correct thing to do. Meaning, you should have asked what someone else thought."

"Like Uncle Caleb."

Mr. Ritchie smiled. "Exactly. And if he thought it was what needed to be done, then you could go forward with it. But that way, you would have double-checked."

"*Ooooh* . . . I get it," Jackson said with a nod.

And so the conversation went. Jackson hung on Mr. Ritchie's every word and asked lots of questions, while Ginger took her spot on top of the toilet tank. Equally entranced. The trio stayed long after Mr. Ritchie had to go wait on another customer.

Caleb smiled as he watched his nephew and his fascination for the inner workings of a toilet. While most kids his age were still telling "potty" jokes, Jackson now understood how a potty actually worked, and for that matter, he could probably take one apart and put it back together again. Much to his amazement, Caleb was surprised by the joy he felt from watching Jackson learn something new.

Is that what it felt like to be a parent?

He certainly hoped to find out for himself someday. Soon. But first he wanted to complete the "wife" part of the equation, before fatherhood came into the picture.

Yet the very second those thoughts entered his mind, he felt the sudden impulse to look up and toward the aisle. And that's when he saw her. The same beautiful, young woman who had been seated next to Kayla during the electricity and wiring class. Right away, Caleb's pulse began to pound, and he had that same instantaneous reaction to her that he'd had before. And every fiber of his being told him to go talk to the woman. If nothing else, he needed to know who she was, and whether she was married or had someone in her life.

If he didn't at least try, he knew he would regret it.

So he smiled at her and started to walk in her direction, when he heard the words that made his heart stop. "Uncle Caleb, help! Ginger knocked something into the toilet. I think it plugged up the S-trap."

Without giving it a second thought, Caleb spun on his heel and raced back to his nephew. "Coming, buddy."

After all, he'd messed up once by turning his back on Jackson, and he sure wasn't going to make that mistake a second time.

So he returned to the toilet and plumbing display, and quickly reached down and grabbed the huge bolt that Ginger had so happily knocked into the bowl. Before it reached the S-trap.

Then he turned around to look for the pretty woman again. But she was gone. Practically vanished into thin air. Which, oddly enough, left a strange aching inside his chest. Something that made no logical sense whatsoever.

And now he couldn't help but wonder, who was she and where did she go?

But most of all, he wondered if he'd ever see her again.

Chapter Twenty

As she hurried out of Mr. Ritchie's store, Libby did her best to breathe through her heartache and bite back the tears that stung her eyes. It was hard to believe that, over six months after she'd lost Devin, such a sweet and adorable moment could trigger so much sorrow within her. Worst of all, she couldn't seem to look away from the scene, and she was absolutely drawn to the little drama as it played out. Like metal to a magnet.

There they were, a guy around her age—a very good-looking guy, at that—explaining the inner workings of plumbing fixtures to a little boy. And the whole time that Libby watched them, she couldn't help but think how that could have been Devin instead, with a young son of their own. In an instant, she became acutely aware of how much she longed for that kind of life, the life *they* were supposed to have. A life where they would take their own children to Mr. Ritchie's store or to the museum or to just about anywhere on the weekend.

She was also acutely aware that she'd been robbed of that very life. And though she hated to use the word, she suddenly realized how "unfair" it was.

She sniffled a little, then forced herself to take some nice, deep breaths. "You're okay," she told herself over and over again as she got into her car. "You'll get through this."

But she needed to do far more than just get through this. Someday, somehow, she needed to get past it, too. Painful as it may be. That meant, like it or not, it was time for her to look reality straight in the eyes and face the facts.

Fact number one? Devin was gone, and she would never be raising a family with him.

And fact number two? Losing Devin did not mean that she, Libby, couldn't have a family someday. Obviously, that aspect of her life was still very important to her, and maybe even more significant than she'd realized. Otherwise, the scene at Mr. Ritchie's store never would've affected her so much.

Though she had to admit, what she'd witnessed had been so touching and heartwarming that it was almost like watching a movie. At first, she'd thought the pair were father and son, given the way they were obviously so bonded. But then she heard the child say, "Uncle Caleb." Something that made the situation all the more poignant, knowing this man had taken his nephew under his wing. It also meant that "Uncle Caleb" must have been babysitting today. And apparently, there was some backstory as well, an "incident" involving an overflowing toilet that accounted for this lesson in plumbing fixtures. Of course, it probably wasn't all that funny at the time, but hearing them talk about it now was pure comedy.

On top of that—literally—they had a beautiful, orange kitten with them, one who sat on the top of the toilet tank and knocked a big bolt right into the toilet bowl. And certainly added to the complete cuteness of it all. From what Libby could gleam, the kitten was probably about the same age as Merry. And after living with her own overzealous little cat, Libby knew full well what kittens were like at that stage.

"A kitten like her would be a perfect friend for Merry," Libby murmured as she drove out of the parking lot. "Those two would definitely be partners in crime."

If only she could find a kitten just like that adorable, orange one. So far, she'd gone to a few cat adoption events and seen several young cats. And while there were plenty of cute kittens who needed good homes, none of them seemed quite right for Merry. Because Libby's little calico was going to need a highly energetic and highly intelligent friend to keep up with her.

Especially now that Libby had completed her welding class, as well as her lampworking class, and was about to set up her own shop in her garage. Where she'd have more room to create lamps and light fixtures to sell in her Libby's Lights business. And with the welder and the lampworking lamp that she'd just ordered at Mr. Ritchie's store, it wouldn't be safe for Merry to hang out with Libby in the garage anymore. Not while she was using that equipment. Which meant little Merry would be stuck in the house by herself a lot more than she used to be. So finding a friend for her had jumped up higher on Libby's priority list.

A priority list that absolutely amazed Libby these days.

What a different person she'd become. Not only was she turning her garage into a workshop with new equipment on the way, but she'd also ordered a gigantic list of supplies from Mr. Ritchie, things she would use to create even more unique lamps and light fixtures. Plus, she could now spout off terms like "sheet metal" and "soda-lime glass" and "welding wire," and she actually understood what each of those things was supposed to be used for. Frankly, it was mind-boggling. If someone had told her a year ago that she'd be doing things like this, she never would've believed them.

But her ever expanding business had also forced her to make another tough decision—to sell Devin's car. Because a bigger workspace wasn't the only "bigger" thing she needed. It had become blatantly clear that she also needed a bigger car. An SUV. To haul her completed works to Mr. Ritchie's store, and then to haul supplies back to her place. The money from the sale of Devin's car would go a long way in paying for her new vehicle.

Still, she knew it was going to be hard to say goodbye to Devin's beloved car. *Really* hard. And painful. Yet she also knew that Devin would've approved wholeheartedly of her "light" business.

It was one of the first things she mentioned to the Merry Widows that evening, when she met the group for dinner a half an hour later.

"I'm so glad you're able to move on like that," Bridget told her with a smile as she tucked her auburn hair behind her ears.

"It takes a lot of strength and courage on your part. I don't know how you do it."

Libby shook her head. "Me, neither, if you want to know the truth. I feel like a child learning to navigate the world all over again. And because I sort of feel like a child, I just keep telling myself 'baby steps, baby steps.' And then I take one little step at a time."

Evelyn Carstairs, who had joined the group for the first time, nodded. "That's all you can do. And I know it sounds strange, but you've got to find some joy in your life while you're going through all this. And if creating your lamps makes you happy, well, then I think you've got to run with it. For me, it's being around animals that makes me happy."

Caroline swiped her perfectly highlighted, blond and brown hair from her forehead. "But don't you find that lots of people judge you if they see you being happy? Especially while you're still a new widow?"

"Very definitely . . ." Tessa spoke up, with sparks in her green eyes. "I've heard it many times. 'How can you laugh at something when you just lost your husband? Do you have ice water in your veins?'"

Caroline was already nodding. "I get that kind of stuff from people, too! People I barely even know, if you can believe it. Sometimes they actually say something, and sometimes I just get 'the look.' Either way, it's all pretty judgy."

"Oh, the look!" Tessa echoed, smoothing her dark hair that hung over her shoulders. "I know 'the look!' I've gotten it many times. It's so weird, but everyone seems to have an opinion on how you should be grieving. I've read that back in Victorian days, widows were expected to wear black and go through years of mourning. Otherwise, they were considered socially 'inappropriate.' Can you imagine?"

"For me, it's been the opposite," Evelyn put in. "I get the 'When are you going to move on with your life?' speech. People tell me, 'It's been years since your husband died. Haven't you gotten over it yet?' Never mind that we were married fifty years."

Bridget sighed. "I've gotten both. 'Move on' and 'How can you move on?' Sometimes in the very same day. How about you, Libby?"

"I got a lot of that at first," Libby told them. "From total strangers, mostly. At the grocery store and post office and things like that. I think most of those instant advice givers get their information from talk shows," she told them with a chuckle. "So now I'm really selective about who I confide in, and who I even tell that I'm a widow. Otherwise, I've pretty much just kept to myself and stayed focused on making my lamps. Though I have to say, I've also met people who've been in my shoes. People who have lost a loved one and gone through grieving themselves. And they've really helped to steer me in the right direction," she added, immediately thinking of Mr. Ritchie.

"It's wonderful to find people like that," Bridget said as the waitress brought soup for two of the women and salads for the other three. "I haven't met anyone like that, except for the women in this group. And I can't even tell you how much I appreciate all of you."

"Me, too. I'm so thankful for our group," Libby gushed as she dribbled raspberry vinaigrette over her salad. "Because we understand what each other is going through. When other people don't."

This brought forth nods and murmurs of "So true," and "I agree," from the other women.

"At work, everyone treats me with kid gloves," Libby went on. "Like I'm a delicate flower who must be handled with care, or I'll wilt and die."

"And yet you're quite the opposite," Evelyn said. "You're a very strong person."

Bridget speared some large pieces of Romaine with her fork. "It takes amazing strength to go through all this. Though at least, Libby, it sounds like the people you work with have your best interests at heart."

Libby took a sip of her wine. "Yes, they do. And I guess it's better to have them treat me with kid gloves than to stand in judgment."

Evelyn dipped into her soup. "In general, I think people my age are better at dealing with widows, since there are so many of us. But with you girls being so young, I don't think other people know how to handle it."

"I think that's true," Caroline agreed while she ate her salad. "Because I don't *know* how to handle it myself half the time. So, I guess, how are they supposed to know?"

"I think our situation sort of scares people," Tessa told them, picking up her wine glass. "Like they're afraid they might be in our shoes one day. And they want us to act how they think *they* would act if they were in the situation. So that widowhood doesn't look so awful, and like it's just a phase that someone goes through. And gets over."

"Interesting theory," Caroline noted and then took a sip of her wine.

"Could be true," Libby added, grabbing a grape tomato. "But any way you look at it, we're widows, not lepers. And personally, I don't want to be treated any special way. I just want to be treated like a regular person."

Caroline shook her head. "I think all the crying makes it hard for them to treat us like everyone else."

"Yup, those sudden, uncontrollable crying spells don't help," Libby said with a sigh. "I hate those."

Evelyn grabbed a roll and buttered it. "That crying part should die down after a while."

Libby took another sip of her wine. "I sure hope so. I still have those moments when I'm about to burst into tears. Then I work hard to fight them off, so I'm not crying around everyone else. I don't know why, but I hate the way people react to me when I'm crying. All that sympathy makes me feel sort of pathetic."

"To be honest, I think it's nice that people pay attention to me when I cry," Bridget told them, swirling the wine in her glass. "They never did when Dalton was alive. People always buddied up to him, and I always felt like I was invisible. But now people notice me. Especially men . . . when I'm crying," she added with a smile, raising her eyebrows.

Evelyn turned her attention to Bridget. "Hmm . . . it makes me wonder if those people are right for you. If they only pay attention to you when you're crying, and they acted like you were invisible before."

Bridget frowned. "Maybe not. Though to tell you the truth,

they were mostly Dalton's friends."

Libby dug her fork into her salad. "I'm not sure those people are good for you either, Bridget. But it's hard to tell. Because I've just found that whenever I'm crying, the whole conversation suddenly becomes all about me and Devin's death. The whole group can be having fun, but once that topic is on the table, the entire mood changes. I hate that. I'd rather keep having fun and escape the world of grieving for a while."

"Yup," Tessa said with a nod. "I think others feel sort of obligated to drop what they're doing and feel sorry for you right then and there."

"Exactly," Libby agreed. "And honestly, I don't want to talk about Devin's death all the time. I want to talk about other stuff, and I want to hear about my friends' lives, too. I could hardly believe it, but I didn't even know my best friend was dating a new guy. And I didn't know some other friends were expecting their first child. Probably since all our conversations had been focused on me. And they didn't want to tell me about the good things going on in their lives because they were afraid it would upset me. It wasn't right. Relationships have to be give and take. Even while you're grieving."

Tessa nodded. "Absolutely."

"Yes, but I do like all these big, strong men coming to my rescue . . ." Bridget added with a smile as she finished the last of her salad.

"Are you ready to start dating again?" Caroline asked her.

Bridget wiped her mouth with her napkin. "No . . . well, maybe. I don't know . . ."

That made Caroline laugh. "I'm not ready to date at all."

Libby laid her fork across her salad bowl. "I'm not sure where I stand on that subject at the moment."

"I'm ready," Tessa told the group, as the waitress took their bowls and plates. "I just want to move on. I'm hoping to invite you all to my wedding in a year."

Bridget's eyes went wide. "Wow! You're a mover and a shaker."

Tessa shrugged. "Why not? Why should I spend the rest of my life suffering because Blake died suddenly of a heart attack? I deserve to be happy. He may not be here to enjoy life.

But I am."

"All very true," Caroline said.

Tessa took another sip of her wine. "We keep saying that we're 'not ready.' But what does that even mean? And honestly, what's stopping any of us from dating right now?"

"I think I can answer that one," Evelyn explained as their entrées arrived. "I think it all boils down to guilt. I felt guilty every time I had a dinner date with a man after I lost George. I felt like I was cheating on him. Even though I knew full well that I wasn't."

Libby dug into her spaghetti. "I felt guilty when a guy simply asked me out. Especially since I seriously considered going out with him."

Caroline raised her hand. "Total guilt here, too. I had one date, and it was a disaster. Though I'm not sure it was entirely my fault. I'm pretty sure the guy targeted me because I'm a widow. He seemed to think that Cole had a really big life insurance policy, and that I was rich now. *Really* rich."

"I was targeted, too," Evelyn said. "George *did* have a big life insurance policy and men landed on my doorstep within days of his death. Young men, old men, it didn't matter. They acted like I'd just won the lottery."

"Me, too, I was definitely targeted," Tessa agreed after she took the first bite of her lasagna. "But that just means I'll have to weed through the muck and find a great guy. Because I fully intend to get remarried. And I'm not going to waste any time, either."

"No guilt on your part?" Caroline asked.

Tessa shook her head. "Not one bit. I figure my late husband wouldn't have waited around to start dating again if I passed away. And from what I've learned lately, I'm not sure he was such a faithful husband while he was alive. Judging by some of the women who showed up at the funeral."

"I can see where you're coming from," Evelyn reassured her and took a bite of her chicken parmigiana. "If that was the case, you might get over his death a lot faster than the rest of us. I hope you meet someone soon."

"Who asked you out, Libby?" Bridget wanted to know.

"A very good-looking guy," Libby told them with a smile.

"And I didn't exactly say no. I only said, 'not yet.' But to be honest, I doubt he'll still want to go out with me when I *am* ready. Because I didn't exactly handle it well. I sort of freaked out."

Caroline laughed. "I don't think I'll ever meet someone as wonderful as my husband was."

"I know the feeling," Evelyn went on. "But I think we've got to be careful. It's easy for a widow to idealize her late husband. So no man ever measures up again."

"And all people have their flaws," Libby murmured. "Even the guys we were once married to."

Tessa wound spaghetti around her fork. "*Especially* the guy I was married to. I plan to do better next time."

"My husband set the bar pretty high," Libby added. "It would be hard to top a guy like Devin. But if I should ever meet the right guy, how does a person know when they're ready?"

Evelyn nodded. "Good question."

Libby raised an eyebrow. "Because marriage is still something I want in my life. That, and a houseful of kids. And I want that house to be nice," she added with a laugh.

"Me, too," Caroline put in.

"So do I," Bridget agreed.

"I'm not sure about the 'kids' part," Tessa told them. "Kids are not a deal breaker for me. Mostly, I just want a guy that I love and loves me back. If we have kids, great. If we don't, fine."

"I've already raised a family," Evelyn added. "But I really miss the companionship of a man. I miss being part of a couple. Men just have a whole different perspective on things. Sure, men and women have their differences, but I've always liked how men and women can complement each other."

On this point, they all agreed.

Then they went on to talk about work and shopping sprees and any other subject that came up. By the time dinner had ended, they were thoroughly "talked out." Afterward, they hugged goodbye and promised to meet again.

Libby drove home that night with her mind racing on overdrive. Funny how the Merry Widows had so much in common, and they were going through such similar things. Yet they had such completely different approaches to it all. Tessa could hardly wait to get remarried, maybe as kind of a do-over. And the rest of the bunch were holding off, dipping their toes tentatively into the dating world.

So now, Libby couldn't help but wonder, was it time for her to start thinking about stepping into the wide, wild world of dating herself?

The thought of it sent shivers up and down her spine. Because she remembered all the ups and downs of dating when she was younger. Not to mention, all the drama. As she recalled, she had a lot of fun and met some interesting people. But she also remembered plenty of lousy dates.

Until she met Devin.

So was she even ready to face all that again?

And for that matter, if and when she was ready to start dating again, how would she ever meet the right guy?

Chapter Twenty-one

Caleb did his best to relax the tension in his shoulders as he drove to his parents' house. He could hardly believe it, but here he was again—practically avoiding a conversation with his mom. And he had to say, he was doing a first-rate job of it. Getting by with texts and emails only. Ever since the night of the great ceiling situation. But this morning, it was very likely he would run into her in person, since his dad had insisted that Caleb swing by and pick him up. After all, they were taking his dad's big, high-dollar boat out fishing, so it only seemed fair that Caleb did the driving to the marina.

And now as he pulled up to his parents' house and parked his truck, he felt anxiety rise in his chest, wondering how the interaction with his mom might go. But mostly, he questioned why he was uncomfortable talking to his mom at all. She'd always been one of his biggest supporters, especially when he was in the Army. With every phone call and every letter, she had never failed to say she was proud of him.

Which more than likely was the root of the problem now, and the reason why he'd been avoiding her. Because frankly, from what he could see, he'd been falling short of the mark lately. With his track record of dating the wrong women, he was the only son who hadn't settled down yet. Then there was his fiasco with Fallon and his botched babysitting job with

Jackson. Which truly made him wonder if his mom might think she'd raised three great sons and one major dunderhead.

But any way he looked at it, he couldn't avoid her forever. No, it was time to face the music. So he took a deep breath, got out of his truck, and strolled up the walkway. Then he knocked on his parents' front door and walked on into their home. With any luck, his dad might be all ready to go, so there wouldn't be much time for chitchat with his mom.

But he couldn't have been more wrong. Because his mom was right there to greet him with a big hug and a smile.

"How's my favorite vet?" she asked him. "And what, no Ginger today? I was looking forward to babysitting my beautiful grandcat."

Caleb shook his head. "Nope. I let her go home with Jackson last night after he worked for me yesterday afternoon. Sweeping and cleaning up on a job site. So he's going to be watching her all day while I'm out fishing. Jacob thinks it would be good for the kid to have the responsibility of a pet. And they're using Ginger for a trial run. If it works out, they'll get the kids a pet of their own."

She nodded. "It's wonderful how you've taken Jackson under your wing lately. It's made such a difference for him." She smiled again and motioned for Caleb to follow her into the kitchen.

"Glad to hear it," he murmured as he walked behind her. "He takes all this construction stuff pretty seriously."

"So I've been told. I also heard you had some fun and games when it came to babysitting," she added with a chuckle.

Caleb smacked his palm to his forehead. "Seriously, Mom, I don't know what got into that kid. I'd already put him to bed, and I thought he was sound asleep. I've never heard of a kid doing something like that."

This made his mom laugh as she pointed to the coffee pot. "Help yourself. Jackson probably isn't like most kids. But he's not that unusual for this family. Or rather, your dad's side of the family." She stood behind the kitchen island and went to work on half-finished ham sandwiches that were spread across the counter.

Caleb poured himself a cup of coffee and added cream.

"He's not? What do you mean?"

Just as his dad walked in with fishing poles. "Nope. He's not unusual at all. You've met your Uncle Chad, right?"

Caleb took a sip of his coffee. "Well, sure. Nice guy. He's a little stiff and serious, though. But really smart." He grabbed a box of plastic sandwich bags from a drawer.

His dad gave his mom a knowing smile. She winked back, and never missed a beat as she slathered a layer of mustard on the bottom halves of crusty buns.

"Chad is a very serious guy now, as a grown-up," his dad went on. "But when we were kids, he wasn't like that at all."

Caleb started bagging up the finished sandwiches. "Really? Uncle Chad?"

His dad laid the fishing poles across the island stools. "I think your Uncle Chad was about ten, and I was a couple of years younger when Houston got one of its rare, big freezes. One that lasted a full week. And Chad got the bright idea that he could warm things up if he let hot water run across everything. So he filled up the bathtub and let it flow over. We lived in a pretty small house at the time, and it didn't take long before that water ran over the tub, headed down the hallway and right out the front door. Then it started rolling down the walkway. My dad was at work and my mom had just taken some soup over to the neighbors who had the flu. She couldn't have been gone more than half an hour."

Caleb choked on his coffee. "Are you kidding me? Why haven't I ever heard this story before?"

"I think you have, but it probably didn't hit home like it does now," his dad suggested. "Anyway, my father had to replace all the flooring on the first floor. And believe me, your Uncle Chad had to spend all his free time helping. Plus, he earned money by doing odd jobs for the neighbors, to pay for the new floor. But nobody could use the front walkway for a week. It was like an ice-skating rink."

Caleb's mom grabbed a huge bowl of potato salad from the fridge. "That's just one of the things he did. Another time, he decided to jump off the roof and grab onto a tree branch."

"A dead tree," his dad added with a laugh. "One that was scheduled to be cut down. He was testing some theory he had about using a cape to fly."

Caleb wrapped up the remaining sandwiches. "Seriously? What happened?"

"The tree branch snapped and went straight through a window," his mother told him. "But thankfully, Chad didn't. Instead, he hung on for dear life as that branch went down. He let go and dropped to the ground just before it hit the plate glass window."

Caleb's mouth fell open wide. "Uncle Chad? The perfectionist engineer? The one who worked for NASA and helped design stuff for outer space?"

"One and the same," his dad said as he packed the sandwiches and potato salad in coolers.

Caleb could hardly believe his ears. "He did . . . he did all that?"

His dad grabbed a big plastic container, lifted the lid to see brownies inside, and then nestled it safely inside one of the coolers. "Yup. He and Jackson are cut from the same cloth. But your grandmother never gave up on your uncle. She recognized what a talented, creative kid he was. So she just steered him in the right direction."

Caleb's mom was already nodding. "And she gave him lots of love, while providing a whole lot of structure for him. Not to mention, disciplining him when it was needed. As you can tell, it paid off."

"Wow . . ." Caleb murmured, amazed. "I never knew."

His mom grinned. "Still think your grandmother had it so easy?"

"No," Caleb said, shaking his head. "No, I do not. Not after taking care of Jackson. He's a great kid. Super-smart, and always, always, always asking questions. But wow, someone's gotta keep an eye on that kid twenty-four seven. It would be a major job. Full-time and then some."

"So you see why your grandmother was a hero, too," Caleb's mom went on. "And she wasn't some damsel in distress who needed to be rescued all the time. In fact, I think she was busy rescuing her kids and her home on a daily basis."

"Message received, Mom. I know you sent me over there to babysit so I would learn something," Caleb added with a sheepish grin. "And believe me, I did. So how did you know Jackson might pull something?"

"Because . . . he's Jackson," his mom said as she shut the lids on the coolers. "And thanks to Daphne and Jacob's love and determination, and now your added help, Jackson will turn out to be a fantastic young man when he grows up."

"Yup, he will," Caleb said as he picked up one of the coolers. "Thanks for making all this food for us, Mom. You went to a lot of work."

"Happy to," she said with a smile. "Just make sure you keep the potato salad on ice."

"Will do," he told her before he and his father started carrying things to his truck.

When they had it all loaded up, his dad put his arm around his mom and kissed her goodbye. "Plan on fresh fish for dinner."

"Redfish?" she asked him, wrapping her arms around his waist and leaning into him.

"I'll do my best to catch some," he promised. "Then I'll grill them up nice and crisp with my special seasoning."

"Sounds perfect!" came her instant response. "Have a good time today. Who is the rest of the group going with you?"

"The Sorry Saps Society," Caleb told her. "And Matt."

She laughed and nodded. "Well, you may not have landed the big fish that you wanted. But I hope you land lots of smaller ones today."

"Me, too," Caleb added.

Then he and his father headed to his truck, and Caleb drove them straight to the marina. Funny, but he'd been going fishing with his dad since he was old enough to remember. On a small craft when he was young, and later, as the years went by, on his dad's big boat. But no matter how or where they went, it never got old. In fact, some of his best memories revolved around fishing with his dad. And someday, if he ever had kids of his own, he planned to carry on that tradition, and take them fishing, too.

Though today, it was purely a male bonding trip. And the rest of the guys arrived at the marina only seconds before Caleb and his dad did. They all pitched in and helped to load up the boat in a hurry, and not long after that, they were headed out through Galveston Bay toward the Gulf of Mexico.

Amazingly, they couldn't have asked for a more perfect morning. While it was pleasantly warm already, the breeze from the ocean kept the temperatures nicely cool. The sun shone overhead and bounced off the ocean waves, while the scent of salt water filled the air with the promise of a great day.

Right away, laughter rang through the group.

"So glad we finally found a day when we could get together," said Reggie, who had changed out his usual dark-rimmed glasses for a pair of aviator sunglasses. His light brown hair was already showing signs of becoming sun bleached.

"Great day to be on the water," Finn put in, as he rubbed sunscreen over his face and bald head, before donning a baseball cap and sunglasses.

C.J. also slathered sunscreen over his fair skin, which would likely turn as red as his hair if he didn't have it protected. "It wasn't easy with our work schedules."

"Thanks again for taking us out today, Mr. MacKnight," Armando added as he pulled the rim of his own cap lower on his close-cropped dark hair.

"Happy to," Caleb's dad hollered back from the helm in the pilothouse just slightly above them. "But please call me 'Nate.'"

And so they did. Then after a short trip out, they found a good spot and started fishing right away. Caleb caught a few nice redfish before lunch, and others caught snappers and more. Around eleven o'clock, Caleb and his dad set up a lunch bar below deck. Then the men filled their plates with sandwiches and potato salad and brownies. All but Nate grabbed a beer, and everyone found a seat on the main deck.

"This is delicious," Richard exclaimed. "Maybe I need to add ham sandwiches and potato salad to my lunch menu at the restaurant."

"Please thank your mom for us, Caleb," Matt added. "That was extremely nice of her to send all this food."

Which was followed by murmurs of "Oh, yeah," and "That's right," and "Give her our thanks."

"But strangely enough, there is one other person we have to thank," Finn said with a big grin as he raised his beer bottle.

"Because, without her and her conniving schemes, none of us would have met. And we wouldn't be having this fun fishing trip. So, I say, let's give a toast to the woman who brought us all together."

C.J. moaned and Richard rolled his eyes.

But Reggie laughed. "Only she doesn't know it . . . ."

"That's right, she has no idea!" Caleb said, grinning along with him as he raised his own beer. "To Fallon!" he toasted.

"You mean, Kinley," Matt corrected.

"To Kinley!" The whole group now echoed, raising their beers and clinking them together.

"May she rot in jail," added Armando.

Which brought a chorus of, "Hear, hear!"

"Wait . . . we have one more toast we need to make," Reggie said with a laugh as he raised his beer once more. "To the Sorry Saps Society. Along with Matt and Nate."

"Hear, hear!" they repeated.

"Hey, speak for yourself," Caleb's dad put in, laughing. "I married my high school sweetheart, and she's still the greatest gal on the planet."

"My late wife was pretty fantastic, too," Finn added. "Which is why I still can't believe I got taken in by this 'Kinley' person. Though I knew her as Crystal. I guess I was just pretty lonely. Otherwise, I'm not sure I would've let her in like that."

"I hear you," Armando added. "I still wonder how I got sucked in like I did."

"Well, c'mon," C.J. said. "The girl is gorgeous."

"Stunning, actually," Richard confirmed.

Reggie nodded. "Oh, yeah, definitely the kind of woman a guy wants on his arm."

Caleb glanced at one of the fishing poles. "Beauty and a good body made a great first impression, but I think there was something more that hooked us in."

C.J. took a sip of his beer. "Probably. When I look back now, I realize the girl was a flatterer."

"Most definitely," Caleb agreed. "She hung on my every word."

"She laughed at my jokes," Reggie put in. "Nobody laughs at my jokes. Probably because my jokes aren't really funny unless

187

you're a tech nerd like me."

Finn grabbed another brownie. "She acted like everything I said was so fascinating to her. Whenever I talked about oil field subjects, like pumping units and horizontal wells and root cause failure analysis, she acted like it was the most interesting stuff in the world."

Caleb rubbed his forehead. "Oh, yeah, she did the same thing to me. She was the only woman I've ever met who seemed interested in construction stuff. Like electrical panels and framing and rooflines. And all the details that go into building a house. A really nice house, that is."

"All that may be true," Matt put in. "But I'm still not sure it was enough to really manipulate you guys like she did."

"It was the crying," Armando suggested.

C.J. sighed. "Oh, yeah, definitely the crying."

Finn raised his hand. "Yup, it was the crying here, too. I didn't know what to do with that. Especially since I'd been grieving my wife. And I'm not afraid to admit it, but I did some crying of my own after she died, and I felt pretty bad if people walked away from me when I did. So I made sure that I held Crystal, or rather, Kinley, and let her cry."

"The same thing happened to me," Richard told the group. "And I felt sort of obligated to take care of her. Especially after she started hinting about suicide."

"Me, too . . ." Caleb put in. "But there's another thing. Apparently, I'm a rescuer. And I have a bad habit of rescuing women. Or, at least, I did. I'm trying to change all that."

Finn tilted his head. "Okay, I guess I'm probably a rescuer myself. But sometimes a woman needs to be rescued. If they're in danger. I pulled a woman out of a car once when she'd driven into a ditch. During one of our floods. Because I was stronger than she was, and I saved her. I guess all those hours at the gym really paid off."

"I once saved a woman from a guy who was trying to attack her," Matt told them. "She was no match for that guy, and I was."

"But it's not just women who need to be rescued," Armando added. "I saved a kid once in a swimming pool. When I was a lifeguard."

Richard finished his beer. "I worked for a fire department for a while. I saved kids and dogs and old men, and you name it. And a guy who was in a car accident."

"I saved a little, orange kitten once," Caleb said with a huge grin.

Which made the whole group laugh, with echoes of "Good job," and "Way to go."

Now Caleb held up his hands in defense. "Okay, okay! But I really like that kitten," he laughed. "She's my pet. In any case, I guess we're all rescuers. That much is clear."

"And there's a time and a place for rescuing," Matt added.

Caleb frowned. "But maybe that's the difference. They were all people and animals who really needed to be saved. And Kinley wasn't. But what is a guy supposed to do when someone threatens to commit suicide?"

"Get professional intervention," Matt jumped in. "Call the police, call a mental health agency, or something. Let someone who is trained in that field deal with it. They can even put someone who is suicidal on a seventy-two-hour mental health hold. Which would have been interesting in Kinley's case," he finished with a chuckle.

"Since she wasn't who she said she was," Nate said, looking at his son. "But I agree, there is a time and a place to rescue. And as a man who's been married for a long time, I've learned my wife doesn't need to be rescued on a regular basis. But it sure is nice to jump in and help her out sometimes. And lighten the load a little. Especially since she does the same for me."

Something they all agreed with. Right before they got back to fishing. Though deep in his heart, Caleb was still painfully aware that rescuing women had gotten him into a lot of trouble. And he certainly wasn't going to make that mistake again.

The rest of the day passed in comfortable companionship and conversation that flowed easily. Everyone caught plenty of fish, and by midafternoon, they'd all had enough sun and salt for one day, and they were ready to get off the water. So Caleb drove the boat back, while his dad joined the other men and helped to clean the fish. They had everything cleaned and wrapped and sorted by the time Caleb steered the vessel into the marina again. He was close to their slot when he spotted something that made his heart stop. Or so it felt. He immediately cut the power to the engine and idled in the water.

"Hey, guys!" he said in a loud whisper from the helm. "Take a look at who's on the dock up there! Getting ready to go on that huge boat. The one with all the bells and whistles."

"Are you talking about the babe in the bright pink bikini?" asked Richard with a grin. "The one who . . ."

"You mean that gorgeous woman standing there?" Finn started to say. "Oh . . . wait a minute . . ."

C.J. gasped. "You've gotta be kidding me."

"Fallon," Caleb said just barely above the sound of the motor. "Or Kinley."

"Holy catfish, it's her, all right," said Reggie.

"Let's go over and see how she reacts when she sees all six of us," Finn suggested through clenched teeth.

But Matt held out his arm. "Hold on there, gentlemen. This could be the opportunity we've been looking for. I suggest we play this right. Everyone, stay low and don't look her way. Make sure you've got on a hat and sunglasses. And Nate, why don't you jump in the pilothouse and take the helm. So she won't see Caleb."

"Got it," came Nate's immediate response. "Wow, that guy looks like he's about my age. And she's really playing him for all he's worth."

"Of course she is," Armando murmured. "She's an expert at playing on men's emotions."

"Which is perfect for us," Matt told the group. "Everyone, keep staying low. I'll jump out and grab the lines while we dock the boat. I'll get it secured enough to go talk to the guy."

"Huh?" Caleb whispered.

"Trust me," Matt said with a grin. "Kinley has no idea who I am. So she won't think a thing of one man asking help from another."

Then before anyone could protest, he stepped on the dock and tied the lines to moor the boat. A few minutes later, with a wide smile, Matt made his way over to the tall, heavyset man with Kinley, as they were getting ready to board their boat.

Matt smiled at Kinley and waved to the man. "Excuse me, sir," he drawled in his best Texas accent. "Could I get a hand over here for a moment? I've got a problem with one of my lines, and I could sure use your help."

That's when Kinley pouted and arched her back, jutting her chest out front and center. "Oscar, you promised we would leave right away."

The man was clearly dazzled by Kinley's posture. "It'll just take a minute, Lauren. Then I'll be right back, and we'll have the whole evening and night together. Why don't you go on in and make yourself at home? There's a nice Sauvignon Blanc chilling in the refrigerator. Go ahead and pour us a glass."

"All right," she conceded, keeping up her pout. "But don't leave me here lonely. You never know when some other guy might come by and pick me up."

Matt nodded to her. "I'll have him back in a jiffy, ma'am. Don't you fret none."

With that, the man named Oscar headed toward Nate's boat with Matt, while Kinley stepped onto Oscar's boat.

And Matt didn't waste any time as they walked along. "Oscar, I'm going to level with you, and I'm going to say this quick. My name is Matt Doychek, and I'm a private investigator." He quickly pulled out his P.I. license and flashed it at Oscar.

Oscar stopped dead in his tracks, pulling his baseball cap from his head and ruffling his dark, thinning hair. "Wait a minute, buddy. What kind of scam are you trying to pull here?"

"I'm not, but she is," Matt explained. "You may know her as 'Lauren,' but her real name is Kinley Karnowski. And she's a con artist from Chicago. So, if you don't mind, would you please keep walking with me?"

"All right . . ." Oscar muttered and slapped the cap back on his head. "You've piqued my curiosity. What's going on?"

"I investigated her on behalf of one of my clients," Matt went on. "A client who was scammed by her. He's sitting on this boat up here. Along with his father and five other guys who were also scammed by her."

"Okay, this I gotta see," Oscar told him.

"You won't even need to get on the boat to hear their stories. Then we're gonna need your help."

"Let's see what they have to say first."

"Fair enough," Matt said as they approached Nate's boat, where the rest of the group was still hunkered down.

Caleb was the first to wave. "Hiya. Welcome to the Sorry Saps Society. A group I hope you never have to join."

The rest of the men quietly nodded and murmured in agreement.

"Hopefully we caught you in time," Richard told him. "Before she conned you, too."

"Because you're a marked man," Reggie added. "Just like we were. Whatever you do, don't let her near your business."

"How do you know I own a business?" Oscar asked.

"Because she has a type," Matt told him. "A specific kind of man that she targets for her con."

"Okay," Oscar said. "I'm all ears."

"You are the light of the world. A town built on a hill cannot be hidden." (Matthew 5:14, NIV)

Chapter Twenty-two

Libby raced through her garage and out to her brand-new, cranberry red SUV. Even though she was in a hurry, she couldn't help but pause for a few seconds and take a quick glance around. It had only been a matter of months since she'd set up her workshop in her garage, and much to her complete shock, she'd already outgrown the place. Especially now that she'd been making mixed-media lamps and light fixtures. Pieces that combined vintage jewelry and old silverware and other items, along with sheet metal sections that she'd cut, shaped, and welded, before embellishing with lines of decorative weld beads. Plus, she'd also attached art glass shapes that she'd created with her lampworking, which included everything from glass roses to leaves to elegant multicolored teardrops. With all those elements combined, and so many stunning details on each one of a kind piece, these days she was designing and creating lights that were absolute works of art.

And thanks to her sales at Mr. Ritchie's store, her work had also been "discovered" by the owner of a famous art gallery in Galveston. He was so taken with her creations that he invited, or rather, *insisted* that Libby create a collection for a major showing at his gallery.

In October.

Of course, Libby had been over the moon with excitement about it all. And she quickly agreed to do the show, before she had a chance to freak out about how little time she actually had to construct the kind of extra special pieces she would want in the exhibit. Because, without a doubt, she wanted to put her very best work on display. After all, it was such an honor to have her creations shown in a high-dollar art gallery. Something that had not even been on her radar a year ago. And something she had never, ever, *ever* dreamed would happen to her.

That's when she suddenly realized just how crowded her shop was these days. Now, not only did she need to find space to make and house all pieces for the gallery show, but she still had to make things for Mr. Ritchie's inventory, too. Plus, she was pretty sure that her ever-expanding Libby's Lights business would grow even more after the gallery show.

All of which meant she needed more room to work and store supplies.

Thankfully, she'd spotted something online that she believed could solve her problem—an ad for custom homes. Meaning, she could build a beautiful custom home on a nice piece of property and put a fantastic custom workshop right behind it. One with plenty of space to create all the lamps and light fixtures she wanted. And though she knew it was probably unrealistic to expect that something like that could be built before October, it would still help a lot down the road as her business continued to grow.

The only major downside to the whole plan? She would have to sell her house, the house that she and Devin had bought together. And in a way, selling her house felt like she was selling off her memories with Devin. Much like she felt when she'd sold Devin's car.

But lately, it seemed like her house held the wrong kind of memories. Starting with memories of her being alone while Devin was in the hospital, and memories of hours and hours of crying and learning to cope after he was gone. These days, the place felt more like a constant reminder of Devin's dying young. And to be honest, she was tired of that constant reminder. It was time for her to leave all that pain behind and move on. *Really* move on. Into the life she was meant to live.

So she'd called Jessica on a Saturday morning and asked if she'd go look at some custom homes with her.

Jessica reacted with way more enthusiasm than Libby had expected. "Yes, I'd love to! Because I wanted to talk to you today anyway. I've got some big news!"

Words that definitely piqued Libby's interest. "You do? I just saw you at work yesterday. What kind of big news?"

But Jessica refused to say, staying completely cryptic instead. "I'll tell you when I see you. Or rather, *I'll show you* when I see you!"

Libby's mouth dropped open. "*Ooooh*. . . the suspense is already killing me! Something must have happened last night. Something big. Can't you give me a hint?"

Which made Jessica laugh. "See you shortly."

"I'll hurry. I'm dying to know what's going on!"

And now as Libby drove to Jessica's townhome, she couldn't help but smile, so happy to hear her friend bubbling over with excitement. But she had barely gotten on the road when a thought hit her, practically making her swerve into a ditch.

"I'll bet she got engaged!" Libby said breathlessly.

And sure enough, she was right.

Jessica greeted her at the door, flashing a bright, sparkling diamond ring. "Rex proposed at dinner last night! And I said yes. So we're getting married!"

Libby gasped and hugged her friend. "Oh, Jessica, the ring is so gorgeous! And congratulations! He is such a great guy. I am so happy for you!"

An understatement, if ever there were one. Jessica had been such a rock for Libby the whole time that Devin was dying, and then afterward when Libby wandered through her own personal valley of grief. If anyone deserved to have a happy life and marriage, well, it was a kind, thoughtful person like Jessica.

"I know it's fast," Jessica gushed. "But after watching what you went through losing Devin, we don't want to wait. We want to start enjoying our married life now. Besides, I know he is *the one*. I can't explain how I know, but I do. We didn't need years of dating to figure it out."

Libby tilted her head. "Sometimes, you just know when it's right. And you have to seize the moment, so it doesn't pass you by. There are some things you can't overthink."

"Exactly," Jessica agreed with a dreamy sigh. "Anyway, you've got to be my maid of honor! Since I was your . . ." she started to say, before she hesitated. Though they both knew precisely what words were about to come next.

And they also knew why Jessica had left those words unsaid.

But Libby decided her days of being handled with kid gloves were over. Sure, she might still have some moments of grief, but it didn't overwhelm her anymore. Not like it had before. And she wasn't going to quit living life just because she'd gone through such a horrible loss. Besides, it was time she started returning a few favors, and she needed to be there for the people who had been there for her.

So she took a deep breath and finished Jessica's sentence with, "Since you were my maid of honor."

Jessica let out a relieved breath. "Yes. And I couldn't imagine anyone else standing up for me. But will you be okay? Being part of my wedding? If you're not ready, I can understand."

"Are you kidding?" Libby told her. "I wouldn't miss it for the world! So please don't give it a second thought. I'm doing so much better, and from this moment on, it's all about you and Rex. Because I have responsibilities as your maid of honor. Have you decided when you want to have the wedding?"

Jessica's eyes danced with excitement. "The weekend after Thanksgiving. We both love that time of year. And people will already be heading back to town for Thanksgiving anyway. Then we'll have our first Christmas together as husband and wife."

"Sounds wonderful," Libby told her, trying not to gulp when she realized how quickly her calendar was filling up for the fall.

Needless to say, it was going to be one unbelievably busy season.

But maybe "busy" was exactly what she needed this year. Especially around the holidays. In fact, it was that very subject that had dominated the last dinner conversation she'd had with the Merry Widows. Not a big surprise, considering it was a time of year that was known for being painful for people who had lost loved ones. And the Widows had been trying to figure out some strategies to handle it. To be prepared.

So maybe Libby had just gotten her answer. If she stayed ridiculously busy, then she wouldn't have time to dwell on things. Though when she thought about it, this wouldn't really be her first Christmas without Devin. Last year, he'd been in the hospital, and he barely even knew she was there. In a weird way, it was like she'd already lost him, and there had been nothing normal about the whole season.

But this year, between getting ready for her gallery show and making lots of lamps for Mr. Ritchie's Christmas inventory, as well as helping Jessica get ready for her wedding, Libby would barely have time to breathe. Let alone think about things. Especially since she also planned to expand Libby's Lights to include setting up people's outdoor Christmas lights.

With so much going on, frankly, her situation couldn't have been better.

She smiled to herself and then at her friend. "So you have the *when*. Have you thought of the *where*?"

Jessica nodded. "Yes, definitely! I want to get married at Destiny's historic chapel. It'll be perfect. Believe it or not, they have an opening that weekend, since apparently, most people don't have weddings that close to Thanksgiving. So we booked it. Afterward, we'll host the reception right next door at the historic hotel. We'll probably stay there, and our out-of-town guests can stay there, too, if they like."

"You are amazing," Libby told her friend with a chuckle. "You've practically got the whole thing set up. You're way farther ahead than I was when Devin and I got engaged years ago."

"It helps that I've seen so many of my friends go through this. You might say I've learned a lot. And to be honest, I actually started thinking about this right after Rex and I started dating."

"So you knew from the start that he might be the man for you."

"I did," Jessica told her. "From the very first date."

Libby smiled again. "In that case, I think we should go look at wedding dresses this morning. We can look at houses later. Maybe after lunch."

Jessica bit her lip. "Oh, that would be so fantastic! But are you sure you don't mind? I know you invited me to go look at houses, but I am absolutely dying to look at dresses!"

Libby smiled. "I know just how you feel. So let's go. Do you have a shop you want to start with?"

"I'd love to get my dress right here in Destiny. It would mean so much to me."

"Should we head to the bridal shop downtown then?"

"Absolutely," Jessica said with stars in her eyes.

With that, Libby drove them straight to Destiny's most popular bridal shop. Once they arrived, Jessica practically floated into the store, while Libby plastered a smile on her face and steeled herself for what lay ahead. Honestly, she wasn't sure how she would react when she walked into a bridal shop, and the last thing she wanted was to have one of her crying spells. Not during Jessica's big moment of trying on wedding dresses. After all, Jessica had been there for her, and now she needed to be there for Jessica.

But the second she set foot inside the shop, Libby feared the worst. Because her senses were immediately overwhelmed by the whisper of chiffon and tulle rustling in the racks, and the soft scent of roses and perfume. Not to mention, the dazzling bright beauty of all those white and ivory gowns. It was almost more than she could take, and she fought against her feelings with everything she had, determined now more than ever not to let grief ruin the day.

She closed her eyes for a second or two and took some deep breaths, while the saleslady zeroed in on Jessica. After that, Libby sat back and relaxed with the token complimentary glass of champagne. Then she watched as Jessica modeled a variety of beautiful dresses. Thankfully, Libby managed to calm down before too long, especially when Jessica was completely taken with an off-the-rack dress. A dress with a sweetheart neckline and shoulder straps made of dangling flowered lace. The bodice was embellished with 3D flowers and crystal beads, and it had a fuller skirt, with those same flowers cascading down from the waistline. The entire effect was so romantic and whimsical that it was completely breathtaking on Jessica. But the real indicator was the way Jessica couldn't stop staring at her reflection in the mirror.

"You are absolutely radiant . . ." Libby cooed. "You look like an angel in that gown."

Tears formed in Jessica's eyes. "Is it possible I just found my dress? I thought I was supposed to spend weeks searching for the perfect one."

Libby shrugged and smiled. "Maybe not. Maybe you just know when it's right. Like you did with Rex. And you don't need lots and lots of shopping around. Because you know what's in your heart."

"Very true," Jessica said, dabbing at her eyes. "Then I have to say, this is the dress I want to get married in."

"Rex will love it," Libby added as she hugged her friend. "Wait till he sees you in this. The man is going to faint."

"So is this the one?" the saleslady asked with a maternal glance.

"This is the one," Jessica told her.

The saleslady smiled, nodding with amazement. "I'm so glad you came in this morning, because we just got that dress in, and I knew it would sell in a hurry. And that dress is perfect for you. Not to mention, it's a perfect fit. I don't think you'll need a single alteration."

"It's like it was made for you. And it got here just when you were about to go shopping," she added, suddenly feeling thankful that they'd gone wedding dress shopping first, before they went to look at custom houses.

Otherwise, Jessica's dress might have been gone. And it was clear that this was the dress for her. Yet the timing of it all was uncanny, almost like . . . almost like . . . there was some divine intervention involved.

Something she wondered about as Jessica paid for her

gown, and the saleslady boxed it up. Then Libby and Jessica were off to a late lunch, celebrating over chimichangas and sopaipillas.

"I can't believe I found my dress already," Jessica gushed, practically in a dream state. "And I can't believe it's sitting in the back of your car. Good thing you've got such a nice, roomy SUV."

Libby laughed. "I never thought a wedding dress would be one of the first things I'd be hauling in it. But I couldn't be more proud. It's such a glamorous dress."

Of course, they'd taken plenty of pictures, so they could look at them over and over while they ate.

"It's stunning on you," Libby sighed. "Absolutely stunning."

"Thanks for going shopping with me," Jessica said. "I'm so glad you were there. Now let's go find the perfect house for you."

Libby laughed. "It may not be as exciting as wedding dress shopping, but I want to check out three custom builders," she explained as they walked out of the restaurant. "I'm looking for someone who can build a custom shop for me behind a custom home. A shop with central air conditioning and proper ventilation."

Jessica climbed into the passenger side of the car. "For Libby's Lights. I am totally amazed at how much you've grown as an artist. And as a business."

"That makes two of us," Libby said as she plugged the builder's address into her navigation system.

Minutes later, she turned the car into the driveway of the model home of the first custom builder. But her heart sank the second she laid eyes on the place. The builder's style was very plain and understated, without any artistic details at all. And when they went inside for a look, she was even more underwhelmed.

"Not for me," Libby told Jessica.

"Not at all," Jessica agreed as they left and drove to the next model home and design center that had been set up by another custom builder.

A place that could best be described as excessively modern. And "white." Pure white walls, white baseboards and woodwork, white kitchen with white countertops and white cabinets. Though at least the floor was a dark gray color. And thankfully there were a few décor items in turquoise and black that had been placed strategically around the rooms. The light fixtures were all chrome, something Libby had hoped might be repeated in such things as drawer pulls and cabinet handles, but those items were conspicuously absent. In fact, there weren't a lot of details anywhere.

"We specialize in being ultra-modern," the saleswoman with a stark, angled haircut informed them. "Along with being completely minimalist."

Well, if this place was minimalist, Libby decided she must be a "maximalist." Because the whole place reminded her more of a sterile medical institution than a warm and happy home. And it wasn't long before she felt those stark, white walls closing in on her, practically making her feel claustrophobic. So she merely smiled at the saleswoman, grabbed Jessica, and got out of there.

"Wow," she said once they were headed back to her car. "That house is going to give me nightmares. With all that white, how could you even distinguish one room from the next?"

"You got me," Jessica added. "Can you imagine a bunch of kids running around in an all-white house? Those walls would be full of stains, and who knows what else."

"I can't even envision it," Libby said, shaking her head. "Maybe looking at custom homes today was a bad idea. I guess I'm not doing as well as you did with your dress. Not even close."

"Let's just try one more place," Jessica encouraged her. "It might be the one."

Libby nodded. "Okay, but just one more. If it doesn't work out, then maybe this wasn't meant to be."

And a few minutes later, they parked in front of a third model home, one with a sign out front that read "MacKnight and Sons Custom Homes."

For a moment, Libby just stared at the exterior of the classic brick architecture. Then much to her surprise, her heart started to pound, and she suddenly felt a little bit breathless.

She gasped and thunked a hand to her chest.

Jessica touched Libby's shoulder. "Are you okay?"

Libby gulped and nodded. "I can't explain it, but I seem to be having a moment. Like you had with your wedding dress."

Jessica laughed. "Well . . . like you said to me, sometimes you just know when it's right. And you don't need a lot of shopping around."

Libby had a hunch her friend was spot-on, especially after they stepped inside the model home and started looking around. And just kept on looking and looking and looking. Because the whole place was so beautifully appointed with so many wonderful details. Double crown molding and baseboards. Columns with architectural embellishments. Arched doorways. Transom windows. And a beautiful, circular staircase with a Juliet balcony at the top. The hardwood floors were outlined with a darker wood, and the walls were a soft, buttercream color, which only made the white woodwork pop even more.

Jessica turned to her friend. "I think this is your kind of place."

"I think so, too," Libby barely managed to breathe, still so entranced by it all that she could hardly think straight. "God is in the details. And this house certainly has plenty of those."

Of course, she could easily spot those details and the builder's artistic touches all over the place. The model they were in was a two-story home and probably a lot bigger than Libby needed. But she knew those same touches would end up in any home she hired this company to build.

A very trim saleslady wearing a navy pencil skirt and a white blouse strolled up to them. "Welcome to MacKnight Custom Homes. I'm Daphne MacKnight," she said with a smile. "If you have any questions, I'm happy to help."

That's when Libby realized she'd heard that last name before. "Are you related to Kayla, by chance?"

Daphne nodded with enthusiasm. "Oh, yes, Kayla is my sister-in-law. Though honestly, she's more like my real sister by now. We're all very close."

But before Daphne could say more, a young couple interrupted them, asking about the possibility of adding another bedroom.

So Daphne simply nodded to Libby and Jessica, saying, "There are cookies and sweet tea in the kitchen. Help yourselves." Then she took off with the young couple, pointing to the ceiling and explaining how another bedroom could be added.

"What do you think, Lib?" Jessica asked as more and more people made their way into the model home.

Before long, the house started to get crowded.

"I think I'd love a house that was built by this company," Libby said, feeling more breathless by the moment. "But when I look at all that's gone into this place, I wonder if it would take a lot of time on my part. Because I imagine there would be lots of decisions to make on a home like this. And I don't know if I would have time to do all that until after Christmas."

"I can see that," Jessica agreed. "I've heard that having a house built is practically a full-time job."

"I've heard that, too," Libby told her as she turned in a circle, taking it all in. "So maybe I should just get some brochures and information today. And then look at building after New Year's. When I have more time to devote to it. But regardless, I think I've found my builder."

Jessica glanced at the coffered ceiling in the living room. "I think you have, too. And I can hardly wait to come over for dinner. You might even have a new beau by then."

Libby gave her a sideways glance, right before she took a brochure and some sheets with sample floor plans. And as they walked back to her SUV, Libby was the one with stars in her eyes now, just thinking about owning a house like the one they'd just seen.

She carefully stashed the brochure and floor plans in the car's console, so she wouldn't lose them. Then she started the car and headed down the street, while she and Jessica chatted away about all the fantastic details of that home.

But they had barely driven a block away when a beautiful, orange kitten came strolling into the street, right in front of Libby's SUV. The longhaired kitten froze in place and stared up at them while Libby slammed on the brakes, stopping the car just a few feet in front of the little feline. Without hesitation, she put her car in park and ran out to check on the cat.

But the kitten merely looked up at her and started to holler. And holler and holler and holler.

"Is it hurt?" Jessica wondered as she joined Libby. "I know we didn't hit it."

"I know we didn't, too," Libby said. "But this kitten is having an absolute conniption. I wonder if she's just scared."

Jessica crinkled her brows. "She sure doesn't look scared. She actually sounds sort of, well . . . demanding. Bossy."

"Either way," Libby said. "I don't think we should leave it alone."

"Let's bring her into the car."

And so they did.

While the kitten just kept on having her conniption.

Even so, the beautiful kitten made absolutely no effort at all to get out of Libby's arms. In fact, she seemed perfectly comfortable there.

"I honestly can't tell if there's something wrong with this cat or not," Libby said in her most gentle voice, hoping to calm the little feline.

"But where did she come from? There aren't any houses around here. Aside from that model home. Maybe this kitty is just lost." Jessica reached over and petted the talkative cat. "Hey, look! She's got a tag. And it says 'Ginger.'"

"Thank God. Do you see a phone number?"

"Yes!" Jessica read off the numbers while Libby grabbed her phone and tapped them in.

A few seconds later, the phone rang a couple of times and then went to voicemail. "Hi, you've reached Caleb," said a decidedly masculine voice. "Please leave your name and number, and I'll get back to you as quick as I can. Unless this is a scam call, and then don't bother. Anyone else, go right ahead. I'll be happy to call you back."

Libby laughed before she left a message. "Hi, no scam call here. I got this phone number from a collar tag on a cute, orange kitten that we found in the middle of the street. Her name is Ginger, and she's acting sort of . . . well . . . unusual, so I'm going to hang onto her just to make sure she's okay. Could you please call me back and I'll drop her off to you? My name is—"

Beep!

Libby's mouth fell open wide. "Wait a minute. I didn't have a chance to leave my name."

"It shouldn't be a problem," Jessica assured her. "If he wants his cat back, he'll call you right away. But what should we do in the meantime?"

"Hmmm . . . I already told the owner I'd hang onto her, so I guess I'll take her home and feed her. And give her water. To make sure she's all right. Can you hold her while I drive?"

Jessica nodded and carefully took the kitten into her arms. "Do you think Merry Anne will mind?"

Libby put the car in gear. "Ha! Merry Anne will love it. I think these two will be thick as thieves."

Jessica cringed. "Oh, no. I just realized, this is exactly like Bert suggested. Ginger and Merry Anne."

Libby rolled her eyes and laughed. "Too funny. Maybe this is meant to be. Because I've been trying to find a friend for Merry for a while. But none of the adoptions have gone through."

"Oh?" Jessica cuddled the longhaired kitten, who kept on talking and now sounded like she was telling Libby how to drive.

Libby turned onto the main street. "The first kitten got sick before I could pick her up, and the foster mom of the second kitten decided she didn't want to let her go. So she kept her."

"Maybe this kitty will end up joining your family," Jessica suggested.

"Maybe . . ." Libby murmured.

Yet as she drove them home, she couldn't help but feel like there was something very familiar about this very demanding and very adorable little cat.

Chapter Twenty-three

Caleb took a quick glance at his phone as it vibrated to let him know that a call had come in. But he didn't recognize the number, and since he was supposed to stay off his phone anyway, he let it go straight to voicemail. It was probably nothing but another phone scammer, even though his phone didn't warn him with the usual "Scam Likely" message. Either way, he made a mental note to check for a voicemail message later when he could. Just in case it happened to be something important.

As for right now, he and the rest of the Sorry Saps had been told in no uncertain terms to keep their phones on silent and their mouths shut. Otherwise, there was no way the police detective would have allowed them to be there at all, watching a cluster of monitors in a nearby room while the sting went down.

At least, they hoped the sting would go down. To be honest, Caleb was pretty nervous about the whole thing, considering his own experience with secretly trying to get Fallon, or Kinley, to repeat her blackmail demands so he could get it on tape. Though at least they were way ahead of the game this time, since Matt had convinced his friend, Detective Benny McGregor of the Destiny Police Department, that Kinley was a con artist who had committed real crimes. And they weren't simply "he-said, she-said" situations. Not when the same thing had happened to six different men. But Matt had sealed the deal with Benny when he offered up the prospect of gathering rock-solid evidence, the kind that could hold up in court.

So here they were, Caleb and Matt and the rest of the Sorry Saps, playing a waiting game at Oscar LaMorre's perfectly decorated and well-constructed mini mansion. They'd arrived early to help set things up, after riding out together in Richard's restaurant delivery van, so there wouldn't be a lot of cars around the place. The van was now safely covered and hidden inside Oscar's oversized garage, where it would never be noticed.

Richard had also been happy to contribute the food for the gourmet meal that Oscar was supposedly preparing for Kinley tonight, as their ruse to lure her over.

"Her last meal," Richard announced before he took charge in Oscar's kitchen. "As a free woman."

Or so they all hoped, while they quickly scarfed down a very early pizza dinner themselves. They were extra careful to dispose of every bit of trash while Richard finished preparing the meal for Oscar and Kinley. Then Richard put his chef's apron on Oscar, so it would look like he'd been the one who had cooked the elegant dinner.

"Easiest meal I've ever cooked," Oscar joked.

"I'll go set the table," Caleb told the bunch.

"Do you know how?" C.J. razzed him.

"Sure," Caleb said with a laugh. "I come from a family of four boys, and our mom made us learn how to do this stuff. She said it could come in handy someday, and it turns out she was right. It is coming in handy."

Which only brought about more good-natured ribbing as he headed to the ornate dining room. Of course, Caleb knew all that joking was only there to break the tension. And tonight, there was a lot of tension to break.

He made a beeline for the china hutch, and right away noticed how nicely the china and crystal glassware were displayed. No doubt the work of Oscar's late wife. Clearly, these things had been very special to her, just like his mom's things were special to her. And as Caleb did his best to position plates and utensils and wine glasses, the mere idea of Fallon eating off them made him sick to his stomach. He thought of the very last time he'd seen her, when he'd taken her out to dinner and tried to get her to give up the game. And he remembered how hard it had been to act natural, since it was the first time he'd been face-to-face with her after he'd learned the truth.

What an actor he had been that night. Though his nerves were running rampant, and his anger threatened to blow, he'd managed to keep it together. Somehow.

Now he hoped that Oscar could do the same. It was a lot of pressure for the guy, though it seemed like a part of him was actually enjoying the whole setup.

And Caleb had to admit, Oscar had been a real godsend for all the Sorry Saps. Someone must have really been smiling down on them that day when they spotted Oscar with Fallon, only seconds before the two were about to leave on his boat. Thankfully, Oscar had been very receptive after hearing a quick rundown of their stories that afternoon. And he'd played along perfectly, acting completely casual when he returned to Kinley. From what they'd heard later, he had taken her out on his boat and pretended like nothing had ever happened, even though he was well aware by then that she was out to scam him. He also had no problem setting up another date with her. Of course, it probably helped that she had dollar signs flashing in her eyes, blinding her to any cues that he might be on to her.

The next night, Caleb and Matt and the Sorry Saps had filled him in on how her con worked, when Oscar joined them all for dinner.

Once he'd heard the whole story, Oscar leaned back in his chair. "Now that you mention it, that's exactly her style. She keeps the conversation focused on me and my investment firm. Most women's eyes glaze over when I talk too much about high-yield, short-term investments. And bonds and bull markets. Unless they happen to be in the industry. But not Lauren, or rather, Kinley. She acts like it's the most fascinating subject in the world. And she also claims to be a widow, probably since she knows I lost my wife a year ago."

"So she's playing on your vulnerabilities," Finn confirmed.

"Like she did with me. That woman is a heat-seeking missile when it comes to finding men who've lost their wives."

"She and her partner probably read the obituary columns," C.J. suggested.

"It's very likely," Matt confirmed. "In any case, Oscar, what do you say? Would you be willing to keep up the ruse and help us catch her?"

"Oh, yeah," Oscar said as he raised his beer. "I'll do it. For all the sorry saps out there."

To which the whole group laughed and raised their glasses.

"Don't forget," Oscar added. "You guys are saving me from going through the same thing that all of you went through. And thanks to you, I'll be careful to document every single interaction she has at my office. Or anything that could be construed as work related. Not to mention, I'll do my best to interrupt whenever she tries to act like she works there. I've already had to maneuver her out of my office a few times when I was with clients, and she decided to join in on a session."

"Let me guess," Caleb said. "She acted like she was an expert."

"Oh, yeah, she most definitely did," Oscar confirmed. "And then some."

"Just watch out for her crying phase," Matt warned. "That's her number one trick. It's how she managed to manipulate everyone here."

Words that brought forth nods and groans from all the men.

"I'll keep my eyes open," Oscar assured them. "And you'll be the first to hear when it starts."

Then after a few months of watching and waiting—with Matt keeping a close eye on things—Kinley did start her crying routine, along with her subtle suicide threats.

Now tonight, the whole group was sure she was going to take the next step with her con job. And they were ready for her. The table was set, the meal was simmering, and the police were in place.

"We'd better head to our hideout," Matt told them, glancing at the oven clock. "And join Benny and his bunch."

Reggie patted Oscar on the back. "Good luck, bro."

"You can do this, Oscar," Caleb assured him.

"Break a leg," Finn said with a chuckle.

Matt grinned and shook his head. "Maybe not the best sentiment, considering who we're dealing with."

"How about, 'Dude, you got this,'" Richard put in.

"All right, all right," Oscar conceded. "You guys get out of here. Go hide. Her Uber should be here any minute now."

So Matt and the Sorry Saps left the kitchen and joined the police in a large room that had been Oscar's wife's sewing room, where she had made custom gowns and dresses. Which meant the men had to fit in between dressmaker mannequins and bolts of fabric and sewing machines.

Stuff that had already been moved once to make room for the police monitors and recording equipment. Yet as Caleb glanced around, it suddenly dawned on him that Oscar had probably kept his wife's work area exactly as it had been on the day she died. In fact, he guessed he'd simply shut the doors and left things as they were. And who could blame the guy? It must have been great to be married to someone who had so much passion for her work. For life. Someone so artistic and creative.

The kind of woman that Caleb might want to consider finding for himself someday. After all, given his passion for his own work, it might be nice to share that with someone who had the same passion for her work, too. Someone who was very different from the type of women that Caleb usually dated. Like Fallon. Or rather, Kinley.

Detective McGregor raised his hand, signaling that Kinley had just arrived. And sure enough, they spotted her on the first monitor.

The room fell completely silent.

Right away, chills raced up and down Caleb's spine, and he felt queasy just seeing her on the screen. She was dressed to kill as always, and she waltzed in wearing the same black, one-shouldered dress that she'd worn the night that Caleb had made his fake proposal. He really hoped that wasn't a bad sign. And for once, he said a silent prayer, asking God to help make this operation go well.

"I thought I'd cook for you tonight," he heard Oscar say smoothly on camera. "Since you've been so down lately. After losing your job last month."

"Oh, that is so sweet of you . . ." she replied, twinkling up at him.

Then he held her chair and got her comfortably seated, before he served the dinner and poured the wine. All the while, she didn't even offer to lift a finger, and instead, simply batted her lashes and smiled at him with great adoration. But shortly after they'd both tucked into their food, she suddenly and very dramatically tossed her head back and drained the wine from her glass.

Oscar looked up, startled, just in time to see Kinley drop her fork onto her plate and then drop her head into her hands. Right away, she started to sniffle and wipe her tears with her napkin.

"And here come the waterworks," Matt murmured while the rest of the men simply nodded.

"What is it?" Oscar asked, still eating his dinner. "Is my cooking that bad?"

"I don't know what I'm going to do," Kinley wailed as she managed to produce a nice flow of tears. "I'm going to lose my apartment. And my car. And everything I have."

Oscar darted a glance in the direction of the hidden camera before focusing entirely on Kinley. "Honey, cheer up! I'm sure you'll find a new job. Have you started looking?"

His response seemed to take her by surprise. "Yes . . . but there's nothing out there. Besides, I need money now." Her tears flowed even faster.

Oscar didn't so much as flinch. "Didn't your late husband have a life insurance policy?"

"Yes, but . . . I spent all that. On the funeral. And other stuff."

"Other stuff?" he repeated.

"Yes . . . he had a lot of bills. Medical bills."

Oscar took a sip of his wine and then nonchalantly dug into his food once more. "Don't you have any savings?"

She immediately turned indignant. "Of course I don't. I'm not rich like you."

Oscar shrugged. "I wasn't always rich. My late wife and I had to work hard for everything we got. And I'm sure if you work hard, too, you'll get by." All the while, he didn't miss a beat when it came to downing his dinner.

Kinley suddenly glared at him, obviously confused. "But I have been working. I've been working hard. I just haven't been getting paid for my work."

Oscar washed down his latest bite of food with a big swig of wine. "Oh, how's that?"

"I've been working for you! After all, you've picked me up several times and taken me to your office."

"That wasn't so you'd work there," he mumbled between mouthfuls. "I was only doing that so you wouldn't harm yourself. You sounded like you were going to commit suicide. I didn't know what else to do."

Now her tears returned. "You mean . . . you mean . . . you don't really care? Then fine. Just pay me the wages you owe me, and I will be gone."

Oscar raised a dark eyebrow and kept on eating. "But honey, I only pay wages to people who actually work for me."

Her eyes went wide. "Aren't you listening? I *have* been working for you. I've been there every day since I lost my job. I've been helping your clients and doing all kinds of stuff."

"No, you haven't."

"That's not fair." She slammed her fists onto the table. "How can you say that? How can you discount the work I've done? When you're so rich, and I'm so poor."

Oscar shrugged. "I'm always happy to pay the people I hire. I even give them bonuses. But I never hired you."

"Keep pushing her," Matt whispered, while the rest of the men nodded again.

"Sure you did!" Kinley insisted, crying all the while. "You brought me to your office lots and lots of days. You told me to show up early for lunch some days. To work for you."

Oscar laughed and took a bite of garlic bread. "No, I didn't."

"That's not true! You took me there to work. You knew I had the personality to make your business a success. It was me who convinced a lot of people to buy into your investments. You're making a lot of money off those investments. Off of my work. Now you owe me."

Oscar sat back in his chair. "I owe you?"

She dabbed at more tears. "Yes, you owe me. All I want is my fair share. What I have coming to me. I want one hundred thousand dollars. That's what you owe me."

Back in their room, watching the monitor, the Sorry Saps gasped. Then they looked at each other. One hundred thousand dollars? That was pretty steep, even for a crook like Kinley.

But Oscar just scoffed at her and forked up some more of his food. "A hundred thousand dollars? Are you crazy? I'm not paying you that kind of money. And there's not a damn thing you can do about it."

That's when her tears dried up so fast it was like someone had turned off a faucet. "Sure I can," she said, her tone turning ice-cold as she gave him a sickly-sweet smile. "If you don't pay me what you owe me, I'll put it up all over social media that your investment house has lost your clients millions of dollars."

Oscar laughed, still eating. "Idle threats. You don't have the brains to pull off something like that."

Kinley's eyes flared. "Oh, I don't, huh? Do you know who you're talking to? I've already got hundreds of fake social media accounts set up. Sock puppet accounts. I can put out thousands of posts in a week, all claiming to be people who've been hurt by your firm. Then other people will share those posts. I can even make some go viral. And I can ruin you."

Oscar feigned shock. "What are you saying?"

"Listen up, you moron! If you don't pay me one hundred thousand dollars, I'm going to ruin your company. I've done it before, and I can do it again."

That's when Detective McGregor nodded. "We've got her. That's all we need."

And seconds later, Caleb and Matt and the rest of the Sorry Saps continued to watch the monitors, and they could see the look of complete shock on Kinley's face when Detective McGregor and a couple of uniformed officers entered the dining room. They could even tell that Kinley had turned completely pale, right before she jumped up and tried to run away. Only to be caught by a female officer who grabbed her and took her down, quickly slapping handcuffs on her.

Minutes later, after she was read her rights, Kinley was led away.

Caleb and the others didn't emerge until Kinley was safely restrained in the back of a patrol car. They knew the police would also be picking up her partner at the same time.

Matt grinned, though it was obvious he'd been sweating bullets. "Oscar, you deserve an *Oscar* for that performance. You were great."

"Yeah, you did good," Caleb told him while everyone shook Oscar's hand.

Then there was a whole chorus of "Way to go," and "Nice job."

"I don't know what happened to me in there," Oscar told them. "Something just took over, and I was cool as a cucumber. I guess I was thinking about how she'd scammed and conned so many people. Now here she was, trying to con me, too. And I simply wanted her to go to prison, where she couldn't hurt anybody else."

"Amen," Caleb told him.

And that night, or rather, very early the next morning, as Caleb left the guys and finally headed home, he tried to put his finger on the mix of emotions that seemed to be vying for attention in his brain. Joy, sadness, and who knew what else was in there. Yet mostly he just felt relief, knowing that she wouldn't be able to scam anyone else. And relief in knowing that their sting was over, and they'd caught her in the act. But with that relief came an overwhelming, completely consuming sense of fatigue. He barely made it home and crawled into bed. And since he'd left Ginger with Daphne and Jacob and family for the weekend, he knew she was in good hands. So he dropped his head onto his pillow and fell fast asleep.

It wasn't until the next morning that he remembered to check his voicemail.

And he completely froze the second he listened to the first message, one from his sister-in-law, Daphne. "Caleb, I am so sorry. We were completely swamped at the design house today, and Jackson was keeping an eye on Ginger. But when he took a bathroom break, I guess the girls opened her pet carrier and accidentally let her out. And when Jackson returned, he couldn't find her anywhere. In fact, we still haven't been able to find her. He has been frantic. We're all frantic. And we're still looking for her. Again, I am so sorry . . ."

After that, Caleb didn't even listen to the rest of the messages. Instead, he was up and showered and out of the house in world-record time, not even bothering with coffee or breakfast. He joined Jackson and Jacob and Daphne at the design house, hunting everywhere for his orange kitten. Finally, he gave up and took Jackson with him to have posters made up with Ginger's picture, front and center.

"I only left those girls alone for ten minutes," his nephew told him with tears in his eyes. "Ten minutes! That was it. I just went to the bathroom. And my sisters let Ginger out of her pet carrier because they wanted to play dress up with her. They were going to dress her up in doll clothes. But Ginger doesn't like to play dress up. And she ran away from them," he said, throwing his hands in the air and shaking his head. "You know, a guy just can't turn his back on little kids for a second. They'll do all kinds of things if you do."

Of course, the parallel did not escape Caleb, and a part of him wanted to laugh. But he held back for Jackson's sake.

"I hear ya, buddy," was all he said.

"I'm so sorry, Uncle Caleb," Jackson barely murmured. "I'm sorry I wasn't watching those girls. And I'm sorry I wasn't there to stop them from letting Ginger out. Do you forgive me?"

"You bet I do, buddy. But thanks for telling me you're sorry. That means a lot."

To which Jackson nodded somberly. "My mom thinks you're probably mad at her, too. Are you going to forgive her?"

"Already have," Caleb assured him.

"I wonder where Ginger is right now," Jackson said, his tears returning. "I hope she's okay. I hope she's not scared."

Caleb nodded to his nephew. "You know Ginger. She's never scared of anything. And we're gonna get her back. Now let's get these posters out."

And so they did. They had the whole bunch out within a matter of hours. They also knocked on a few doors and asked if anyone had seen the orange kitten. But no one had, and despite all their efforts, they didn't have a single lead. At long last, they decided to take a break, and Caleb took Jackson out for burgers and fries. And a chocolate milkshake.

But the little boy barely touched his food, too upset to eat. And by the time Caleb took Jackson back to his house, they still hadn't heard a word about Ginger. In fact, it was getting dark when Caleb gave up for the day and headed home. From that point on, he knew it was just a matter of waiting.

Or, at least, he hoped it was.

Caleb glanced at his phone again after he walked in the door, in case a new call or message had come in. But there was nothing. And it wasn't until he was brushing his teeth that it dawned on him—he hadn't finished listening to his messages from yesterday.

So he played them one by one.

Until he reached a message that made his heart skip a beat.

A message from a woman who told him she'd found Ginger. It must have been the unknown number that came in the night before during the middle of the sting at Oscar's house.

And now he wondered if it was too late to call her tonight. He paced the floor and debated for a moment or two, but in the end, he took a chance and phoned.

A very sweet, but very drowsy woman answered. "Hello?"

"I'm really sorry to call you so late, ma'am," were the first words out of his mouth. "But I'm returning your call from last night. This is Caleb and I just got your message and I guess you found my cat. Ginger? I sure hope you still have her."

The woman let out a little laugh. "Oh, yes, she's here. She's a beautiful kitten, though maybe a little bit . . . Umm . . ."

"Demanding? A diva?" Caleb supplied.

"That's her," the woman laughed again. "Can I get her back to you tomorrow? I've got to go to work early in the morning. But I've got a pet sitter coming over for a few hours in the afternoon to watch my own kitten for a while. So that means Mrs. Carstairs will be watching your kitten, too. And then I can bring Ginger to you after work."

Caleb's chin practically hit the floor. "Did you say Mrs. Carstairs? She already knows Ginger! She pet sits her, too, sometimes! Maybe she could just drop Ginger off at the hardware store that I go to all the time. Mr. Ritchie's place."

"I know Mr. Ritchie. I'm sure Evelyn wouldn't mind going there at all. It's not far from where I live. I'll ask her to take Ginger over when she leaves my place."

"Wow, that would be great. Thank you so much for doing this. I can't begin to tell you how much I appreciate it."

"Not a problem. I know what it's like. My kitten is about the same age. And the two girls have been getting along like they've known each other for years. But the funniest thing is their names. My cat is Merry Anne."

Caleb rolled his eyes and laughed. "And I have Ginger. Gilligan's Island. Too funny. Anyway, thank you for being a rescuer. And for rescuing Ginger."

"No one has ever called me a rescuer before," she said gently.

That's when he suddenly realized that he didn't even know who he was talking to. "I apologize, ma'am. My mom would kill me for being so rude, but I didn't get your name."

The woman laughed. "She sounds like my mom. And my name is Libby."

"Well, thank you, Libby. I owe you one."

"I am happy to help. And Ginger will be back home by tomorrow night."

"Thank you, again," Caleb said before they got off the phone.

Then he quickly sent texts to Jacob and Daphne, to let them know that Ginger had been found. And so they could let Jackson know, too.

Yet all the while, the woman's name rolled around in his mind. Libby. A name with two *b*'s. Side-by-side. When Kayla had been trying to line him up with a woman, all those months ago, did she say "Gabby?" Or did she say "Libby?"

"Libby," he murmured out loud.

And wasn't that also the name of the company that made lamps and light fixtures that Mr. Ritchie sold at his store? Like the one he'd bought for his mom?

Libby's Lights?

> "No one lights a lamp and hides it in a clay jar or puts it under a bed. Instead, they put it on a stand, so that those who come in can see the light."
> (Luke 8:16, NIV)

Chapter Twenty-four

The opening night reception of Libby's gallery show, *Let There Be Light,* was every bit as elegant as she had imagined. Champagne was served in tall, tapered flutes, while light jazz played softly in the background. The gallery kept their regular lights off, with the only light in the rooms emanating from Libby's lamps and fixtures. The effect was breathtaking and showed her work "in the best possible light," as the gallery owner had joked.

More than one person also commented that Libby looked rather "breathtaking" herself, wearing the same midnight blue gown that she'd worn on her cruise in the spring. Naturally, she was flattered to hear the compliments, but she was pretty sure the phrase "out of breath" was probably a *lot* more accurate.

Either way, she couldn't have been more pleased with how the night was going. Her parents had driven down, and Jessica, Rex, Bert and a very obviously pregnant Candace had shown up, too, all dressed to the nines. It was fun to have them there, though Libby didn't get much time to spend with her friends and family since she was completely inundated with questions about her lamps and light fixtures the minute the doors were opened. And because the gallery had been so gracious in showing her work, she felt it was only right to treat their customers like she would treat her own. Especially since several of the patrons were also interested in purchasing some of her creations. So she played the gracious hostess, in a sense, making time to chat and say hello to everyone who attended her big event.

Amazingly, she'd managed to create twenty-nine pieces for the show, and even she had to admit—it was some of her best work yet. But the pièce de résistance of the whole collection was a large fixture that now hung from the ceiling in the middle of the gallery's adjoining second room. The dragonfly-themed piece, featuring metal work with green, blue, and burnished brass overtones, along with dangling glass dragonflies in the same colors, was the perfect size for a kitchen island or bar. And of all the lights she'd ever made, this dragonfly piece had to be her favorite, and the one she was most proud of.

It was also the work of art that seemed to grab everyone's attention.

A lady who looked to be in her mid-forties waved her over. "Libby, I absolutely *love* your stuff! I'm Alyssa Van Sant, and my husband and I recently built a new house. But we could never find the right light fixture to go over our kitchen island, so our builder simply put up something plain for now, until we found the right piece," she explained, her blue eyes dancing as the words spilled out of her like water tumbling from a cliff. "And now I've found the perfect fixture! This one right here!" she exclaimed as she flipped her long, brown ponytail over her shoulder and pointed up to the dragonfly fixture.

"I'm so glad you like it," Libby said with a smile.

"I do, I *really* do," Alyssa raced on. "I know it's one of a kind, and I'm so scared it's going to sell right away. But I have to ask, since it's so expensive, would you be willing to sell it to our contractor for a contractor discount? I would appreciate it so much, because we've spent a fortune on that house, and we have next to nothing left in our budget. But just so you know, this fixture would have a very good home. And we would tell all our friends that we met you and that you made the fixture and then tell them to buy Libby's Lights and . . ."

By that point, Libby was already laughing. "Say no more. Who is your contractor?"

Alyssa clasped her hands to her chest. "MacKnight and Sons."

The very same custom builders that Libby had been considering herself. And that's when it dawned on her—if she was willing to "work" with MacKnight and Sons regarding this customer, they might use her fixtures in their building projects later on. Meaning, a little discount right now could translate into a lot more sales down the road. Not only that, but it would be an honor to have some of her work featured in such fantastic homes!

She nodded to Alyssa. "I've looked at MacKnight and Sons homes myself, and I absolutely love their style. So, yes, of course, I'd be willing to give them a contractor discount."

Alyssa was obviously overjoyed. "Thank-you, Libby. Thank-you, thank-you, thank-you!"

"Just have your contractor call the gallery right away and complete the order, since they're actually handling the sales. Then they'll mark the piece as 'sold.'"

Alyssa gave her a quick hug. "I'll call Caleb this minute."

"Be sure to send me pictures once you have it in your house," Libby added, smiling again. "I'd love to see it."

"I will! I promise," Alyssa said as she dialed her phone. Seconds later, she said, "Caleb? You'll never believe what I just found . . ."

There was that name again. Caleb. It played over and over in her mind as she strolled to the reception table for another glass of champagne. Could he be the "Uncle Caleb" that she'd seen at Mr. Ritchie's store? The one who was teaching his young nephew about plumbing fixtures? She recalled the scene in her memory, and she suddenly remembered the beautiful, orange kitten who'd been sitting on top of the toilet tank that day.

That's when the pieces finally fell into place. Because that gorgeous cat looked a lot like Ginger, the kitten she had rescued and returned to her owner. Via Evelyn Carstairs.

Were the cats one and the same? If so, that also meant the "Caleb" that she'd seen that day at Mr. Ritchie's store was the same Caleb who owned the kitten she'd found. Not only that, but the Caleb she'd seen in person was a very nice and very attractive guy.

But was he also Alyssa Van Sant's building contractor? With MacKnight and Sons? Needless to say, there was an easy way for Libby to find out. She still had Ginger's owner's number in her phone, from the day she'd called him to tell him she'd found his kitten. That meant she could call him right now and ask him a few questions. To find out if he was the same guy.

But then what? Was she going to ask him out? Maybe for coffee or lunch? And was she even remotely ready for something like that? For that matter, what if he was married? Or had a fiancée?

Somehow, Libby doubted it. He'd sounded like he was solely responsible for Ginger, rather than a wife or a girlfriend being part of the pet ownership equation.

Of course, Libby could start by asking Mr. Ritchie for more information, since he would most likely know. Though if she did, Mr. Ritchie would probably have her set up on a blind date before she even left the store. Especially now that Mr. Ritchie himself had stepped into the world of dating. Apparently, on the day that Evelyn had taken Ginger down to his store for Caleb to pick up, Evelyn and Mr. Ritchie had hit it off. In the span of a heartbeat. And they'd been seeing each other ever since.

That's when Libby decided it might be wise to give it a little more thought before she quizzed Mr. Ritchie about this Caleb. But she really didn't have much of a chance to think about it in the following weeks anyway, not when she was so busy helping Jessica get ready for her wedding. Not to mention, creating the rest of the lamps and fixtures that she needed to take to Mr. Ritchie for his holiday sales. And when she did see him, as she dropped off the rest of her inventory, they barely had time for a quick hello.

"People love these, Libby," he told her. "I'm so glad you're selling them here. They're going to be perfect for Christmas."

"Thank you so much, Mr. Ritchie," she gushed. "And thank you for all you've done for me. You've made such a difference in my life. I don't know what I would have done without you. You and all your wonderful advice. You got me through some incredibly difficult times."

"I'm so happy to hear it," the older man said, with the hint of tears in his eyes. "And I'm so glad I've gotten to know you over the last year. You may have realized it already, but just so you know, I've come to love you like you were my very own daughter. Which means I'm also very proud of the way you've come through all your struggles. On top of it all, you've evolved into an outstanding artist."

Words that *did* bring tears to Libby's eyes—happy tears, for once. "Thank you, Mr. Ritchie. Coming from you, that's definitely high praise. And just so *you* know . . . I love you like a second dad. In fact, I think everyone in Destiny loves you. You've made such a difference in the lives of so many other people, too. God blessed us all when he put you on this planet." Then she gave him a quick hug and kissed his cheek, before she said goodbye and raced off for Jessica's wedding rehearsal.

The next evening, she stood proudly at the altar in her purple chiffon gown, waiting for her best friend to walk up the candlelit aisle and join her future husband. She bit back more happy tears as she kept her eyes on Rex and watched when he saw Jessica for the first time as a bride. That's when tears came to his eyes, too. Because Jessica was a vision of loveliness as she strolled up the aisle in her romantic, flowing gown, looking absolutely radiant in the glow of the candlelight, with her curly, red hair in an elegant updo.

And as Libby took Jessica's bouquet, and stood witness while the ceremony unfolded, Libby couldn't help but wonder if she might be a bride herself one day, for a second time. But could she do something like this all over again? Even after all the pain she'd gone through, watching Devin's horrible illness and decline, and then losing him when he was so young?

Right away, she knew the answer. Though their time together had been brief, she wouldn't have missed it for the world. And a part of her would always love Devin.

But she also knew there was room in her heart to fall in love with another man someday. Because, if there was one thing she'd learned through all this, it was that life could be fleeting. She needed to celebrate each day she was given. So yes, she hoped there would come a time when she was a beautiful bride herself, strolling up the aisle once more.

She was still thinking of it later, during the reception when the few single guys who were there asked her to dance. And especially when the DJ announced the "tossing of the bouquet," and Jessica sent it flying straight into Libby's hands. Then Jessica winked at Libby before she and her new husband took off for their honeymoon. Not long after that, the dancing wound down, and Libby left with a couple of the men's business cards, with requests to call them.

Though she knew she probably wouldn't. Not yet anyway.

Once she got home, she sat on her couch and put her feet up, holding Merry in her arms. Thanksgiving was in the books, and she had survived it all. Her first year as a widow. And honestly, she'd been so busy she barely had time to even realize what time of year it was.

But she still had Christmas coming up. And once again, she planned to stay so busy that she wouldn't have a chance to dwell on her situation. Or think about being lonely.

Merry, on the other hand, had been completely lost and lonesome ever since Ginger had gone back to her owner.

"Well, little one," Libby murmured to Merry's multicolored, furry face, "our next task is to find you a friend. How does that sound?"

Merry purred up to her. Just as Libby's phone sounded.

It was Evelyn. Would she be the next bride to walk down the aisle?

Libby answered the phone with a smile. That was, until she heard Evelyn's voice crack as she sniffled back tears.

"Evelyn, what's wrong?" Libby asked.

"I'm afraid I don't have good news, my dear young friend. But I wanted you to hear it from me," Evelyn said softly. "Before you heard it on the news, or somewhere else . . ."

Libby's heart skipped a beat. "Oh, no . . . what is it?"

"I know you and Mr. Ritchie were close," Evelyn went on, openly crying now. "You were like a daughter to him."

Suddenly, Libby had a hard time breathing. "No . . . not Mr. Ritchie . . . I just saw him yesterday and he was fine . . . Just like always. He is the sweetest, kindest soul on the planet."

"Yes, he most truly was. He was always thinking of everyone else. But I'm afraid he's not with us any longer, dear one. Because our beloved Royce passed away this evening."

"No, no, no . . ." Libby murmured, biting her lip as the tears started to come. "I can't believe it . . ."

"It's a huge shock, I know. It was all very sudden. But know that he didn't suffer. The doctors said it was a stroke and there was nothing they could do."

"Please, tell me this isn't true. Tell me this is just one big nightmare."

"Oh, how I wish I could . . ." Evelyn barely managed to get out before she started to cry even harder. "But I'm afraid it's true. He's gone home now. He's in God's hands. And though he's in a better place, we will always miss him. There will never be another man like him."

And that's when Libby began to openly sob.

Chapter Twenty-five

Caleb fought back tears as he and the rest of his family sat pushed together in a couple of pews in the middle of the huge stone church. Not surprisingly, the place was packed. It was a good thing they'd gotten there early, otherwise they probably wouldn't have found seats. As it was, everyone in the church had been asked to scoot closer together a couple of times. To make room for more mourners. The choir loft in back had even been opened up for more people, with the choir members being relocated to the chancel in front of the altar. Pretty soon, it looked like it would be standing room only in the rear and along the walls.

And even though it was a little uncomfortable, deep down, Caleb was glad to see it. It showed just how much everyone had loved Mr. Ritchie, and what a difference he'd made in the lives of so many people.

Caleb's included.

He still couldn't believe that Mr. Ritchie was gone. What would they do without him? The world would never be the same again.

Caleb touched his fingertips to his eyes, so he wouldn't flat-out start crying. Sure, he knew it was perfectly acceptable for guys to cry at a funeral, but he had no intention of making an absolute spectacle of it. Plus, he was afraid that if he let loose, he would *really* let loose.

From the pew behind him, his mom put a reassuring hand on his shoulder, while Joshua and Jacob both sniffled back tears. Luke, on the other hand, didn't hold back, and Kayla cuddled up to him, clutching his hand to give him comfort.

In fact, it seemed like the whole place was quietly weeping or dabbing at tears. And with the church now bursting at the seams, the organist began to play *Oh, God, Beyond All Praising* while the choir belted out the words with heartfelt vigor, and the processional strolled slowly up the center aisle.

Thin, gray-haired Pastor Mooreland moved over to the podium next to a large, cascading bouquet of lilies and looked out onto the congregation, waiting patiently until the music had finished. "Good morning," he said in a voice of pure kindness. "Even though this is a sad occasion, I'm glad to see a full house here today, all to pay their respects to such a great human being and my personal friend, Royce Ritchie. As you can see by this turnout, he was one of our community's most beloved members. And though we're here to celebrate his life, that doesn't mean we can't mourn his death at the same time. No doubt, we're all going to miss his reassuring voice and his wonderful advice. To say that he had an impact on the lives of so many people around us is probably an understatement bordering on blasphemy. But our loss is Heaven's gain."

Pastor Mooreland paused for a moment, fighting back tears of his own. "I knew Royce for most of my life. He was a good man when we were young, but over the years, he grew into a *great* man. Though he wasn't in a role that our society might deem important. He wasn't a senator or a celebrity or a doctor or anything like that. No, Royce Ritchie ran a hardware store and lumberyard. He worked with everyday people. All kinds of people. And yet, what made *Royce* so important was the way he made everyone *else* feel important. Because he acted like each person who walked through the door of his hardware store mattered. He cared about them all. He talked to them, and he listened to them. In a fast-paced, cellphone-addicted, impersonal world, Royce Ritchie gave people the kind of care and attention that they *really* needed. The kind you can't get from social media or a chat room."

The Light

The preacher paused and glanced around the congregation. "But don't forget that Royce certainly went through his own share of hardships and loss. Especially when his beloved wife passed away many years ago. Yet instead of letting those bad times tear him down, he managed to turn things around and become an even better person. He learned from the trials and tribulations that life handed him, and he used his own pain to help others. His empathy knew no bounds. Royce could put himself into other people's shoes better than anyone I've ever met. He was known for giving truly excellent advice, often based on his own personal experience and pain. And he became a light in the darkness to so many."

Pastor Mooreland stared at the floor for a moment, clearly fighting to keep his composure, before he looked up and went on again. "And when you think about it, isn't that what really made Royce Ritchie such a great man? The fact that he took the time to listen to people and encourage them? He always found ways to bring out the best in people, and to help them move on from their own tragedies."

Now the pastor took a deep, ragged breath. "So this morning, as we celebrate his life, a life well lived, many of us are wondering how we will go on without him. But maybe that's not the question we should be asking. Maybe we should be wondering if it's our turn to step up to the plate and become the next Royce Ritchie. Maybe it's time for us to be like him and make a difference in the lives of other people. Who do you know that you could support and encourage? Whose life can you impact in a big way? Because, if you will take the time to do just that, I think it's the best way to truly honor Royce's legacy."

Caleb's thoughts immediately turned to Jackson. He was such a terrific, gifted kid, and he had so much potential to do important things in life. But he was also a kid who was going to need more guidance than most, probably even more than his parents could give him. So maybe Caleb could take on a Mr. Ritchie-like role for his nephew. And maybe he could help other gifted kids, too, possibly by teaching some very basic classes on building and construction. Like the things that Jackson was so interested in.

But was Caleb up for the challenge?

As the choir sang *On Eagle's Wings*, he recalled some of the advice that he had received from Mr. Ritchie over the years. And that's when the light broke through and something suddenly dawned on him. In all the years that Mr. Ritchie had given him advice, the older man had never jumped in and "rescued" him. No, he had simply listened to Caleb and steered him in the right direction. And then Mr. Ritchie had continued to encourage and support him. But he never treated Caleb like he was helpless or a lost cause. Or incapable. No, it was quite the opposite.

And maybe that was a big difference between rescuing and encouraging. By "rescuing" someone, someone who wasn't actually in harms' way, it pretty much gave the message that the person was incapable. Helpless. But by "supporting and encouraging" someone, it gave the message that they were, in fact, capable.

And when Caleb perpetually rescued the women he dated, it also sent the message that he was a big sap who could be taken advantage of. And plenty of women had done just that. Women who weren't really all that helpless and incapable. No, the truth was, they were *so* capable that they knew how to manipulate him to their own advantage. Hence his relationships had never worked out. And he was a perfect target for women like Fallon.

But now, as he glanced at his brothers and their wives, and he thought of his parents sitting behind him, he realized their relationships didn't involve one person doing all the giving and the other person doing all the taking. Instead, they were two-way streets. Partnerships. With each partner bringing their own skills and assets to the marriage.

A much, much better idea than what Caleb had been doing.

Pastor Mooreland smiled and addressed the congregation again. "As you've probably guessed, I could go on and on about Royce. But instead, in true Royce Ritchie fashion, I'd like to hear what other people have to say. So I'm going to invite anyone who wants to say a few words to come up to the podium. Please keep your thoughts to a minute or two, since there will probably be more than a few takers. And form a line on the right, please."

Right away, Caleb felt his father shuffle around behind him, and start to work his way out of the crowded pew. He also noticed plenty of other people practically jump up and head toward the altar. And a line started to form, something he found amazing, considering most people's fear of public speaking. Especially in crowds as big as this one. Yet there they were, willing to forego their own fears for the sake of singing Mr. Ritchie's praises.

Caleb didn't know the first three speakers, but he agreed with all the kind words they had to say. He even had a feeling that Mr. Ritchie might be looking down on them now, smiling. He noticed Mrs. Carstairs in a front pew and wondered how she was doing. Then he spotted Matt in the line, along with his father, both with bowed heads and hands clasped before them, waiting for their turn to speak.

Even so, none of those people caught his eye the most.

Instead, it was the beautiful, young woman in line behind his father that grabbed his attention. He was sure he recognized her, though he'd only seen her a few times at Mr. Ritchie's store. Once when he'd been teaching Jackson about plumbing fixtures, and another time when Kayla had been taking a class on electricity. And just like before, he had an instantaneous reaction the second he saw her. A reaction he couldn't explain, and one that didn't make sense.

After a few minutes of waiting, she stepped up to the podium to speak, looking stunning in her black dress. "Mr. Ritchie was one of the most wonderful, helpful people I have ever met," she began, her voice cracking as she fought back tears. "A year ago, I was watching my husband wither away from cancer and die shortly afterward, and I had no idea how I would go on. But I was so blessed to have met Mr. Ritchie, who had already gone through so many of the same things that I was going through right then. He gave me just the right advice, and he guided me through it all."

That's when Caleb's heart started to pound, and he couldn't look away. There was something about her that simply seemed to draw him in.

"But he also encouraged me to use my creativity as an outlet to deal with my loss," she went on. "And he kept gently pushing me to expand my abilities, and to uncover talent that I didn't even know I had. To make light fixtures and lamps. Thanks to his encouragement, I ended up with a whole new creative business, Libby's Lights. It's taken me down a path that I never thought I'd walk. I even had my work shown in a major art gallery, something I never, ever dreamed would happen to me. But it all started because of Mr. Ritchie. Honestly, I don't know how I would have survived the early weeks and months of my widowhood without him. And without him, I never would have found my creative side. God bless you, Mr. Ritchie. I'm glad you're in Heaven right now, but I will always miss you." With those words, she bowed her head and returned to the rest of the congregation.

But Caleb's heart did not return to normal.

So this was Libby.

The same woman he'd seen in Mr. Ritchie's store.

The same woman who'd rescued Ginger.

The same woman who created Libby's Lights, one of which was now hanging happily in the home of one of his favorite clients. The Van Sants. Not to mention, the lamp at his mom's house.

And now he knew—she was a widow.

And she was wonderful.

And . . . he intended to talk to her once the ceremony had ended. To introduce himself.

This time, he'd made up his mind, and that was that.

But it was also when things went haywire.

Once the service had ended, he jumped up right away. But the place quickly turned into pure pandemonium, with people talking and greeting each other and immediately sharing their personal stories of Mr. Ritchie. As the sounds of the crowd rose to the rafters, one thing was clear—Caleb wasn't going anywhere.

Still, he wasn't going down without a fight, so to speak. So he quickly tried to step past the other people sitting in his pew and over plenty of women's purses.

"Excuse me," he said as he slipped by a couple of elderly ladies.

Until finally, he came to a standstill behind a big crowd of mourners who were all trying to get out at once.

"What's your hurry, bro?" Jacob called out from behind him. "Have some respect, would you?"

It felt like hours before Caleb finally reached the back of the church, and then stepped outside into the crowd who'd stopped to talk.

Yet no matter where he looked, he couldn't find Libby anywhere.

She was gone.

Chapter Twenty-six

Libby left the funeral with such a huge jumble of emotions running through her head that she couldn't even begin to process them all. Naturally, attending Mr. Ritchie's funeral brought back memories of Devin's funeral. And it reminded her once again of how precious life really was.

On top of all that was her complete nervousness about speaking in public, especially in front of such a gigantic crowd. In fact, she'd never spoken before such a big group in her entire life. Frankly, it was sort of terrifying.

Okay, make that utterly and *totally* terrifying!

At first anyway.

But while she stood at that podium, with her knees knocking and her hands shaking, she reminded herself of why she was there. She was doing it for Mr. Ritchie. And she knew he would have encouraged her to stand up tall and boldly say her piece. More than anything, she did not want to let him down. Not when she remembered all the people who got up and spoke at Devin's funeral, and what a difference it made to her. So she wanted to do the same for Mr. Ritchie's family, and to honor the man who had meant so much to her. Even with the terror of talking to such a large group, she wasn't going to let that fear stop her from saying what was on her heart.

Especially since she had a lot to say. Without Mr. Ritchie,

her year of grieving would have been much, much rougher. And without Mr. Ritchie, she might not have discovered the artist within her.

She was going to miss him terribly.

It was amazing how life could turn on a dime. One day she was attending Jessica's elegant wedding and the next she was speaking at Mr. Ritchie's funeral.

At least she'd had that wonderful final moment with him the day before he died, when she heard him say that he loved her like a daughter. And she'd had the chance to tell him that she loved him, too. Just knowing that was a comfort beyond belief.

Oddly enough, it was also a comfort to be part of such a large group, all celebrating and grieving the life of one fantastic man. She'd even run into Evelyn on the way out, and they greeted each other with a hug.

"You were wonderful up there," Evelyn told Libby.

"Thank you," Libby said. "You have no idea how scared I was, talking in front of such a big crowd."

"Well, it didn't show," Evelyn said as they followed a line of mourners heading for a side door.

"How are you holding up?" Libby asked her.

Evelyn sighed. "Honestly? Not the best. I'm glad I met Royce, and I'm glad I got to spend the time with him that I did. We hit it off so quickly and so easily, that I truly believe we would have gotten married if he'd lived."

"*Oooh. . .*" was all Libby could manage to say. "I'm so sorry."

"Me, too, dear. For all of us. We were all blessed to have known him. I only wished I had met him sooner."

"You don't find people more wonderful than him," Libby murmured. "Will you be at the next Merry Widows dinner?"

Evelyn shook her head. "Not this time. I'm leaving for Nevada in the morning, and I'll be staying with my daughter and son-in-law until the New Year. So I'll be spending Christmas with them and the grandkids."

"I hope you have fun."

"I will, dear. And you, too. But Libby . . . there's something I need to tell you."

"Okay . . ."

All of a sudden, Libby's breath caught in her throat, and she wondered what Evelyn was about to say. She could tell by her tone that it was serious. And she also noticed her older friend seemed to be hesitating, as though she were picking her words carefully. Surely Evelyn wasn't sick or dying herself, was she?

Libby took a deep breath and put her hand on Evelyn's shoulder. "What is it?"

"Well, we're both widows, and we've talked a lot in our little club about moving on. And finding someone else to love."

"Yes . . ." Libby said with a nod.

"And most of the women say they're not ready to move on."

"True . . . I guess I've been in that camp myself."

"So let me just say that, after losing Royce . . . well, I think there's a very big lesson in all of this. We spend so much time grieving, and maybe we even use it as an excuse for not getting out there again. Me included. But I'm not sure it's the right thing to do. I think maybe we all need to seize the day."

"Carpe Diem?" Libby added.

"Exactly. I'm just saying that, if you find someone you love, don't hold back out of fear and guilt for the one you lost. They would want you to be happy. And you're a young woman. If you keep telling yourself that you're not ready, you could miss out on something wonderful. Take it from me. I wish I had met Royce a long time ago, but I was too stuck in my grieving, and too busy telling myself that I would never meet anyone again."

"I know where you're coming from," Libby said slowly.

"And yes, this probably isn't the time for advice," Evelyn went on. "But I feel like I need to say it anyway, so you don't make the same mistake that I made. Because, if you were to find another someone, please don't hold back. Don't let your being a widow ever stop you from finding love again. Every single day matters. Every hour counts. Don't let the pain of the past stop you from having a fantastic future."

Words that stuck with Libby long after she left the church. And now she couldn't help but wonder if she had been holding back. Letting fear and guilt rule her.

But it was something she would have to ponder at a later time. Because right then, she needed to go home, change clothes and get her game face on. She had three appointments in the afternoon with potential customers who were interested the newly expanded aspect of her business—Christmas light decorating. One person was interested in lights for a home, another for a business, and amazingly, one man was looking for someone to decorate a large party boat for a Christmas parade. Besides all that, she needed to get her own Christmas lights up and sequenced, so she could use them as a sample for other customers.

But as she drove to her first appointment that afternoon, her mind suddenly turned to the people she'd seen in the audience while she was at the podium at Mr. Ritchie's funeral. Or rather, one person in particular that she thought she'd seen while she was standing up there.

The guy who'd been at the hardware store, teaching his nephew about plumbing fixtures. And from what she had gathered, he was the same guy who had called her late one night after she had rescued his cat.

Caleb.

He was sitting in a pew with a whole bunch of people. Men and women. Was one of those women his wife? Girlfriend?

Libby would probably never know.

And yet, for some strange reason, that very realization sent pangs of sadness racing through her heart.

* * *

Chapter Twenty-seven

Caleb could hardly believe it. Here it was, so close to Christmas, and he was sitting on a hard, wooden bench in the back of a courtroom. Along with Matt and the rest of the Sorry Saps. As well as Oscar, who had basically become a member of the Saps, though he wasn't really a sorry sap at all. In fact, he was quite the opposite, having rescued them and any other man who might have been one of Kinley's future victims.

And though the group had been joking around on the way over, they now sat stone-faced as Kinley was led before the judge for her arraignment. And what a different Kinley she was now. With no makeup, stringy hair, and decked out in an orange jumpsuit and cuffs, she hardly resembled the woman that Caleb had once dated.

Even so, there was an aura about her that he would have known anywhere. And he felt sick to his stomach the minute he saw her.

After that, he had a hard time focusing on the interaction between the lawyers and the judge. But he did catch a few key phrases. No bail. Flight risk. Would remain in jail until her trial.

All good news, as far as he was concerned.

It was over not long after it began. But just as Kinley was about to be led away, a police officer entered from the back of the courtroom, and the door shut behind him with a loud "*whoosh!*"

That's when Kinley jumped, and her head spun around so fast that Caleb thought she might get whiplash. For a few seconds, she stared straight into Caleb's eyes. Then her gaze went from one Sorry Sap to the next.

Her reaction to the men was startling. She went pale for a moment, clearly surprised by the sight of them. But then her eyes turned dark, and the expression she gave was one of a monster. She smiled a sickly-sweet smile, all the while staring at the men with so much anger and evil that Caleb felt like someone had punched him in the gut.

Especially when he suddenly realized that she had run her scam on them for so much more than just money. From what he could tell, she had also scammed them because she enjoyed it. And because, deep down, she hated them. Why, he wasn't sure. But somehow, they must have represented something to her, and she felt they deserved whatever she dished out.

The realization was unnerving.

And it left Caleb and the rest of the men shaken by the time they all walked out of the courtroom and went to lunch.

"Did you see . . .?" C.J. started to ask.

"Oh, yeah, we saw," the rest of the group chimed in.

"I still don't understand why," Finn added.

Matt shook his head. "We may never understand why. *She* may not understand why. Even years of psychotherapy may not help her to understand why. But my guess is that Kinley is simply a sociopath. She enjoys doing what she does, and she enjoyed fooling people. Plus, I'd say she liked having that power over men. And she hit them where it hurt the most."

"In their wallets?" C.J. joked.

Caleb laughed and jumped in. "Nope. In their hearts. And in their heads."

To which all the men agreed.

After that, they were silent for a while as they ate their lunch, with each man lost in his own thoughts. Later, Caleb had a hard time returning to work.

Especially after he got a call from Matt.

Who had just gotten a call from his friend, Detective Benny

McGregor.

"You're the first one I phoned," Matt told him. "Since you were the one who started this whole process. But I wanted you to know, Kinley just took a plea deal. She rolled on her partner. She'll still be going to jail, but she'll be up for parole a whole lot sooner. And he'll be in prison a whole lot longer.

"One more act of aggression toward yet another man," Caleb murmured.

"You got it," Matt agreed. "It gave her some power in a situation where she's basically powerless."

"It's sickening, isn't it?"

"Yup, it sure is. But just know this, Caleb. You actually took a leap of faith when you stepped into my office. Because it set things in motion to catch her. Thanks to you, we've gotten her off the streets where she can't hurt another person again."

Caleb let out a low chuckle. "Well, thanks for saying that. But you did the heavy lifting."

"I think you did a fine job yourself," Matt went on. "You've got a lot to be proud of."

Though oddly enough, Caleb didn't feel all that proud at that moment. He mostly just felt discombobulated. His head in a swirling mass of emotions. Yet he had no idea why.

But he knew someone who could probably help him figure it out.

So he drove straight to his parents' house. His mom had been watching Ginger for the day, and now he found them together just as he walked in. And what a scene it was. His mom was putting up a huge Christmas tree in the tall foyer. And Ginger was smack dab in the middle of the artificial tree, climbing to her heart's content.

Something his mom didn't seem to mind at all. In fact, she kept on smiling and cooing to the little cat. She even pulled out her phone and snapped off a couple of photos.

"Isn't she adorable?" his mom asked with a laugh.

"She is that, Mom."

Then she snapped a picture of Caleb, too, before giving his face the once-over. "So . . . pretty rough today?"

Caleb gave her an exaggerated nod. "Rough is the word. And weird. But it's also a relief. Somehow, I just feel better knowing that Fallon is no longer out there. But at the same time, I don't feel better at all. She really put me through the ringer. She threatened me and our family. Plus, she hurt some guys who are now my friends. And it wasn't like she was destitute or something and did it for the money. No, she did it simply because she wanted to hurt us."

His mom motioned him toward a chair in the living room. Then she took the opposite chair while Ginger hopped into his lap.

"It's hard to understand something that doesn't make any sense at all," his mom said softly.

"You can say that again."

"And no matter what you do, you may never understand it."

"You've got that right," he said as Ginger began to purr. "I just wish I could quit thinking about it."

"Easier said than done. But there is one thing you can do. Probably the hardest thing of all."

"What's that?" he asked, taking a deep breath.

"You could forgive her."

That's when Caleb's mouth fell open, and he had a hard time breathing for a moment or two. "You can't be serious, Mom . . ."

She nodded to him. "Oh, but I'm afraid I am."

"Fallon doesn't deserve to be forgiven. After all she's done. Who knows how many people she's hurt."

His mom glanced out to the foyer. "Well, you're right, she doesn't actually *deserve* your forgiveness. And forgiving does not mean forgetting, or that you shouldn't still pursue justice. No, the forgiveness is for you, not her. So you can let go. Otherwise, her crimes will continue to haunt you and hurt you for as long as you let them. And it could prevent you from having a real relationship with a woman. And from having a healthy, happy marriage."

Caleb sighed and closed his eyes. "I don't believe this."

"I know," his mom said gently. "Sometimes it's the hardest thing in the world to do."

"Okay . . . so how am I supposed to forgive her?"

"Well, I'd suggest that you find a nice, quiet place. All by yourself. No noise, no interruptions. So you can have some

Cindy Vincent

alone time with God. Then ask Him to help you, and tell Him you forgive her."

Caleb hung his head and rested his chin on top of Ginger. "I honestly don't know if I can do that, Mom."

"It won't be easy, I know. But until you do that, I wonder if you can really move on."

Unfortunately, Caleb knew full well that his mom was probably right.

"Arise, shine, for your light has come . . ."
(Isaiah 60:1, NIV)

Chapter Twenty-eight

Libby could not have imagined a more perfect night for a Christmas boat parade. The stars twinkled brightly in the navy blue sky, and a full moon hung suspended directly over Galveston Bay, reflecting light that shimmered on the water below. And while the strings of pixel lights that Libby had rigged up and ready to go on the vintage boat would put on quite a show—dancing and racing and flashing to the music in an amazing spectrum of colors—they still couldn't compare to what was happening in the heavens above.

Regardless, the boss of the company who owned the large boat was pleased with her work. "This is fantastic, Libby," he had told her repeatedly the night before, after she turned on the light show and the music so he could preview the whole thing.

Naturally, she was happy that *he* was happy. And she hoped it might translate into more business down the road.

So tonight, while he stayed on the shore so he could watch the entire parade, she remained on the boat, ready to start the show once they had entered the parade route in the bay. But she was also ready to troubleshoot if any issues came up.

And besides all that, she hoped to drum up more business by wearing her new company jacket, one made of purple fleece with the name "Libby's Lights" appliqued on the back in big, yellow satin letters. She had personally embellished the jacket even more, by sewing in a strand of multicolored twinkle lights, powered by a battery pack from inside her front pocket. Though the lights weren't waterproof and wouldn't hold up in rain or heavy spray, thankfully, that wouldn't be an issue tonight since the sky was perfectly clear. And she knew her jacket would make quite a statement when she turned the twinkle lights on. Something she intended to do once the parade was well underway. It was the perfect marketing tool, and something she would wear all season long. Especially for her inland light show reveals.

Though tonight, she did notice one minor issue with her new jacket—namely, she didn't have room for a life preserver underneath. And if she wore one on top, it would cover up her business name on the back. But looking around, she quickly noticed that nobody else on the boat seemed to be too strict about those regulations. Including the costumed dancers who were warming up and the jovial three-person crew who were manning the large boat.

So Libby simply went about her business, making sure that everything was working just fine. All was well as they cruised from the marina and officially entered the bay, and she started up the light show and music. While the dancers began their routine, Libby wandered about the boat, checking to make sure her light strands were all secure. Especially after the boat was hit by a few wind gusts.

Something that hadn't been in the forecast.

Not that she was too concerned, considering she'd used three times as many heavy-duty zip ties, or cable ties, as she needed, to hold the pixel strands in place. In case of any unexpected weather. And since cable ties were about the strongest thing out there, she knew she was in good shape.

Before long, the wind gusts died down and she truly started to enjoy herself. She walked around and marveled at the rich colors of the pixel lights. Blue, purple, red, teal, turquoise, lime green, bright pink, and white. Running back and forth across the strands. Then fading up and fading down. And flashing, before they all turned one solid color and then turned the full range of colors. All in time to the music. It was mesmerizing. She took a few quick videos, so she'd have something to share at next year's Christmas lights conference.

The thought of it made her smile. And she was about to activate the lights on her jacket, when a huge gust of wind hit the boat. Right away, she glanced out to the front, to the bow pulpit, just in time to see four of the cable ties suddenly snap. All at once. Right in a row.

She could hardly believe it. Sure, she could envision the remote possibility of *one* tie breaking. Maybe. *But four*? The odds of something like that happening were, well . . . astronomical!

And now her heart began to pound as she noticed the loose section of the light strand blowing wildly with another big wind gust. If those pixel lights were smashed against something, they would be broken and couldn't be repaired, not while they were out here on the water. Which meant a whole section would go dark, and not having lights on the front of the boat would ruin the entire effect of the show.

That meant she had to get them tied back on, one way or another. And fast. So she grabbed her supplies and carefully made her way out to the bow pulpit. She turned on her phone's flashlight and set it on the deck, facing upward, to help her see what she was doing. Then she reached out past the railing, ready to grab the flapping light string and fasten it safely back into place.

But she couldn't quite reach it.

So she moved a little closer, bending over the railing and reaching out some more. And then some more. She had barely managed to wrap her fingers around the light strand when a gigantic gust of wind hit the boat, making it lurch suddenly to the starboard side.

Libby immediately reacted by grabbing onto something solid, something that would hold her, like the railing. And for a split second, she believed she had, since her hand had wrapped around something firm. But she looked down in time to see that she'd only clutched a life ring in its metal holder. And with the force of her hand grabbing it and the boat correcting itself, the most she'd managed to do was to pull the life ring from the holder. And instead of steadying herself, she went tumbling, tumbling, tumbling, overboard.

Straight into the bay.

She hit the water with such force that she instantly lost her grip on the life ring and went completely under. The sudden burning of salt water filled her nostrils as she fought her way upward. Then adrenaline started to course through her veins, helping her kick and swim for all she was worth. Once she'd reached the surface, her first thought was to get out of the path of the oncoming boat. But thankfully, her spectacular fall had landed her far enough away that she managed to avoid being run over. She spotted the life ring nearby, so she swam toward it and grabbed onto the edge.

And with more kicking, and by fighting with everything she had against the waves, she got her arm around the floating ring and pulled her upper body up onto it and out of the water. Then she pushed her wet hair from her face and tried to get her bearings.

Right away, she became acutely aware of two things. Two things that could be dangerous. First, the water was a lot colder than she'd ever imagined. Even though she was technically near the Gulf of Mexico, known to be a warmer body of water, it wasn't exactly like being in someone's swimming pool. And second, she noticed how heavy her clothes felt now that they were weighted down with water.

In the distance, she could see the top of the tall boat gliding away from her with its pixels still flashing and blinking and moving. Had anyone seen her fall? Somehow, she doubted it. Not with the loud music playing and the dancers performing their routine while facing the shore. Unfortunately, she'd fallen off the other side of the boat, so she was probably the last person anyone would've noticed, especially since she'd gone over in a flash. That meant it might be a while before someone even realized she was missing and start looking for her.

Which also meant they wouldn't know *where* to start looking for her.

She groaned and dropped her head onto the top of the life

ring. She could hardly believe it. Here she'd had her first job decorating a boat, and it had already landed her in the brink. Something that didn't exactly bode well for any future decorating jobs.

But that was something she'd have to deal with later. At the moment, her top priority was to get help. So she tried hollering to get someone's attention, but it wasn't long before she realized that idea was pretty futile. Considering how loud the music was on all the boats, it wasn't likely that someone was going to hear her. Not to mention, the boat that she'd been on was a long way away and continuing on down the parade route.

That's when she realized one more danger—she was smack dab in the middle of the path of the parade boats. Which also meant she could get run over. So she kicked with her legs and swam against the waves, until she felt pretty certain that she was out of the direct path of the parade. On the other hand, she didn't want to move too far away, since she still hoped she could get someone's attention by screaming and waving when a boat went by. Unfortunately, she also realized that she was on the far side of the parade, which meant she couldn't swim to shore without crossing through the parade route.

But it wasn't long before she realized she had an even bigger problem—despite all her efforts to swim against it, the current had started to carry her farther out into Galveston Bay. Which would eventually take her straight into the open waters of the Gulf of Mexico.

On top of it all, one fact kept ringing through her head—it was extremely hard to spot someone who had fallen overboard.

Especially at night.

And especially if no one even knew that person had gone over in the first place.

Chapter Twenty-nine

Forgiveness. The word played over and over again in Caleb's mind as he dropped a fishing line off the back of his dad's boat. From where he sat, anchored in Galveston Bay, he could see the boat parade in the distance. Yet he was still far enough away that the music wouldn't bother him.

Or prevent him from doing what he'd come out here to do.

He rubbed a hand over his face as doubts flooded his mind. Now that he was here, he wondered if he could actually go through with his plan. His mom's suggestion. Like she had said, it was probably the hardest thing of all to do. So, could he really forgive Fallon? It was definitely something that fell into that whole "easier said than done" category.

Even so, he couldn't forget that his mom had a point. A very good point. That unless he forgave Fallon and let her go, he could never really move on with his life.

And there was nothing he wanted more at this moment than to move on from Fallon, or Kinley, and the turmoil she had created for him. It was the reason he'd come out to the bay tonight. Because yes, he'd decided to take his mom's advice and find a quiet place to do a little praying. And the only place he knew of where he could truly find that kind of peace and quiet was out on the water. That's where he always went when he needed to think. And this time, to pray, as well. Something he hadn't done a lot of lately.

But would God even hear him? Since he didn't exactly "tune in" on a regular basis?

Hopefully, the answer to that question was yes. Because Caleb wasn't only hoping to forgive Fallon. No, the truth was, he was hoping he might find something more out here tonight. Maybe some answers. And maybe some guidance on what direction he should take with his life.

He glanced out across the water to the boat parade. And his eyes were immediately drawn to one boat in particular, one decorated with a wider range of colors than he ever imagined possible when it came to Christmas lights.

Of course, he'd forgotten that the boat parade was tonight when he'd driven out to the marina earlier. But he figured it out in a hurry when he pulled into a very packed parking lot. It was a miracle he'd even found a spot at all, and after he parked his truck, he made a beeline to his dad's boat. He managed to back out of their slip and maneuver out into the bay just as the parade boats were starting to line up. The sight of them made him smile, and though the sun was only starting to set, he could still see the boats were all decked out in their Christmas finery. So if the "prayer and forgiveness thing" didn't work out tonight, well, at least he knew he'd be in for a good light show.

And by the time he had his boat in position in the bay, the sun was down, and a bright, full moon had started to rise in the twilight sky. Not long after that, the sky turned a beautiful, dark blue, and stars began to sparkle in the heavens.

Which meant the lights on the boats weren't the only lights on display tonight. Especially when the full moon rose even higher, reflecting a vivid, golden light across the gentle waves of the water.

Truth be told, despite a few strong gusts of wind, the night couldn't have been more beautiful.

Yet somehow, it didn't exactly seem fitting for his task at hand. Instead, it seemed like the weather should have been just as stormy as the emotions swirling inside of him. Emotions he wanted to unload and leave behind in the waters of the bay.

Though once again, it all hinged on his ability to forgive a woman who had hurt him and turned out to be nothing but a con artist. A crook. And he needed to forgive and let go so he wouldn't spend the rest of his life feeling traumatized by what she'd done.

But there was something else his mom had said that really hit home with him. Probably since he knew she'd been right. Hanging onto the pain that Fallon had inflicted could prevent him from having a happy marriage someday. And Caleb still had dreams of finding the right woman and falling in love. Real love. Someday, when he met the woman of his dreams, he wanted to be ready for a relationship. And he wanted it to work. But in order for that to happen, he needed to put the past behind him first, so he would be ready to look forward to his future with someone else.

Especially since there was a woman who had been in his thoughts lately. Ever since he'd seen her at Mr. Ritchie's store, and then later, at his funeral.

Libby.

He had so wanted to meet her that day. And for that matter, he *still* wanted to meet her. But how? Sure, he knew he had her number in his phone. But if he just called her out of the blue, would she think he was some kind of stalker or something? Besides, she didn't even know who he was or what he looked like. Or anything about him at all. And when it came right down to it, he didn't even know her last name.

No, the only proper way to meet her would be face-to-face. In person. But he wasn't sure how to make that happen. He thought about asking Mrs. Carstairs to help out, but she wouldn't be back until January sometime. And normally, he would've worked something out with Mr. Ritchie, and asked him to make the introductions. Of course, Mr. Ritchie would have been happy to.

But obviously, that was no longer an option.

Caleb felt a pang of pain in his chest just thinking about Mr. Ritchie being gone. He missed the man terribly, and it was going to be a strange Christmas without him. Though at least the man's legacy would live on, since his son and daughter-in-law and family had decided to take over the store. It would be a big move for them—literally—since they would be packing up and moving in from Waco. Not to mention, pulling their kids out of school and enrolling them locally. Amazingly, they also had a son who was about the same age as Jackson. One who was just as smart and mischievous. The two boys had hit it off immediately and were now as thick as thieves. Caleb only hoped they'd use their superpowers for good and not for evil.

And Caleb intended to offer as much encouragement and support as he could to the new Ritchie family. No doubt, everyone in Destiny would do the same.

Caleb let out a deep sigh before he reeled in his fishing line and cast it out again. It would be nice to catch something tonight, to make this whole "big moment" a little less depressing. Though to be honest, fishing was only helping him to procrastinate. Something he needed to quit doing. Because sometimes, like they say, a guy just has to jump in with both feet.

So he secured his line and, once again, tried to set his mind on his purpose for coming out here tonight.

Forgiveness.

Like it or not, he had to do this.

Then he took a deep breath and looked up at the bright, full moon that seemed to be holding court among the stars. "Okay, God," he said out loud. "You probably already know why I'm here. Since you can see everything. I need to let go of a person who hurt me and my family and some friends of mine. And to tell you the truth, I'm not sure how this is supposed to go. I'm kind of new at this."

But before he could say more, there was a tug on his line. So he grabbed the rod and reel and eased the line taut. Then he gave the fish some slack before he reeled it in a little more. Whatever was on the other end of the line must have been pretty good-sized. And a real fighter.

So Caleb repeated the process a few more times. Letting it run a little and then reeling it in. After a good half an hour, he finally brought the fish up. He was tired and sweating and felt like he'd just had a good workout. Yet all that struggling and fighting to reel in that fish had somehow made him feel better.

That was, until he saw the fish he'd caught.

"Oh, good Lord, that thing is ugly," he hollered.

Sure, he'd heard about Black Drums before, but he'd never actually caught one himself. Or seen one up close, for that matter. Especially an old one. And now, as he watched the slime ooze from the fish's scales, he was completely grossed out by the big whiskers attached to the fish's chin.

"And now I know why they call these fish 'Big Uglies,'" he said with a laugh. "But you know what, Fish? I've got a better name for you. I think I'll call you Fallon instead. And guess what Fallon, I'm throwing you back and letting you go."

And with that, he removed the fish from the hook and dropped it back into the water.

Chapter Thirty

Libby hollered for help again, though she knew her attempts were in vain, since no one would be able to hear her. And by now, she was beginning to wonder if she would ever be saved. She couldn't believe she'd actually fallen off a boat, and that she was now drifting out through Galveston Bay. Which would eventually take her into the Gulf of Mexico.

If only there was some way she could get someone's attention.

But she couldn't come up with a single idea that would help. She'd already checked the life ring for a whistle, but there wasn't one. And she'd looked for a water-activated light, but the ring didn't have one of those attached, either. That meant she was stuck floating around in the water until she could get someone's attention. Or until someone found her.

Helpless, warm tears started to fall down her cheeks. Was this going to be it for her? Was she going to die out here in this cold water, all alone? Devin had died young. Was she about to join him?

Much as she loved him, she wasn't ready to die, too. The idea of her life being over was just too sad, and so incredibly disappointing. She didn't want to go. Not yet. Not when there was still so much she wanted to do in her life.

She wanted to get married again. She wanted to have a

family. She wanted to spend time with her friends and *their* growing families. Plus, there were all her newfound artistic skills. She wanted to make more and more lamps and lights. And she wanted to add glass creations and metal pieces and much more to beautiful light fixtures that would hang in people's homes. Who knew how many creations she could make over the years? She might even learn more skills to add to the skills she'd already acquired in the last year.

On top of it all, there was Merry. The idea of never seeing her furry little face again was heartbreaking. Who would take care of her little kitten?

Was everything in her life about to come to an end out here in the water?

Would they even find her body?

The thought of it was more than she could bear.

"Help me, God! Please help me!" she cried out into the night.

The light, came the words into her head.

Like a still, small voice.

"The light?" she repeated. "There is no light. I already checked."

The light, she heard again.

"Wait a minute," she murmured, remembering the battery pack and the strand of twinkle lights she'd sewn into her jacket. "I do have a light, but there's no way that would work now."

After all, the lights sewn into her jacket weren't waterproof. They weren't designed to work after they'd been completely submerged for who knew how long she'd been in the water. Which meant they were way too waterlogged to ever light up.

Still, there was no harm in trying.

So she reached around the life ring and found the edge of her jacket. And then her pocket. Her fingers were a little numb, and she fumbled a few times trying to maneuver her hand in the water and find the battery pack. But after a few tries, she did, and she even managed to move the switch on the battery pack to the ON position.

In a split second, the lights sprang to life. To top it off, they were flashing and twinkling just like they were supposed to.

Joy immediately rose in her chest.

"There is no way that should have worked!" she gasped.

Much like the light of her bedside lamp never should have gone on, either. Again and again. Every single time she turned it off, during those days when Devin was dying in the hospital.

After all, she knew exactly how electricity worked now. In the natural anyway. She had taken classes on it and used electrical connections in her work. So she knew full well that the Christmas lights she'd sewn into her jacket should not have gone on.

That meant the source of those lights could only be, well . . . supernatural.

From above.

And that meant God was really there. And right here, too. All around her, for that matter.

She glanced at her lights and then up at the light of the moon and the stars and whispered, "Thank you."

"Therefore, if your whole body is full of light, and no part of it dark, it will be just as full of light as when a lamp shines its light on you." (Luke 11:36, NIV)

Chapter Thirty-one

"Okay, so maybe that wasn't so hard," Caleb said as he dipped his hands into the water and washed off the slime from the big, ugly fish.

And sure, he may have let the fish go, the one he'd named Fallon, but had he actually forgiven the real Fallon? Or rather, Kinley?

Probably not.

Yet it was the reason he'd come out here tonight, and he still needed to get the job done. Fully done. And as a guy who didn't like to leave a job unfinished, he knew he needed to take this next step. So he took another deep breath of the fresh, salt air, and looked up into the endless sky bursting with stars.

All ready to say the words.

And that's when his tongue seemed to be tied up in knots. Could he do this? *Really* do this? Because the truth was, he didn't exactly feel like forgiving Fallon.

Wow, it was amazing how hard something like this could be.

He slapped his palm to his forehead and groaned. How could a con artist and criminal like Fallon have so much power over him that he couldn't even manage to utter three little words? And if he didn't say what he'd come out here to say, that basically meant she'd won. Even though she was no longer *in* his life, she would still be *affecting* his life.

And he was allowing it.

But that needed to end. Right here and right now. So one way or another, he needed to take this final step.

"No guts, no glory," he muttered.

Then he focused on the stars and the moon above, stood up straight and mumbled the words, "I forgive her."

And though he'd stated it, he had to admit, his words sounded half-hearted at best. Even to his own ears. And he was pretty sure they wouldn't count.

So he tried again, this time in his regular voice. "I forgive her."

And then he said it once more, a little louder this time, just to make sure it took. "I forgive her," he repeated. "I forgive her, God. What she did was horrible, but I forgive her. I really and truly forgive her."

Then much to his amazement, he suddenly felt lighter and more relaxed. He couldn't say he was oozing with happiness, exactly, but he did feel a sense of relief.

He took another deep breath and kept on gazing up at the stars. And while he certainly felt better after taking that difficult step, he knew full well that he hadn't accomplished *everything* he'd set out to do. Meaning, there was one more step he needed to take. After all, he wasn't where he wanted to be in life yet. He was still single, and he didn't have a family. And on and on and on. Obviously, he wasn't doing so well on his own, and a little divine intervention could go a long way for a guy like him.

"Hello, God. It's me, again. Caleb," he said, pausing as he realized God probably knew his name. "Anyway, God, while I'm at it, I could really use some help down here, if you don't mind. Would you help me find the love of my life? The woman of my dreams. You know, the woman who is supposed to be my wife? Because I'm not doing so well in that department."

But he had barely spoken the words when another word popped into his head. It came to him so quietly, but with such firmness it nearly knocked him over.

Rescue.

"Rescue?" Caleb repeated with a laugh. "Sorry, but I quit doing that. Rescuing is what got me in trouble in the first place."

One more.

But Caleb shook his head. "No way. I'm not rescuing again. I've learned my lesson. Besides, there's nothing out here to rescue anyway," he said. "Which basically means I'm just losing my mind and hearing things."

The light.

Now Caleb dropped his head into his hands. "Oh, that's just great. The light. As in 'move toward the light.' Isn't that what people hear when they're dying? Maybe you misheard me, God. I didn't say 'light.' I said 'wife.'"

Wow, he could hardly believe it. He may have come out here to forgive Fallon, and to ask for God's help, but now he was just getting a bunch of nonsense inside his brain. Maybe it was time he called it a night.

So he threw his hands up and hollered, "Okay, thanks anyway, God. I'm going to head back to the marina now. Where hopefully, I won't be hearing more voices telling me to do things that don't make sense."

The light.

There were those words again. What someone would probably refer to as a still, small voice. And this voice was being rather insistent. Kind of like Ginger when she wanted something. Except this voice was probably just some kind of hallucination brought on by the stress of dealing with Fallon.

And yet he heard it one more time.

The light.

What if that really was the still, small voice of God? Well, if nothing else, it wouldn't hurt to look around. For . . . something. So he moved to the edge of the boat and glanced around the water, looking mostly in the direction of the shore.

And that's when he saw it. Not far in the distance, but quite a way from the boat parade. Were those . . . Christmas twinkle lights? Red, green, yellow, blue. Out here? Sticking up just above the waterline? Blinking and flashing?

Or maybe they were nothing but a reflection from one of the boats in the parade. But he quickly realized that wasn't possible, considering how far away those parade boats were.

Then he wondered if someone had simply lost a set of lights from their decorated boat, and maybe they'd floated out this far.

But what was the power source for those lights?

As far as he knew, nobody had invented twinkle lights that could withstand all that water.

No, the most likely scenario was that he'd simply graduated from hearing things to seeing things.

But either way, there was no harm in checking it out.

So he did. He fired up the boat and moved forward slowly to come alongside those lights.

And that's when he spotted the life ring.

And the woman who was hanging onto that life ring, with a strand of Christmas lights twinkling all around her.

His jaw dropped when he spotted her. What was she doing out here? And how were those lights even working? Though if nothing else, she appeared to be completely real and not a hallucination at all.

But more importantly, she needed to be rescued from the water. And quick.

She gave him a weak wave. In return, he honked his horn, to let her know he'd seen her and was on his way to save her.

But that's when things got tricky. Even though he'd once been trained in how to pull someone out of the ocean during a rescue, it relied heavily on speed and timing. You had to be careful not to overshoot the person in the water, so you could grab them. But you also had to be careful not to run them over.

Besides that, he had no idea what kind of condition she was in and how long she'd been in the water. Was she injured? Hypothermic?

Though he didn't waste a single second to find out. He turned the boat in the right direction, set the speed on extra slow and stepped to the back deck. Then, when he knew he was in position, he hit the kill switch on his electronic key fob to

Cindy Vincent

stop the engine. The boat drifted closer and closer, coming almost to a stop in front of her. Then he turned on a spotlight, so he could see her better and keep track of her in the water.

She wiped her long hair from her face and stared up at him, smiling through her tears.

And even though she was totally drenched, she looked familiar to him. Was that . . . could it be . . . Libby?

Not that it mattered at that moment. Whoever was out there in the water needed to be brought in. And now.

With his heart practically pounding through his chest, he quickly managed to catch her life ring with a boat hook and pull her toward the side of his boat. Her hand felt small and cold in his when he finally clasped it, and he could tell she was shivering and weak when he pulled her up and out of the water. That's when he noticed the letters on the back of her sopping wet jacket. Libby's Lights. And it was the jacket itself that was blinking with those Christmas lights.

"I'm Caleb," he told her quickly. "Are you Libby?"

"Thank God you found me, Caleb," she gushed. "And yes, I'm Libby. I don't think I've ever been so happy to see someone in my whole life."

Caleb was pretty sure that went double for him. Maybe even triple.

"Let's get you into something warm," he insisted as he peeled off her waterlogged jacket. "How in the world did you get out here?"

"I was riding on one of the parade boats. One that I decorated," she said through chattering teeth. "I was trying to fix a strand of lights and I fell off. It wasn't one of my better moments."

"Everyone has moments like that," he said with a chuckle as he put one of his big jackets around her. "Trust me."

That's when she gasped and pointed to her own jacket that was now lying in a wet mess on the boat deck. "The lights!"

He looked down to see what she was talking about. "Umm, whoa . . . yeah, the lights went out. Thank God they stayed on long enough for me to see you out there."

She tilted her chin up, and her beautiful, blue eyes went wide as she stared straight into his. "Thank you . . . Thank you

258

so much."

Thank you, he said in a silent prayer.

"Now, we'd better get you warmed up," Caleb told her. "Let's get you into the cabin. I'll crank up the heater. And I know my sisters-in-law have some sweatpants and sweatshirts stowed away downstairs. I think you'd better change into some dry clothes."

"Good idea," she said softly before he helped her down to the cabin below.

Right away, he found her a couple of towels and some dry clothes and led her to one of the berths so she could change. "Do you think you can manage yourself?"

She smiled. "Yes, thank you. Amazingly, I'm a little better already. Now that I'm out of the water."

"That's a good sign. I'm going to make some coffee while you get dried off and change. The coffee will help get you warmed up."

With that, he left her and got right to work in the galley. While the coffee was brewing, he opened up a can of chicken noodle soup, poured it into a pan, and started to heat it up on the tiny stove. And he also turned up the heater for the whole cabin.

She emerged just as the soup was boiling, now wearing black sweatpants and a pink sweatshirt that looked like they fit her perfectly. She'd also found a brush and was pulling it through her wet hair. Amazingly, she looked beautiful, even after her ordeal.

Though she was still shivering.

So Caleb quickly guided her onto the kitchen bench and wrapped a couple of blankets around her. Then he ladled soup into a cup and put it before her. Along with a spoon.

"This will help you get warmed up," he told her. "And I've got creamer and sweetener for the coffee. Does that sound good?"

"Very," she told him as she took a sip of the soup. "This is wonderful. I can't thank you enough. For a moment, I thought I was going to die out there."

He poured coffee into a cup. "I think someone was watching over you," he said with a smile.

"I think so, too," she told him as she accepted the cup of coffee from him. For a second or two, she kept her hands wrapped around it, absorbing the heat.

"Do you need any medical attention?" he asked. "I can get you to the hospital in a hurry if you want me to."

But she just smiled and shook her head. "This soup and these dry clothes are really doing the trick. I'm pretty sure I'll be fine once I get warmed up. Besides, I really don't like hospitals."

"Bad experience?" he asked as he poured a cup of coffee for himself.

She nodded. "You could say that."

That's when the reason why suddenly dawned on him. "I know I've seen you before. Did you speak at Mr. Ritchie's funeral?"

"I did," she said sweetly. "It was pretty nerve-wracking. But people spoke at my late husband's funeral, and it meant the world to me. So I wanted to do the same for Mr. Ritchie's family."

"I'll bet they appreciated it. Especially now that his son and family are moving in to take over the store. And I've got a pretty good guess why you don't like hospitals."

She gave him a knowing nod. "If you heard me talk there, then you probably know that I'm a widow, and that my husband died of cancer. And Mr. Ritchie helped me through all that. He was such a wonderful man. I still can't believe he's gone. But I think I saw you in his store one time. With a little boy?"

Caleb laughed. "My nephew, Jackson. The perfect storm of terror and intelligence. I love that kid, but wow, he's a handful."

She smiled. "I kind of gathered that. But he's such a cute little guy. Along with the cat. Was that Ginger?"

His eyebrows shot up. "It was. And you would know that because . . . because, you're the one who rescued Ginger."

She nodded. "My kitten, Merry Anne, still misses her."

"I hate to tell you, but Ginger is kind of a terror, too," he added with a laugh.

She laughed in return and took another sip of her coffee.

Caleb slipped into the bench across from her. "I saw the name 'Libby's Lights' on your wet jacket. So you must be the one who makes all those light fixtures and lamps. They're fantastic. I bought one for my mom. She loves it."

"And I think one of your customers bought one of my light fixtures at my gallery show. Alyssa Van Sant. So that means you must be part of MacKnight and Sons. I went to your model home once. It was gorgeous."

"Glad you liked it. That house was one of mine."

Her jaw dropped. "Wow! You do wonderful work."

He blushed just a little. "Thank you. So do you."

"So which son are you?" she asked as she finished her soup.

"I'm number three. Out of four. And I'm the black sheep since I'm the only one not married and starting a family."

"Oh. And no . . . umm . . . girlfriend?" she asked shyly.

"Nope. I got out of a very bad relationship about a year ago. And I guess you could say, it was so bad that I haven't dated since."

"I can understand. I haven't dated, either, since my husband passed away. Almost a year ago."

And so they talked on. About who they both knew. And about all the surprise connections between them. Then once Libby was warmed up, Caleb made them each another cup of coffee and they went topside to watch the rest of the Christmas boat parade.

"There is something I've been wondering about," Caleb told her as they sat on chairs on the back deck. "The lights in your jacket must be some seriously waterproof Christmas lights."

She shook her head. "But they aren't at all. They're just regular old twinkle lights. Incandescent, even."

"Wow . . . and yet they stayed lit in the water."

"Well . . ." she started to explain. "You might say, there's a little more to the story. I hope this doesn't freak you out. But when I was in the water, I cried out to God and prayed for help. And the words 'the light' just suddenly popped into my head. So I reached down and turned on the switch to my battery pack. I could hardly believe it, but those lights went on. In the natural, they never should've worked."

Caleb's mouth dropped open. "I think I know what you're

saying. Because you weren't the only one out here praying."

She leaned toward him. "You were, too?"

"Yup. Let's just say, I was looking for some answers. And the same thing happened to me. I heard 'the light,' too. Inside my head. And then I looked around and I found you. Out there in the water."

Her beautiful blue eyes went wide. "That's pretty . . . amazing. Miraculous."

"Yeah. I'll say."

Then for a moment or two, they just stared quietly up at the night sky. Letting it all sink in.

"What do you think it means?" she asked softly. "What happened to us tonight?"

Caleb took a deep breath. "Well . . . I think it means we should take the plunge. No pun intended."

To which she just laughed.

Then he reached over and took her hand. "I think we should go out to dinner. And get to know each other. Since Ginger and Merry Anne already do. Though Mrs. Carstairs is out of town, so we won't have a pet sitter."

"Maybe they won't need one if they have each other."

"I like the sound of that."

"Me, too."

Now he stared straight into her eyes. "So, what do you say? Are you free tomorrow night? For dinner?"

Her smile was angelic. "How could I possibly say no to the man who just saved my life?"

Epilogue

A year and a half later, Libby and Caleb were married in a huge church wedding, with his family and her family and their many friends there to celebrate with them.

Naturally, Libby set up a light display for the outdoor reception and dance that rivaled even the best movie set. She also had the idea of seating the Merry Widows and the Sorry Saps together, and the whole bunch seemed to hit it off beautifully. In fact, while the night went on, she even heard talk of them forming a new, collective group called "The Merry Saps." Though Mrs. Carstairs had to leave before the reception was over, since she was pet sitting both Ginger and Merry Anne, who were now happily playing together as sisters.

And when it came time for the last dance of the evening, a slow dance, a slight breeze blew through the party, and Libby shivered in the night air.

So Caleb immediately took off his tux jacket and wrapped it around her shoulders. "Does that remind you of anything?"

She laughed. "One of the scariest nights of my life. Which also turned out to be one of the best nights of my life."

"The night we met," he said as he slid his hand around to the small of her back and pulled her close.

She put her arms around him, and they began to sway to the music. "And the night you saved my life."

He kissed her forehead. "I think you probably saved my life that night, too. Thank God you were where you were . . . and I was where I was. At that exact moment."

"I think we had some serious divine intervention," she told him.

"I couldn't agree more," he replied.

Then she leaned back for a moment and looked lovingly into his eyes. "You know, about that night . . . in a way, it seemed like everything happened so suddenly. And yet, I can't help but wonder . . ."

He nodded. ". . . if we were on some kind of collision course? That we'd been heading for that moment for a while?"

"Uh-huh. Because that one moment changed the destiny of our entire lives."

"You can say that again."

"A destiny moment," she told him, with stars in her eyes.

"A destiny moment," he murmured back and held her tight.

THE END

Discussion Questions

1. Do you believe that Libby and Caleb grew and changed as individuals throughout the book? If so, how did they change?

2. Libby and Caleb both ended up belonging to groups with people who had shared experiences. Do you think these associations were valuable, and how did they impact Libby and Caleb? Have you ever been part of a group like that yourself?

3. How do you think Libby handled her grief? What types of strategies did she use?

4. What role did "light" play in Libby's life?

5. Caleb unexpectedly ended up with a kitten. A very demanding kitten, but one who eventually became a valuable member of his family. Have you ever experienced such an unexpected blessing? Things that started out as annoyances but proved to be otherwise later on?

6. Libby had a lot of support during her time of grieving. Do you know anyone going through grief right now, and is there anything you can do to offer support to them?

7. Caleb knew he had to forgive the woman who had hurt him. Have you ever had to forgive someone who hurt you, when you really didn't feel like it? Has the act of forgiveness ever played a role in your life?

8. What happened to Libby after she cried out to God? And to Caleb after he spoke to God?

9. Libby and Caleb both experienced events that seemed to be chain reactions, where one thing led to another and to another and so on. Have you ever experienced something like that, where one event led to another?

10. Libby and Caleb meet in a Destiny Moment. Can you think of any Destiny Moments that you've had in your life?

About the Author

Cindy Vincent was born in Calgary, Alberta, Canada, and has lived all around the US and Canada. She is the creator of the Mysteries by Vincent murder mystery party games and the Daisy Diamond Detective series games for girls. She is also the award-winning author of the Buckley and Bogey Cat Detective Caper books; the Tracy Truworth, Apprentice P.I., 1940s Homefront Mystery series; the first Maddie Montgomery mystery; and the daily devotional, *Cats Are Part of His Kingdom, Too*. She lives in Houston with her handsome husband and an assortment of fantastic felines, where she does her very best to follow God's plan for her life . . .

Printed in the USA
CPSIA information can be obtained
at www.ICGtesting.com
CBHW011658010524
7763CB00005B/15